Praise for *A Heaven to Die For*

Encouraging, creative, and inspiring.

— Joey Buran
Senior Pastor of Worship Generation,
1984 Pipeline Masters Champion

A Heaven To Die For is a compelling story with twists and turns. It strikes a wonderful balance between the earthly realm with its laws of nature and science, and the spiritual realm—miracles and God's mighty power. While getting lost in the story and the mystery, I was practically encouraged in my faith and in how big and awesome our God is. It's a rare treat to read something that both entertains and concretely encourages me in my faith.

— Darren Mettler
Member of the OC Supertones rock band,
Associate Pastor, Pacific Coast Church,
San Clemente CA

From the moment I heard Scott's idea for this book, I've been eager to see it.

— Jeff Gerke
Author and Artist,
Founder of Marcher Lord Press

A HEAVEN to Die For

A HEAVEN to Die For

A Novel

The First Adventure of The Light Waves Series

Scott Mohr

Contributions by Melissa Mohr

Deep River Books

A Heaven to Die For

Published by Deep River Books
Sisters, Oregon
www.deepriverbooks.com

ISBN-13: 9781940269900

Library of Congress: 2016934294

Printed in the USA

Cover design by Joe Bailen, Contajus Designs

Contents

Special thanks for invaluable feedback, advice,
and counsel:

Sherri, Darren, Mark, Joey O., Lynne, Marlene, Crystal,
Barbara, Rachel.

1

Exhilaration

Axel ran his fingers through his shaggy blond hair and rubbed his sapphire blue eyes as he pulled out of his driveway. "Smells Like Teen Spirit" played through the speakers as Saturday's early morning fog pressed up against the windows and coated the fading paint of his Toyota pickup, his one good headlight barely cutting through the darkness. Silence blanketed the neighborhood, but a stampede rumbled through Axel's mind and his heart galloped inside.

He tuned the radio to the local news station and turned up the volume when the weather report came on.

"A high surf advisory has been issued for coastal communities today. Fourteen- to eighteen-foot waves generated by a violent storm in the northern reaches of the Pacific are expected to hit from Point Conception to the Mexican border. Water safety officials are closing many beaches due to the high tides and dangerous surf conditions."

His truck cruised down the main beach road. *Where should I sit in the lineup? Northwest swell. Stay south of the lifeguard tower. Yeah, stay to the south. Major closeouts just up the beach from there. Paddle an extra stroke down the face. Need that extra push today.*

Daylight dawned as he pulled into the already crowded parking lot. A heavy mist clung tightly to the coastline as adrenaline junkies headed toward the water. Frosty air slapped him in the face the second he opened the door.

Axel loved the danger of riding big waves. Living on the edge. Flirting with mortality. Far from put off by the weather report, he thrived in moments like this. Life-threatening situations made him feel alive and vital—in fact they drove him. The problem was there were never enough of them, especially during the last eight months since he'd graduated from high school. The realization that he'd probably spend the next forty or fifty years drudging through a career of aimless sales jobs had taken its toll and left him dreading his humdrum future. And the problem wasn't simply with his chosen vocation—chasing corporate prosperity in any form just didn't motivate him.

He stepped into his full wetsuit, pulled the sleeves over his sturdy arms, and then peered out to sea, but the fog masked the raging fury of the waves. Only the sound of the behemoths crashing in the distance reached his ears.

After locking his car, he walked through the grainy sand to the water's edge. The air felt salty and damp; the taste of the ocean dusted his lips. He almost gasped as he stepped into the icy water, his breaths becoming short and shallow.

He sprang forward onto his board and paddled vigorously through the frequent waves of turbulent white water, each one more daunting than the last. At about forty yards out, he collided with some as burly as an iron horse that thrashed him in torrents of swirling saline.

The vicious current worked against him, shoving him far to the south and way out of position. *Keep pushing. Keep pushing. Right arm, left arm, right arm, left.*

Moments later, he stopped and sat up on his board, shoulders sagging, gulping in air. Finally, a lull in the swells. He hadn't thought the sea was going to give him a break like this today.

Suddenly the fog opened up, creating a canopy around him with the water completely calm. Waves of light pierced through the gray ceiling above, and the dark teal surface of the ocean gleamed as smooth as glass.

His eyes widened as the beauty of the moment stilled the adrenaline racing through his veins, and he dropped his chin to his chest. *Lord, this feeling I have right now. So pumped and alive. So unlike anything else in my life. I'm so tired of the sleepless nights. And my meaningless routine, so barren of anything fulfilling to strive for. Lord, I want to experience more of this, and I believe you want that for me. But I . . . I don't know how.*

He sat in silence for another few moments. Then, without warning, another dose of furious white water burst upon him. Wave after wave pounded him and twisted him about as he clung to his board. He paddled on fiercely, alone at sea. After some time, the sun burned through a patch in the fog and pointed him to a handful of surfers in the lineup.

He pulled up next to Mick, one of the other regulars. "Any shape to these waves, brah?"

"Most of them are walls, mate," Mick replied, scratching his crew-cut white hair. "No place to go, but a few will give you an open face to work with. You'll need to be in the right spot, though, or you'll get totally drilled. One guy almost drowned. Boards are breaking everywhere."

Axel flashed him a grin. "So we could die today?"

"Seriously, it's possible. The sets are fifteen or sixteen feet and heavy, and there's even bigger rogue waves mixed in."

Axel nodded. "I feel the need . . . the need for speed!" he said in his best Maverick voice, and he paddled away.

Within minutes, a set of three monstrous waves lined up and eclipsed the horizon. Axel and the others scampered frantically toward them, striving to clear the oncoming giants before they broke. Salty ice water stung his bare hands and face and sloshed into his mouth.

His heart raced as he moved safely over the first peak and glanced back. Some hadn't made it out far enough. Churning white water ripped them from their boards and punished them in the roiling fury.

Axel positioned himself to take a run at the second wave of the set. It looked like there was a makeable shoulder to the right. Maybe.

He turned the nose of his board toward shore and glanced quickly to his left. No one there. *Go hard. Go hard!*

The enormous swell lifted him and surged him forward. He jumped up and planted his feet as the wave grew steeper and steeper, shooting him down the face with a hair-raising rush of speed.

Wind blasted him in the chest.

He made a long arcing turn and looked up at the mountain of water above. "Yeeah!" he shouted, sensing it towered more than three times his height.

The wave raged beneath him, shooting him mercilessly toward the shore. He turned his board up the face and then rotated back toward the bottom again, sending spray high into the air.

His eyes bugged as he descended the crest. Alarms went off in his head. It was going to close on him, crashing down from all sides. This could drown even the strongest of watermen.

There was no possible escape route. Axel gritted his teeth and lowered his head as the deep blue darkness consumed him.

The entire weight of the lip came booming down like a ton of bricks, discharging him from his board, snapping his leash and driving him downward into the murky depths below. The tumbling force tore at his limbs and threw him around like a rag doll.

An eternity seemed to pass, yet he continued to plunge, seeing only white turmoil. Turning over and over again. Becoming dizzier and dizzier.

The ocean relaxed its grip for a moment, and he swam madly toward the surface. Pain devoured his chest. His head was about to explode, and pressure mounted upon pressure. The hue of the water became darker and darker. *Lord, help me. I'm going the wrong way!*

He reversed course as blackness crowded into his vision, giving one final desperate kick toward the light above.

Moments later, his head emerged into the open air, gasping and wheezing. He sucked down a couple of breaths. No time to relax; more white water would be coming. He turned frantically and set his sights out to sea, but thankfully, no more waves approached. That had to be a miracle. Appreciation to God poured forth from his soul as he turned his gaze skyward toward the soupy mist.

A large section of his fractured board floated a short distance away. The ocean must have devoured the rest of it. He swam over, climbed on, and limped his way toward shore, disappointed that he was done for the day. But what was up with that lull during the paddle out? Was God saying something? Was it some kind of sign?

After trudging through the gritty sand to his car, he dried off with an old towel, changed out of his wetsuit, and drove the few minutes home.

Oddly, he ached all over. He didn't usually get headaches, but his temples now throbbed. He took a couple of ibuprofen and poured the last of the milk over his bowl of Cheerios. The final spoonful made its way into his mouth as warm beams of sunlight cut through the cracks of the blinds, stretching across his face and shoulders. There was only one place to be on a day like this.

With the pain relievers beginning to take effect, he loaded up his beach chair and headed back to the ocean. The church crew would be there. They always were on weekends when the weather was nice.

Axel padded barefoot down the stairway to the sand and located the familiar cluster of umbrellas, then walked over and sat down next to Francisco.

Francisco smiled up at him in welcome. "Man, I was hoping you'd come down."

"Couldn't pass up the beach on a day like this."

Francisco had been Axel's mentor since his junior year of high school, pouring God's truth into his life months before Axel had chosen to follow Christ. Married with two children, and a fellow surfer, Francisco always made time to discuss whatever questions or doubts Axel had. Axel really admired his stability and maturity, especially the brotherly love he always showed.

Francisco pushed his long, dark hair away from his forehead. "Did you get in this morning?"

"Yeah, it was heavy. Busted my board on the very first wave. What about you?"

"Me and some of the guys went south where it wasn't so crazy. Only about five or six feet, but really fun."

Axel gazed off into the distance. "God really got my attention out there today."

"In what way?"

"I don't know how to explain it. There was this surreal moment when I was paddling out. It was like I was in his presence, and I felt so alive. I know it sounds weird, man, but I just don't understand why I never feel like that in the rest of my life."

Francisco leaned on the arm of his beach chair. "I think I know the answer, but you probably don't want to hear it."

"Try me. I'm open to just about anything at this point."

"Frankly, it's not that hard. What it comes down to is depending on God . . . for everything . . . all the time."

Axel shook his head. "Not really following you."

"You're always moving from one daring experience to another, thinking that's where you'll find satisfaction. You find stimulation in those kicks for a while, but then you need more and more and more just to keep your high. It's like a drug for you. I know it sounds too simple, but God truly is the only thing that can satisfy you. I think if you seek his will, you'll be blown away by what he has for you."

Axel smirked. "What? The church knitting club?"

Francisco laughed. "No, I'm not saying that. But listen to you. You have this idea that life in Christ isn't exciting. For me, as I've depended on him, he's taken me places I'd never dreamed of and given me this amazing sense of purpose."

Somehow, Axel hadn't happened upon that bridge yet. He'd started down the road with Jesus and was extremely grateful for his salvation, but the valley between his Christian experience and verve seemed to have no crossing. "That sounds really cool, but I can't seem to make it work. And from what I can tell, heaven doesn't even sound all that great. It's definitely way better than the alternative, but frankly, I don't see a lot to look forward to. I've spent a lot of time thinking about it ever since I lost Arielle, wanting to know what she's going through and all."

"I know you miss her a lot, man."

Tragedy had robbed Axel of his best friend, his constant companion, the love of his life. Daily, he'd reminisce about Arielle's dazzling brown eyes, her sleek midnight-black hair, and her smooth olive skin. He remembered her laughter, her compassion, the way she believed in him. But the memories were all he had left of her. Killers still at large had taken her life during a trip to visit family in Israel right before the start of Axel's senior year, and authorities had offered no explanation. Her death ripped Axel's heart out, and he still hadn't recovered. "Yeah, way more than I ever imagined," he said softly.

Francisco stirred his toe in the sand. "So what do you think it's like up there?"

Axel ran his hands through his hair and blew out a breath. He recalled most of what he'd heard from their pastor and a few of the things he'd read. It was a fairly short list. "Well, it sounds like there's all this singing and standing around the throne of God—but then what? I mean, I'm sure seeing God face-to-face will be mind-blowing and all, but I can't imagine doing only that forever. It seems like it could get kind of monotonous, and I don't even like singing in church."

Axel glanced out into the water to see a massive set of waves approaching on the horizon. Couldn't eternity be more like that? Like wave after wave of intensity and excitement. That was a heaven he could get into!

Francisco reclined back in his chair again. "I'm sure there's more to it. I stand in awe of God's creative genius in new ways every day. I don't think we'll be disappointed when we get there."

"You know I love the Lord, but I wish I could be more like you, just trusting it'll be like you say. I want to know if there'll be some kind of exhilarating role for me to play there. It's just kind of how I'm wired."

"I don't know the details, Axel, but I can tell you this—God *is* light. There's no darkness in him at all. And he's made his light 'shine in our hearts to give us the knowledge of the glory of God in the face of Christ.' Waves of his light shining in our lives, now and forever, where we'll know exhilaration and purpose beyond anything we can imagine."

Francisco's wife, Nina, turned toward them from a few beach chairs down the row and smiled. "Axel, is he giving you surfer theology again? Just remember that not everything in God's kingdom involves waves."

They laughed. Francisco dug his feet down into the warm sand, and Axel followed his lead. The beach was the best spot for a nap, and he soon dozed off.

A short time later, he woke up with the headache throbbing in his temples again. Maybe sleeping it off in the darkness of his bedroom was what he needed. So he said good-bye to the church crew and headed home.

The pain increased as he drove. Was this what a migraine felt like? He knew his heart was still beating in his chest, but it felt like it pounded inside his head.

Every street sign blurred until he could hardly read them at all. He blinked a couple of times to clear his vision and rubbed the back of his neck. No relief.

He finally reached home and moved quickly toward his bedroom, but a rush of nausea veered his course to the bathroom, where he vomited uncontrollably. He collapsed to the floor as darkness overwhelmed him.

2

Connection

In the parking lot of her regular coffee shop, Holly sat inside her car with the windows cracked, drinking a small cup of coffee. No cream, no sugar, just simple and black. It was a tad burnt this Saturday afternoon, but that didn't matter. Every sip was like taking in a deep breath or rolling back her shoulders, unraveling her full checklist of chores for the day.

Today wasn't unique. She had already exercised, dressed the kids, fed them lunch, and dropped them off at her mom's house. She'd made calls to coordinate rehearsals for the children's Easter musical at church and mailed the remaining invitations for Taj's seventh birthday party. They were late, but that didn't matter. She had sent them to Aunt Alana and her cousin Axel, along with Uncle RJ's family, even though they probably wouldn't come. Aunt Alana and Axel rarely showed up at family events, and Uncle RJ suffered with health problems. That didn't matter. There was an unwritten rule—family members always get invitations, even if they don't show.

She turned the coffee cup around in her hand, her eyes following the last sip as it swirled in a ring, and then she set it in a cup holder and started the car. She glanced in the mirror at her long, golden-blonde hair with side-swept bangs and her sandy complexion, and then shifted her five-foot-six-inch frame in the seat. Her friends were probably waiting for her at the beach trail.

After she pulled out of the parking lot, the light turned yellow and then red. "Father . . ." she whispered, but the words seemed to bounce off the ceiling. "Father . . . are you there?" She stared at the steering wheel. God seemed so far away—distant and untouchable. She felt like a little girl sitting on the floor after a hard day, reaching for her daddy to pick her up and hold her.

But no one was there. No one had been there for weeks.

The light turned green, and the birthday party popped back into her head. She hadn't even called the bakery yet.

A black sedan persisted in the rearview mirror. It had been parked at the coffee shop and was following her a few car lengths back. Was she just being paranoid? Again? Others probably wouldn't have even noticed. Maybe that's what a short-lived career as an investigator got you. A lifetime of irrational fear.

Holly pulled into the beach parking lot and looked around. No sign of that car. Must have been imagining it.

She slid out the door and strolled toward Lynne, Vicki, and Bianca as they waited for her at the mouth of the trail. Clouds floated above the sea, swirling their bright whites and soft grays together.

"There you are," Lynne called. "Come on, Holl."

At that moment, her cell phone rang. The display read AUNT ALANA. She was late already, so she let it go to voice mail. She hoped it wasn't another crisis involving her cousin. Drama just seemed to follow Axel around.

Holly picked up the pace and jogged toward her friends. "Three weeks is way too long to wait. I'm so glad we can finally do this."

The four decided to walk on the damp, low-tide sand rather than take the beach trail. The fog had burnt off, giving way to rays of bright sunshine that bounced off the water on this magnificent winter afternoon.

Vicki gestured at Holly's sunglasses. "So mysterious! Where'd you get 'em?"

"Oh gosh," Holly said, laughing. "They were on sale downtown at one of the surf shops. You know the one where those two little dogs always lay out front? And these are trendy. Trust me."

"Trendy? You look like a secret agent again."

"You know it wasn't like that at all. It was all deskwork and papers, and definitely no adventure. I was an analyst, a nerd, remember? I just *wished* I was James Bond. Hard to believe that was ten years ago."

Holly's life had flip-flopped dramatically since those days. The independent, crime-fighting superhero had transformed into a full-blown stay-at-home mom. She had married her husband Derek at twenty-five, became pregnant with Brianna, and then left her government agency job at twenty-six. Taj arrived two years later, and by then Holly had studied cookbooks and home magazines like they were criminal reports. She knew domestic like the back of her hand.

As the friends continued strolling down the beach, they slid into their usual pairs. Vicki and Bianca always walked slower. Holly set the pace, and Lynne came alongside.

"I've always wondered, do you ever miss your work at the agency? You never really bring it up, but when Vicki teased you about your sunglasses it got me thinking."

Holly sighed. That was a time when she and the Lord had shared the same apartment. "Miss it? Sometimes. But I'd never trade Brianna or Taj or Derek for anything. Besides, it's not the work I miss, but more the closeness I had with God back then. I had more time to read my Bible and live every day just following him. Now I barely have time to think about myself, let alone God. He seems so far away. But I know he's there. Have you ever felt that way?"

"Sure, doesn't everybody? I think having some doubt from time to time is just a part of life."

"What do you do to get over it?"

"To be honest, and this is the hard part, I get over myself."

Holly scrunched her forehead. "Really? I'm not sure I even know what that means."

Lynne smiled. "I'm always thinking about the things I need to get done, like if I don't do them myself they won't get done right. It was worse when the kids were younger. I would always catch myself getting lost in my routine, and then I would be distracted from paying attention to anything other than me—even God. My whole relationship with him becomes about me too. So . . . I just get over myself. Remember that it's about his love, not about what I'm doing right."

Holly looked up at the coils of clouds above her. Now wasn't the time to cry. But when was it ever the time to cry anymore? Lynne put her arm around Holly's shoulder, and they walked in silence.

After a few moments, Holly pulled out a tissue and wiped her eyes. "I always need to control everything."

"When I give things over to the Lord and realize it's not all about me, I start to feel his presence again," Lynne said. "Psalm 31 helps me a lot: 'But I trust in you, O Lord; I say, 'you are my God.' My times are in your hands; deliver me from my enemies and from those who pursue me. Let your face shine on your servant; save me in your unfailing love."

She made it sound so easy. "I wish I could turn everything over to him, but I keep hanging on."

"I know what that's like, trust me. But try giving all those little things over to him, even if it has to be one little thing at a time. You'll get that closeness again."

A slight smile turned up the corners of Holly's mouth. She wasn't alone in the ring after all. Others wrestled with the same quandaries she did, and having a close friend like Lynne in there with her gave her all the more hope. "Thanks, Lynne. You don't know how much I appreciate this."

After the four friends returned to the parking lot, Holly walked to her car and wiped the sand off her shoes with her tissue. She waved to the others as they drove past and then started the engine. Time to think about her to-do list again.

Holly tuned the radio to the local praise music station and pulled out onto the road. She paid no attention to the intersections she crossed as Lynne's words swept through her mind. After a mile or so, she needed to change lanes and glanced casually at the rearview mirror.

Her heart rate jumped immediately. The black sedan was definitely following her again.

Her thoughts spun. Who could it be? It didn't make any sense. She inhaled deeply.

Come on now, remember your background. Remain calm and gather the facts. Dark-haired male, baseball cap, sunglasses, facial hair, BMW. Definitely no one she recognized. *Stay calm. Change course; maybe he won't follow.*

She turned into a neighborhood. The black car veered around the corner right behind her. A few more turns and it stuck close behind, now almost on her bumper. A drop of nervous sweat inched down her forehead, and she white-knuckled the wheel.

Suddenly, her phone blared out its ringtone on the seat beside her. She glanced down. Aunt Alana again, but grabbing it was out of the question.

"Lord," she whispered, "please, please protect me right now."

She cut out of the neighborhood into a business park. Only a few cars lined the streets. Now she really was alone.

She pushed harder on the accelerator, but the black car continued to close in. Its engine growled louder and louder. Its front grill and windshield now filled her rearview mirror. SMASH!

Holly's neck whipped forward. She tried to hold the wheel steady, but it didn't respond. All four screeching tires lost traction, and her car spun out of control as she headed broadside toward a concrete marquee.

CRASH! She jerked sideways and the airbags burst out.

She opened her eyes to a blur of color and white dust. Her surroundings swirled, and she felt smothered in airbag chemical odor. She raised her head to peer out through the shattered windshield.

"No!" she screamed, scrambling to unbuckle her seatbelt. The black car had made a U-turn and now raced back toward her.

The driver aimed a pistol at her from his window. Holly ducked to the floor as shots rang out. Bullets cut through the windows and doors of her car, shattering glass and ricocheting off the sides, covering her with debris. Then the black car sped off.

Holly huddled on the floor. Her ears rang, and her body stiffened. A misty haze impaired her vision. She ran her hands over her sweater and jeans. No blood. No pain.

Soft beams of sunlight caressed her face through the window as a warm and gentle breeze blew her hair. The radio station still played, filling the car with praise, as if the voices of angels sang from on high: "Deliver me from my enemies and from those who pursue me. Thank you, Lord, for saving me in your unfailing love." She let the words sink in. God was with her.

Sirens screamed in the distance. Slowly, she pulled herself up into the seat, brushing off pieces of glass and plastic. Her hands trembled so violently that she could barely grasp her cell phone on the floor. She hit speed dial to call Derek and waited. One ring, two rings, three rings.

"Hey, sweetie," he answered.

Holly sobbed into the phone. "Derek, someone rammed into my car and was shooting at me, and I don't know who it was. I'm so scared, Derek, I—"

"What? Someone shot at you? Really? Are you okay? Where are you?"

"Derek, I need you. Please come right now." She continued to sob. "I'm in the business park a couple miles from the beach. Please stay on the phone."

"I'm coming, baby. I promise I won't hang up."

Two deputy sheriffs, a fire engine, and a paramedic unit arrived on the scene. One of the officers walked over to Holly and began asking questions. Her vision was still a little blurry, washing out his features.

She didn't have a lot of information to give him, but she described the episode as best as she could. Firemen pushed forward to extricate her from the wreckage, and the paramedics examined her for injuries. After a few minutes they opened the door, applied a brace to her neck, lifted her onto a backboard, and transferred her carefully onto a stretcher.

Derek arrived at the scene and ran to Holly's side. She reached out her hand for him. His caring grasp never failed to soothe the sting of a crisis. "I'm so glad you're here."

Derek bent over and gave her a gentle kiss, then looked at one of the paramedics. "Is she okay?"

"So far everything looks normal. She should get a spinal exam to make sure the impact of the airbag didn't cause any damage. I'd recommend transporting her in our vehicle, but you can drive her there yourself if you'd like."

"I would appreciate it if you would take her. I don't want to take any chances."

"Ma'am, I have a few more questions," the deputy said. "Are you her husband, sir?"

"Yes," Derek replied.

"Can either of you think of why someone would do this?"

"No," Holly said, her voice shaking. "I haven't a clue."

Derek studied a large bruise on Holly's arm. "The only thing I can think of is that narcotics ring you helped bring down."

Holly shook her head gently. "Derek, that was like ten years ago. It couldn't be."

"Yeah, but those guys vowed revenge, and I bet some of them have been released on parole in the last year or so."

"Tell me more about this narcotics ring," the officer said. He scribbled on his notepad and seemed to have no time for eye contact.

"Holly worked as an analyst for the DEA years ago," Derek said. "Near the end of her time there, she testified at a trial that convicted the leaders of a major narcotics operation. They all got prison terms, and most of them saw her face in court and knew her name—"

"I caught a glimpse of the driver, and he didn't look like any of them," Holly said.

"Babe, maybe it wasn't one of them. They might have hired someone to do their dirty work."

"You should have been placed in Witness Protection," the officer said, glancing up at them with a frown.

Holly still had no regrets about that. Changing her name and relocating to who knows where had no appeal at all, and leaving her family and friends wasn't an option. "They suggested it, but we declined. We just wanted to move on with our lives."

He pocketed his pen. "All right, I have enough for now, but someone from our investigations division will contact you in the next twenty-four hours. I'm glad you weren't seriously hurt."

The paramedics transported Holly to the emergency room, and Derek followed behind. Her neck exam showed no damage, so they picked up their kids from her mom's and went home. Holly collapsed on the couch for the next couple of hours and flipped through some Saturday evening TV shows. Nothing interested her, but it kept her from thinking about her brush with death.

"Mom, your cell phone," Brianna called from down the hall.

"Bring it here, honey."

Brianna bounced into the room and handed the phone to Holly.

"Holly, it's Aunt Alana. I have some bad news."

The hue of the shadows that shrouded her emotions plunged even darker. She didn't know how much more gloom she could take. "What's wrong?"

"Axel is in intensive care here at the hospital. The doctors say he had a severe brain aneurism earlier today. I found him unconscious on the bathroom floor. They're not sure if he's going to make it through the night." Her aunt's voice broke.

"Oh no," Holly said. First the shooting, and now Axel? How much trauma could one day hold?

"They're going to take him to surgery in a few minutes. Please pray for him."

Bloodlines trumped personal adversity. She could rest tomorrow. Besides, she'd seen enough *Law & Order* reruns. "I will, but I'm coming to the hospital. I'll be there as soon as I can."

Holly found Derek in the garage and told him the news, but he continued sanding the rocking chair he was building and shook his head. "That's crazy. You're bruised and battered yourself. You shouldn't be going anywhere."

"I know, but I feel all right . . . really. They're family. I need to be there."

He looked up at her and sighed. "Okay, but I'm driving you."

"But what about the kids? My mom already had them all day, and she's probably going to the hospital too."

Derek dropped his sandpaper and pulled off his goggles. "No arguments, I'm driving. We'll take the kids next door."

Holly quickly changed her clothes and spent a few minutes in front of the mirror while Derek walked Brianna and Taj to the neighbor's house. She grabbed her purse, then went back to the garage and slid into Derek's Corvette.

As they drove, Holly squinted in the glare of the oncoming headlights. She felt her heart beginning to race and her breathing becoming shallow. Images from the afternoon darted in and out of her mind, prompting her to clutch tighter to the armrest. Maybe Derek was right about those drug dealers.

Derek glanced over at her. "You okay?"

"Yeah. I'll be fine." She gave him a forced smile. "Really."

"Maybe we should head back home."

"No, I need to be with Aunt Alana. I'm just a little tired."

She took a couple of deep breaths and pulled her phone from her purse. Moments later the headlights of a car shone in her outside mirror. Fear gripped her stomach. *Calm down. It's just a car following too close.*

The car moved to pass them on the left. She shifted in her seat, but it drove on without incident.

Breathe. Relax.

A few blocks later, another car sat on their bumper, following even closer. She looked back over her shoulder as they passed under a streetlight. A man with a beard was driving. Surely it was only a coincidence.

Her self-talk wasn't helping. Panic rushed through her veins. She clutched Derek's arm and closed her eyes.

"What's wrong?" he blurted out.

"That car . . . behind us."

He stared in the rearview mirror, his eyes fixed upon it. Seconds passed.

"Derek, the red light!" she screamed.

Derek slammed on the brakes as a car barreled toward them from the left. He whipped the wheel in the other direction, and the tires squealed. Sliding. Sliding. Completely out of control.

CRASH! A violent collision sent them careening across the intersection into a light pole. Holly blacked out at the moment of impact, entangled in a heap of twisted metal.

3

Validation

RJ opened his eyes as wide as he could, straining to see more, to capture it all—if that were even possible. Multitudes of angels moved in unison above him like billions of salmon in a rushing stream. They circled continually and separated in the center to reveal four magnificent creatures, each one somehow graced with the face of a man, the face of a lion, the face of an ox, and the face of an eagle. Nothing on Earth, not the most dazzling of sunsets or stars through a telescope, could have fascinated him more.

He veered his focus upward. A vast expanse glistened like ice and stretched high above the multitude of angels. The figure of a man on a towering sapphire throne sat even beyond that. The greatest words that came to mind—"majestic" or "glorious" or "magnificent"—seemed nowhere near worthy of describing the figure. *Have my eyes ever truly been open before this moment?* It was as if he'd just been born. He parted his lips, but no sound came forth.

Burning light blazed around the figure on the throne. His upper body glowed like heated metal and his lower body like fire. RJ had never seen anything so radiant.

The figure motioned with his hand. *Is he calling to me?* Before RJ could gesture back, a young man appeared and knelt in the midst of the brilliant rays, worshiping, exalting the one enthroned on high.

The young man looked familiar, but even as recognition struck, questions pressed into RJ's mind. Could it really be his nephew kneeling there in the blinding glory? The one who seemed to wander in and out of a serious relationship with God? Maybe he'd made some changes. Maybe he'd finally taken his faith seriously.

Suddenly RJ awoke, no longer in the midst of the dazzling glory. Instead, beige walls surrounded him, with one of the lights burnt out in the corner, and his doctor and nurses stood around his bed. What a disappointment.

His tall and willowy wife, Marie, also stood next to him holding his hand, her chestnut brown eyes and medium-length mahogany brown hair as stunning as always. She stroked his forehead. "Darling, I'm so relieved to see your eyes open again. We thought . . . I'm just so thankful you're still with us."

"What happened?" he said.

The doctor glanced up from his clipboard. "You slipped off into a coma for a few hours. Your vital signs were at critical levels—"

"—but you're back with us now," Marie said. She smiled down at him with love and worry radiating from her soft gaze.

RJ blinked a few times. Marie picked up his glasses from the side table and slid them onto his face. He turned toward the window and saw his son Gerry giving him a "hang loose" sign with his hand. RJ gave him a half-smile back.

Rory, his younger son, stood up from a chair in the corner. "Keep fighting, Dad. You're gonna beat this thing."

The IV monitor beeped, sending one of the nurses scurrying. Moments later she returned with another bag of solution and attached it to the pole.

"You had such a peaceful look on your face," Marie said.

RJ cleared his throat. "I . . . I must have seen a vision, but it seemed so real. The most beautiful place I've ever seen—like heaven. Light—waves of breathtaking light—in every color imaginable, shining in all directions."

"Your imagination still works wonderfully, dear."

RJ frowned. Imagination? No—no, he was sure it hadn't been. "I don't think I was imagining it . . . and Axel was there."

"Axel? That is odd. You haven't seen him for a while."

"I know, but he was there, worshiping."

Marie stroked his hand. "Dreams can be so bizarre."

"No, really, I swear, it wasn't a dream. It was as real as you holding my hand."

"All right, RJ," the doctor interrupted. "You'll have time to describe more of it for us later, but right now you need rest." He scribbled a few more notes and left the room with the nurses not far behind.

Marie shook her head. "It's been such a challenging six months for you. I'm so proud of you . . . of how you've battled it."

"Yeah, Dad," Gerry said. "You've braved all of the treatments and procedures. You've been a real inspiration to us."

"Thanks, son," RJ replied, smiling. They were good people, his family—the best a man could want. But their praise made him a little uncomfortable. It wasn't his doing, really, if he'd been courageous. "It means a lot to me, but I want you all to know that death doesn't scare me. I trust the Lord for whatever's going to happen, whether in this life or the next."

"You've been solid as a rock," Marie said. "In your service for Christ, in your career, and in how you've lived your life."

RJ smiled up at his wife. "There were a lot of good years before they kicked me out. Hopefully, I made a difference in the lives of some of those young people."

"You did, darling. The administration at the high school just couldn't handle your faith."

He chuckled. It was a miracle, really, that he could laugh about it. That was one thing about cancer: it brought perspective. RJ's first love was God, and then Marie and the boys, but science and marrying it with Scripture ranked right after that. And the school board didn't just hand him a pink slip after accusing him of preaching Christianity in the classroom. Instead, they made every effort to humiliate him, to make an example of him. They took their case to the public, smearing him in letters to local papers and carrying picket signs in front of the campus. They deemed his career a failure, slamming his teaching as "not real science," and it had left him devastated.

"The Lord walked me through that storm," he said. "I'm not bitter. I've forgiven them."

"How can you forgive them for what they did to you?" Rory said.

RJ exhaled weakly. Nearly seven months had gone by, and the kid still sounded angry. "Son, when we hate, we turn into the very thing we despise. We need to forgive so we can look forward to better times. Otherwise we live resentful, miserable lives in the past."

"We don't need to relive that nightmare right now, Rory," Marie said. She looked down at RJ, and he squeezed her hand. "So much good came out of your work, darling, not the least of which was the impact you had on Axel. I don't know where he'd be if it weren't for the things you taught him. His mother is so grateful for how God used you in his life."

RJ now struggled for each breath. He was so tired and just wanted to let go. "Axel was a slacker most of his life. Just bored, I guess."

"But he thrived in your class at the end of his senior year, darling," Marie said. "You opened his eyes to a whole new perspective on his relationship with Christ. You can be proud of that."

"Not proud. Happy."

RJ pictured his nephew at the start of last spring's semester. Depression had seeped from Axel's eyes, having lost his girlfriend Arielle just months before. Her passing had cast a dimness over Axel's heart, but it also sparked a desire in him to know more about life beyond this earth. For that, RJ was grateful.

Quantum physics and string theory had ignited Axel's interest, along with RJ's references to the Bible. He questioned RJ about the science of Scripture and how it applied to the afterlife, spurring many of their classroom discussions. Looking back, it was probably some of those same discussions that had triggered the administration's hatred.

Axel's journey into the quantum world began with RJ's lecture on the very first day of class. "Many of the things you learned in the first few months of this course could now be classified as history, only scratching the surface of the realities we know about today," RJ had said. "But I had to teach it to you because the district requires it."

He remembered pausing and looking out at a lot of bored faces. There were always a handful of students who paid attention, though, and that motivated him to infuse some zing into his lessons. At the time he had not thought Axel was one of those students.

"Remember those pictures of atoms in your textbooks? Little balls of energy with very small particles flying around them? Well, modern science is now telling us that those pictures don't tell the entire story."

RJ had held up an elastic exercise band, stretching it longer and then shorter again. "We now know that we're made of even smaller things than those particles. At the tiniest levels, we now believe that we consist of little elastic strings of energy, like this exercise band. In the physics of today, this is known as string theory."

The guy sitting next to Axel tapped his foot and stared out the window.

"Someone ask me, 'Why should I care?'" RJ continued.

He strolled back and forth at the front of the room. No one responded. "I'll tell you why. You should care because string theory suggests that we live in an extremely wild and strange universe, far more *bizarre* than anything we've ever imagined before. Are you ready for some shocking news?"

Axel shifted in his chair.

"You see, for string theory to work, we have to be living right now in eleven . . . different . . . dimensions."

RJ stopped and faced the class. "You're familiar with the three dimensions of space, right? First, I can move back and forth. Second, I can move side to side. And third, I can move up and down. And I can move in any combination of the three. A three-dimensional universe. Simple, right? There's also a fourth dimension we live in. Can anyone tell me what that is?"

No one raised a hand. Indifference permeated the room.

RJ held up his wrist and pointed to his watch. "Time. Time is the fourth dimension. Those are the only four dimensions that we experience. So, if string theory tells us we live in eleven dimensions, not just the four I mentioned, then where *are* the other seven?"

Axel leaned forward in his seat, as did a few others.

"Here's an eerie thought. Those other dimensions . . . they exist right here among us. We just can't see them."

Axel tilted his head. He really had the boy's attention now.

"What does this mean?" RJ shouted. "Modern science is telling us that invisible worlds exist right here in our midst. This is not some weird science fiction novel. These aren't the fantasies of some madman. String theory mathematically gives us answers to problems that not even Einstein could solve!"

RJ paused again. The newly awakened interest in the room simmered, and he was ready to bring it to a boil.

"This idea of unseen worlds in extra dimensions should not come as a surprise to us. There's a very old book that tells us much about them, and I'll bet you can't guess what it is."

"The Egyptian Book of the Dead?" one female student called out.

"No, I'm not talking about some book of encounters with ghosts and goblins. And no, I'm not referring to a manual on how to practice mysticism. What I'm talking about is the Christian Bible—the biggest bestseller in the entire world. This ancient text gives us fascinating details about how this vast universe works, and more importantly, about our lives beyond this world."

A lot of grumbling filled the classroom after he dropped the "B" word. Some students glared at him with expressions of disbelief. Others scowled with scorn. He knew they resented his audacity at bringing up religion in a science class, but he had hoped it would pique Axel's curiosity and entice him to learn more about the eternal life Arielle had now taken hold of.

RJ raised his arms to quiet the room. "I know most of you reject the Bible because you think it only tells you what you should and shouldn't do—a book of rules. Or you've been told it's just a collection of outdated stories with no relevance to life today. But within its pages lies clear evidence of extradimensional worlds."

He picked up his Bible from the top of his desk. "For instance, here's an example from the book of Colossians: 'He'—that's Jesus—'is the image of the invisible God, the firstborn over all creation. For by him all things were created: *things in heaven and on earth, visible and invisible, whether thrones or powers or rulers or authorities*; all things were created by him and for him.' And in Ephesians we read, 'For our struggle is not against flesh and blood, but against the rulers, against the authorities, *against the powers of this dark world and against the spiritual forces of evil in the heavenly realms*.' It's describing other beings, invisible beings living in another dimension. This evidence for invisible worlds existing right alongside us was written thousands of years ago—long before modern science made this discovery."

Axel had remained engaged in RJ's class for the rest of the semester. RJ knew he had rocked Axel's world and given him a view of the eternal. He hoped he had motivated his nephew to give more than just lip service to his belief in God as well.

RJ's thoughts returned to the hospital room, where his wife and sons had gathered around his bed, waiting for him to speak again. His voice even sounded weak to his own ears.

"I truly do relish the memories of challenging my students with the truth of God's Word. I wouldn't have done anything differently."

RJ looked over at his doctor, who stood in the doorway motioning for the family to follow him. He could read the expression on the doctor's face and knew what it meant. Courage through treatment was good, but it wasn't enough. The cancer was winning. He knew his time was short.

Minutes later, Rusty, a fellow science teacher from the school, walked into his room.

"You're just too stubborn to let death get you, RJ," Rusty joked as he took a seat at his bedside.

RJ gave him a weak smile. "I'm ready to go. I'm looking forward to seeing the other side."

"You're pretty confident about that extradimensional stuff, aren't you?"

"I just believe what I read in Scripture. Can you grab my Bible over there? I want you to read me something."

Rusty tilted his head back, his complexion redder than his thinning, combed-over hair. "Oh, I see what's going on. You're still trying to persuade me, huh?"

RJ smiled wryly. Rusty had been a good friend even if he was a skeptic. He had never jumped on the witch-burning bandwagon that had so recently unleashed its fury. "That's between you and God. Just humor a dying man and get my Bible. Open it to the book of John, chapter 20, verses 19 and 20."

Rusty reached for the Bible and fumbled through the pages for a few moments, then began reading. "On the evening of that first day of the week, when the disciples were together, with the doors locked for fear of the Jews, Jesus came and stood among them and said, 'Peace be with you!' After he said this, he showed them his hands and side."

RJ slowly raised his hand, index finger extended and shaking. "Think about it. Jesus appeared to his disciples after he rose from the dead. He was definitely in some kind of body, but he went into the room without going through a locked door. I've thought about that a lot. What if his resurrected body had access to other dimensions? He would simply rotate into three other dimensions of space, then he could go right through the walls."

Rusty pulled out a pack of Tic Tacs and popped one into his mouth. "Hmm."

RJ dug deep for the energy to continue. "And take a look at the story of Philip and the Ethiopian eunuch. Turn to Acts chapter 8 for me and read verses 38 through 40."

Rusty found the passage and read, "Then both Philip and the eunuch went down into the water and Philip baptized him. When they came up out of the water, the Spirit of the Lord suddenly took Philip away, and the eunuch did not see him again, but went on his way rejoicing. Philip, however, appeared at Azotus and traveled about, preaching the gospel in all the towns until he reached Caesarea."

RJ cleared his throat. "Wild, huh? He just showed up in another town. But he didn't walk there. He didn't ride there. He just appeared, instantly. I think God moved him through extra dimensions. Can you think of any other way to explain it?"

"Space invaders maybe?"

RJ patted Rusty's arm. "Come on. You're not listening. You haven't even considered the scores of other evidence. Like Elijah's trip to heaven in a whirlwind, Hezekiah's shadow reversal, Joshua's long day, and Jesus's transfiguration in Luke 9. In that one, Moses and Elijah definitely showed up in some kind of resurrected bodies. Where else would they have come from if not another dimension of space?"

Rusty stared at the wall above RJ's head. "They didn't come from anywhere, RJ; it's just a story. A fairy tale."

"RJ, in your condition, you absolutely need to be resting, not talking," a nurse said as she bustled over to his bedside. She stuck a thermometer in his mouth and held his wrist to check his pulse.

Rusty placed a hand on the white sheet that covered RJ's knee. "Buddy, I will give you this, you seem to have more joy and life on your deathbed than most healthy people I know. I'll be thinking about you. You've given me some things to consider."

The nurse took the thermometer out of RJ's mouth. His lips quirked in a half-smile. "It means a lot that you came by, Rusty. I hope to see you on the other side."

✷

The intercom page for RJ's doctor came into Marie's ears like a dagger as she waited in the lounge. "Code blue" weren't the words she wanted to hear. She'd known this moment would eventually come. Her companion of decades was moving on. Yes, she knew exactly where he was going—to their Father in heaven. But that didn't make it any easier.

Tears moistened her eyes as she looked down at the carpeted floor. Her stomach twisted at the thought of losing RJ. Life without him seemed unimaginable, so lonely and dry, but she could barely stand watching him in such pain. She knew she needed to let him go. The tears she had held back finally spilled down her cheeks.

Supported on each side by her sons, Marie labored to put one foot in front of the other as they walked down the long hospital corridor. It was just like RJ to save her the pain of watching him die. He had waited to pass until he was alone.

She stepped through the door, and the room no longer hummed or beeped with alarms. RJ's eyes were closed, and his chest no longer rose and fell with the breath of life. But a strange, warm peace hovered in the air, wrapping its arms around her. Her beloved was now at home with his Lord.

4

Transition

Voices echoed around Axel, all of them unfamiliar. His entire body groaned. His head throbbed and his limbs tingled. He felt an impulse to twitch, but something inside held a firm grip, keeping him from any kind of shift or response.

His bed began to roll forward, and the lights dimmed. *Where am I going?* Into a tunnel or a corridor maybe? The bed made a number of turns, and harsh lighting stung his eyes beneath their lids. Sharp icicles pressed against his skin, frozen and raw. A chill draft crawled across his face, and the smell of sterility smothered him, followed by a sharp beeping and a soft humming and even more voices murmuring and gathering around.

Then, all of a sudden, silence. A vacuum void of any tumult. The shackles released, and the pain fled like a bandit. Light doused his eyes, brilliant light, and his arms and legs tingled no more.

Where was the hospital bed? Where was the floor? *Very bizarre.* He stood suspended in some kind of space, but could he even call this "space"?

Something else seemed different too, but he couldn't put his finger on it. He felt a freedom to move in ways he'd never been able to before, like boundaries had been removed. As if up and down, back and forth, and side to side no longer stood as the only options. *Strange* didn't even begin to describe this.

Dazzling beams of colored light ribboned around his fingers and up his arms, all in turquoise and indigo and sapphire—the colors of the sea. He followed them with his eyes, mesmerized. The calming colored rays wrapped around him and continued out into the expanse, connecting to something—or someone. A deluge of warmth and love pulsed through them, rousing every niche of his soul to euphoria.

5

Aspiration

Some thirty years later . . .

Axel stood marveling once again at the glory and majesty of God the Father as he sat veiled in brilliant light upon his mountainous throne. Out of nowhere, a heavy hand tapped Axel on the shoulder from behind.

"Come, Axel," Abiron said, his voice deep and rumbling. "We have an important task ahead of us."

Axel jumped. The warrior angel stood much taller and wider than he did, and definitely more daunting. Pure white linen clothed Abiron's body, and he wore a golden belt around his waste. Straight black hair hung down his back, and his muscular arms and legs shone like burnished bronze, reflecting the light swarming down from the throne above. His eyes blazed like torches.

"I'm ready for our next mission," Axel said. His mind snapped back to the only other time Abiron had taken him under his wing, about four years earlier as those on Earth would measure it.

Axel had raced away from the throne through the three extra dimensions of heaven's expanse and glanced back at the multitude of angels and resurrected believers as they reveled in worship. He realized he'd traveled farther out than he ever had before. Throughout his life in the heavenly realm, he'd taken great pleasure in darting through the expanse at high velocity, weaving in and out of the beams of resplendent light and cornering instantly at ninety-degree angles. The term "G-force" had no bearing there.

After a few moments a murky-grey vapor appeared directly ahead, completely blanketing the horizon in front of him, ominous and imposing. He came to a gliding stop and surveyed the mysterious haze. It was the first time he'd seen anything other than waves of light beyond the throne area in the expanse.

"You won't be able to get through unless you know how to navigate the passageway," someone with a low tone said.

The voice had to be Abiron's. Axel turned, confirming his suspicion. The warrior angel stood beside him. "Where does it lead?"

"To the dimensions that intersect the physical universe."

"So that's the road to Earth?"

"Correct. The route through that barrier is only given to a certain contingent of the Lord's servants. Conflict with the realm of spiritual darkness lies right on the other side."

"I imagine you pass through there quite often, then."

"I do, and it has been granted for you to accompany me on this particular mission. This is a very special privilege. Only a limited number of resurrected believers have made this journey. It was the Lord's will for you to join me. You will need to keep this strictly to yourself and will not be able to share your experience with anyone else. Can I have your assurance on that?"

"Absolutely. It stays with me." Zeal to share in the angel's valor and gallantry had absorbed Axel like a sponge on a spill from the moment he'd met Abiron. Passion had seeped into the pores of his soul, filling him with a desire to join Abiron's angelic contingent and fight spiritual battles against forces of evil. Maybe, just maybe, this was his initiation.

"Okay, then. Stick close by. We have an urgent prayer request to answer. When I instruct you to stay in a certain location or to move from one place to another, you will need to comply immediately and do exactly as you are told. Do you understand?"

Axel straightened up his posture and extended his arms down the sides of his swank pure-white garment. "I'll do whatever you need me to do."

Abiron flashed away toward the grey barrier, and Axel came right alongside. Without hesitation, they entered the murky haze. Immediately, a shrill whistling filled Axel's ears. The angel made a sequence of turns through the mist, and Axel traced his path like a pup following his master.

All at once, a bright light flooded Axel's vision, as if a bolt of lightning had struck. He continued to surge forward, but he could no longer see Abiron.

The whistling grew louder and louder, reaching a deafening pitch. The glare scorched Axel's eyes.

Suddenly, the bright light faded, and all he heard was the sound of the wind rushing by. Abiron dashed on in front of him into another expanse with infinite proportions, but this was very different from the one they'd just left. Darkness now surrounded Axel except for countless little points of light out in the distance in every direction. No more brilliant rays, no more throne, and no more singing. Just endless night.

Without warning, an enormous fireball emerged in front of him, becoming larger and larger—a seething celestial monster drawing him in to swallow him alive. An instant later, it eclipsed his entire view. He felt the urge to warn Abiron but quickly remembered that the angel had navigated these parts many times before. *He must know what he's doing.*

Abiron led him right into the center of the blaze and then out the other side. Axel saw only a flash as he passed through and felt only a cool, gentle breeze.

"What was that?" he shouted.

"A star," Abiron yelled back.

"A star? Where are we?"

"In the Andromeda Galaxy."

"We're in outer space?"

"In a sense. More accurately, though, we're in other dimensions right beside it."

"So we could rotate into the universe right now?" Axel said.

"Yes, it sits right next to us," Abiron replied. "We would be very far from Earth, though."

They blazed on past and through stars, meteors and other celestial objects. Moments later, a terrestrial sphere appeared, graced with alluring blue oceans, lush green jungles and forests, and spectacular weather patterns. Axel had only seen this view of Earth in pictures. The real-life perspective put the photographs to shame.

He had spent eighteen and a half troubled years on the planet, followed by over a generation of wonder and awe in heaven. A vagabond who'd emigrated from the mean streets of a destitute country to the palaces of an affluent empire. How could he even compare the two? A life burdened with striving and disappointment on the one hand, and an existence brimming with ecstasy on the other. The contrast was mind-boggling.

Yet he knew he would eventually return to live on Earth again at Jesus's second coming, and he hadn't completely come to terms with the reversal of fortune that would ensue.

Abiron led him around the equator a short distance and descended into the skies above North America, heading straight to an area in its center blanketed with farmlands. They approached the ground, still in the other dimensions, invisible to those in the world, and passed by a small town with cornfields surrounding it on every side. Abiron continued to fly out over a two-lane highway for a few miles and came to a halt, hovering just a few yards above the pavement.

Not ten minutes later, a large flatbed truck approached and passed directly underneath them, heading toward the small town. Axel noted four men in the extended cab and another two standing against the racks in the back. They wore T-shirts with the words "Christian Relief Coalition" stenciled on the front. Food containers and gasoline tanks filled the bed around them.

Abiron began trailing the truck with Axel right beside him. Axel considered asking Abiron a few questions but quickly bit his lip. The situation was obvious. These guys were delivering supplies to the town, and Abiron was escorting them.

Suddenly a Jeep appeared, parked at a ninety-degree angle and blocking the road out in front of them. A tattooed woman dressed in camouflage stood in the passenger seat, and another woman and two men, each one also tattooed and adorned with piercings, flanked the vehicle on each side with handguns drawn.

The flatbed came to a stop, and the assailants walked toward it. Axel prepared to jump on them.

Abiron turned to him. "Do not move, Axel. Observe and take notice."

Axel's shoulders drooped.

Abiron rushed to the back of the flatbed and floated next to a black metal box. He rotated quickly into the earth's dimensions, shoved something into the box's latch, and rotated back out again, all in less than a split second.

At that moment, two fallen spirits darted in from high up in the atmosphere and dragged Abiron away from the truck, but he retaliated and immediately established control, headlocking one under his left arm and clasping onto the neck of the other with his right. Axel let out a cheer.

The assailants continued to walk forward, gun barrels homing in. The four men exited the cab of the flatbed, while the two in the back worked desperately to open the black metal box.

"It's completely jammed," one of them said.

Axel stood perplexed. What did the box contain? Should he help them—but Abiron had jammed the thing. And why wasn't Abiron going after the assailants?

Two other angels arrived and took custody of the fallen spirits in Abiron's grasp. Abiron moved over next to the driver of the flatbed, raised his hands above his head, and gazed toward the heavenly realm.

"AAAHHH!" the flatbed driver screamed. He twitched violently, and a fallen spirit bolted from his body, jetting away into the expanse in the other dimensions. Axel jumped nearly as much. What in the world was going on?

The assailants now stood just yards away. "Put your hands behind your heads, and don't make a move," said the tattooed woman in camouflage.

The men from the flatbed complied immediately.

Axel looked at Abiron and shouted, "Abiron, aren't you going to do something?"

"No, Axel, our work is done here."

Axel looked wildly between the hostages and their armed captors. "What do you mean?"

"Those containers and gas tanks in the back of the flatbed are all empty. These men were going to rob the town and take the plunder away. The black metal box is full of automatic weapons."

"But their shirts say Christian Relief Coalition."

"Good deception, don't you think? The four from the Jeep are the true believers. They were outmanned and outgunned, but the Lord was on their side."

Abiron glided over next to Axel again.

"Boy, was I fooled," Axel said. "How did you know that?"

"They prayed for the Lord's help about a half-hour ago, Earth time, just about when his majesty dispatched me to assist."

The four believers secured the six men from the flatbed, and one of the women made a call on her cell phone. Axel nodded as he watched them. There was no question in his mind that this was what he wanted to do—oppose hatred and wickedness in whatever form it might arise.

"Abiron, I'm ready to join you in these battles against the forces of evil. It's really hard for me to just stand by and watch."

Abiron raised an eyebrow. "That is an admirable desire, Axel, but that decision is not mine to make."

"Can you put in a good word for me with the Lord?"

Abiron laughed. "There is no need for that. I am sure he will thrust you into an integral role of his choosing at the appropriate time."

It wasn't what Axel wanted to hear, but he knew the angel was right.

At that, Abiron sobered again. "The important thing for you to understand is that I operated completely in the Lord's power during this mission. It is in his strength alone that these battles are won."

Axel heard the angel's words, but he cast them off as elementary. *Of course Jesus gives us strength. I learned that a long time ago.* He mused further and said, "Something doesn't make sense to me. This is America, right? Why are vigilantes out trying to rob people of their food, water, and fuel?"

"Evil is rising, Axel, and the world is headed for desperate times."

Axel's thoughts returned to the present, where Abiron had just summoned him again. The angel had taken in Holly, RJ, and the others around Axel with a wide gesture. "You have all been assigned to me for the Lord's return to Earth."

"So the battle of the ages and Christ's thousand-year reign has arrived," RJ said, looking much younger than in the days of his humanity. His short gray hair had been replaced by a sandy shade of brown. His glasses, beard, and bulging gut had all been left behind as well.

"Yes, the prophecies will now be fulfilled," Abiron replied.

Brianna clasped her hands together. "Abiron, I didn't know I'd be going to war. I'm not much of a fighter, and I'm not really interested in becoming one."

"You do not need worry. The Lord will handle everything. All his ways are righteous, and he will not involve you in anything that will be unsuitable for you."

"That's good. I can't handle the sight of blood."

RJ smiled at her. "That won't be a problem either. It won't affect you that way anymore."

Many had now gathered around Abiron. Other groups also met with their lead angels nearby.

Marie rubbed the back of her neck. "I'm curious, Abiron. How much suffering will come from this war?"

"It will not go well for the Lord's enemies," Abiron said. "But their pain will be short-lived. He will take action very quickly. I know that many of you have questions and concerns, and I will have more time to answer them later. I can assure you that our God is in complete control. Please follow me now into the extra dimensions to begin our preparation."

Suddenly, Axel realized Arielle wasn't with them. He'd enjoyed so many great times with her in heaven and treasured every minute of it. Even though earthly marriage didn't apply in the afterlife, he still enjoyed her company immensely, and she cherished his as well. Their love for one another seemed to flourish on in the heavenly realm in even greater measure than before. He appreciated how deeply she understood him and how she never failed to keep him loose with her subtle sense of humor. But he hadn't seen her for quite a while now, and it had really begun to bother him. He felt her absence sharply.

He turned about, but she was nowhere to be found. *I don't want to go without her, but there just isn't enough time to search.* This train was leaving the station. Hopefully she would catch up with them in the next few minutes.

6

Returning

Axel followed right behind Abiron as the warrior angel rotated out to the extra three dimensions of the heavenly realm. His jaw dropped the moment he arrived. *I hardly even recognize this place.* He'd visited here many times before, moving freely throughout the expanse. Not much ever transpired, except maybe a few others going about their business. But now, countless white stallions stood in precisely ordered rows and columns for as far as his eye could see, as if every horse ever created on Earth, and then some, had been imported to heaven and painted glossy white.

Waves of colored light shone down from the throne, beaming through the formation with a spectacular prism effect. Millions of angels and believers rotated into the area, and choirs of angels sang choruses of praise.

"Wow, Abiron. Are these horses real?" Holly said.

"As real as can be," Abiron replied. "They have heavenly bodies just like you do."

"Where did they come from?"

"The Lord created them just for this. It will be like riding a horse on Earth, except that you will fly through other dimensions."

"And I'll bet they're a lot easier to take care of. No mess to clean up, right?"

The angel laughed and nodded emphatically. "Everyone please follow me. Our mounts are waiting."

Axel slid in behind Abiron along with the rest and moved toward the right flank of the heavenly army, passing other lead angels and their regiments along the way. Many from the other groups shouted greetings and encouragement as they went by. Axel drank in the excitement, and it stirred his insides as it made its way down. *This is going to be epic!*

Abiron stopped a short distance back from the front of the heavenly force and elevated onto a tall horse with a slick white coat and impassioned eyes. He placed his feet in the stirrups and said, "Please find the stallion assigned to you and mount up."

Axel counted maybe thirty rows of riders in front of them and scanned the horses in his immediate vicinity, spotting one right behind Abiron's with the word "Axel" engraved in the leather of its saddle. He moved quickly over and climbed aboard.

Holly hopped onto the horse to his right, and RJ jumped on the one right behind hers. But still no sign of Arielle. Surely she would be part of Abiron's group for the return to Earth, wouldn't she?

Brianna smiled from ear to ear. "Riding these horses is going to be a real treat."

"I'm glad you know what you're doing," Taj replied, looking distinctly uncomfortable atop his steed. "You'll need to show me how this is done."

"You won't need to know a thing," RJ said. "These boys will know exactly where to go."

Marie moved up close to her horse and began patting him gently at the base of the neck. "So beautiful," she said over and over.

Abiron's entire team had soon mounted into their saddles, and wild expectations of hurtling headlong through celestial domains consumed Axel's thoughts. He scanned the massive heavenly force. Millions and millions of riders stretched across the expanse, almost all of them behind him. He sat right where he wanted to be, near the front and near the action, ready to engage in the grand finale, the coup de grace, the ultimate conflict in all of humanity's existence. There was no other ticket in town that promised this much adventure.

Derek arched a sly brow and winked at Francisco. "I wonder what kind of weapons they're going to give us."

Taj turned, wide-eyed. "You mean like weapons of mass destruction?"

Francisco burst out laughing.

"What's so funny?" Taj said.

"This is the Lord's battle. Just sit back and watch."

Moments later, the choir of angels ceased from their choruses and the multitude quieted. The light shining down from the throne mutated from multicolored beams into rays of gold, drenching Axel and the masses of horses and riders around him.

With the sound of rushing waters, Jesus emerged on a white stallion at the front of the army. His steed trotted briskly back and forth, agitated and ready to run. Crowns adorned Jesus's head, and his fiery eyes looked out over his forces.

Axel's eyes gravitated to the words "King of Kings and Lord of Lords" emblazoned on Jesus's blood stained robe. *He's definitely dressed the part,* he thought. *Imposing* didn't even begin to describe him.

RJ elevated his arms and shouted, "Your kingdom come, my Lord!"

The entire multitude broke into a riot of cheers. Thunderous celebration rippled through the army, and resounding shouts rang out from every tongue. Eventually, all of their reverence came together in a rousing chant of "Our God reigns!", repeated over and over and over again.

A glistening angel rode to the front and stopped next to Jesus. He lifted his hand, and the praises faded to silence.

"Greetings," he roared, his voice echoing through the expanse. "The Day of our Lord has arrived. The time for his return to Earth has come. His enemies have gathered on the Plain of Esdraelon in northern Israel. Now the sign of the Son of Man will appear in the sky, and all the nations of the earth will mourn. They will see the Son of Man coming on the clouds of the sky with power and great glory."

Not more than an instant later, Jesus raised his fist high in the air. His stallion reared with front legs whirling and dashed off into the expanse. Immediately, the forward regiments raced in behind him.

Axel clenched his reins and watched intently. His passion climbed off the charts. Almighty God had launched his attack against those filled with hatred and wickedness, and the entire creation dripped with the drama.

Each row sprinted away in turn. Some rode standing up, others sat leaning forward in the saddle.

Abiron shouted out as his turn arrived and charged ahead.

Axel's stallion thrust forward and pushed him back in the saddle, reaching full velocity in moments, faster than Axel had ever moved through the expanse on his own. *Yeeah! Go, baby! Go!*

The wind rushed into his face.

Jubilant shouts rang out all around and mixed with the sound of the cavalry's galloping fury. Axel gave Francisco a pump of his fist, and Francisco sent one right back. Holly grinned from ear to ear. Vigor glowed in RJ's eyes.

Suddenly, the murky vapor appeared directly ahead. Axel shortened his reins and shouted, "He-ya!"

The forward regiments headed right into the mist and vanished. Abiron, Axel, and the rest followed in turn. Immediately, the bright light flooded Axel's vision and the whistling filled his ears just as before.

They passed through the haze and emerged into the darkness of the dimensions that intersected the physical universe.

Axel's stallion rushed ahead and then dropped downward in a head-spinning descent, glued to those in front of him. Jesus flattened his path and moved straight out into the expanse with the heavenly force right behind, each one still aligned in perfectly ordered rows and columns, all traveling at freakish speed.

Axel's eyes tracked the Lord. Jesus's glory blazed, and flames raged around him. Brilliant waves of light sprayed the first few rows of riders in his wake.

"Spectacular, isn't he?" Holly shouted.

"Yeah. Awesome. He never ceases to amaze me," Axel yelled back.

Holly looked forward again. "Abiron, does the Lord usually go this way?"

Abiron let out a quaking laugh. "No, he uses other dimensions of time and space. He can be everywhere at once. He is only taking this route for our sake."

"So is this where you fight with demons and evil spirits?" Derek shouted.

"Yes, many battles through the ages."

"Where are they now?"

"Oh they are here, hiding. They will not dare show their faces when the Lord comes around!"

"And what about Satan?"

"Somewhere closer to Earth . . . probably directing his followers."

Holly glanced back over her shoulder. "Oh my, look behind us!"

Axel turned and beheld the swarm of riders following them, all shining in white, reflecting God's purity against the black background of space. Virtue's legions had entered the realm of rebellion, and all hideaways would be exposed. "Stunning," he replied.

Suddenly, Taj shouted, "Hey, the Lord's turning!"

Jesus's crowns glimmered and his eyes blazed as he led the army into a long, gliding turn, still at a blistering pace but now heading toward a particular star. He veered to the right and then around the roaring inferno. Axel recognized the desolate surface of Venus as it came into view, looking completely scorched. A lifeless desert as always.

They passed quickly by the barren planet, and Earth emerged. Axel hardly recognized it. Its appearance had changed drastically from his previous visit with Abiron. No more stunning blue oceans. No more lush green jungles and forests. Just devastated landmasses and mud-red bodies of water. *Man's evil has definitely taken its toll.*

The Lord slowed their pace as they approached, passing by the moon on their left, still in the dimensions intersecting the physical universe. The earth grew larger and larger in front of them, with the blood-tainted Pacific filling Axel's view. He knew his resurrected body couldn't get sick, but nausea filled his soul.

Closer and closer they came. Axel saw a flicker of light, and a gust of wind blew against his face. The air immediately became colder, heavier, and thicker.

"His majesty just rotated us in," Abiron shouted.

"The earth's dimensions?" RJ said.

"Yes, we have arrived."

Axel shook his head. *This is really heavy.* The world had become a totally different place—a sculpture devoid of its original beauty. A masterpiece defaced and scarred, trashed by the depravity of vandals. Almost none of God's original artistry remained.

Jesus descended nearer to the surface, and Axel sensed the temperature rising.

Holly twisted her nose and shouted, "What's that awful smell?"

"I'm afraid it's the smell of death, my dear," RJ said. "All sea life has perished."

"Tragic," Axel replied, mourning as he remembered his many close encounters with dolphins, sea lions, and the like during his surfing days.

Islands came into view in the distance.

"I still haven't figured out where we are," Derek yelled.

"French Polynesia," Axel replied. "That's Tahiti up ahead."

They passed over Papeete, and Axel reminisced about a trip he had made to the island in high school, running through its dense tropical forests and riding the waves of its azure blue seas. But now, boats lay broken on the shore, trees lay fallen, and buildings had burned and collapsed to the ground.

"That must be Australia," Marie shouted, pointing toward the horizon.

Seconds later, the front of the army made its way into the skies over the Aussie nation. Many towns lay desolate and abandoned. Activity seemed nonexistent, even in the large cities. Vehicles lined the roads, but they remained almost still.

"Why is everything just barely creeping along down there?" Holly said.

"Because they are moving in the time dimension of the earth," Abiron replied.

"And we're not?"

"Not yet. We have entered the earth's dimensions of space, but we are still in a different time dimension. We will circle the globe in this time dimension to fulfill the prophecy of Luke 17: 'For the Son of Man in his day will be like the lightning, which flashes and lights up the sky from one end to the other.' And from Revelation 1: 'Look, he is coming with the clouds, and every eye will see him, even those who pierced him; and all the peoples of the earth will mourn because of him.'"

"I don't get it," Derek said.

"Let me try," RJ replied. "Time is moving very quickly for us, making life on earth appear to be almost suspended. We will be able to fly over the entire planet while time stands almost still below us so that when we enter the time dimension of the earth, everyone will see us at once, no matter where they are."

Axel nodded and shouted, "You've still got it, Uncle RJ."

He had always appreciated RJ's insight into the science of it all, even though the administration back at the high school didn't. His uncle had tried to stand up for truth, truth that Axel had now personally experienced. "Boy, those people who brought your teaching career to an end look pretty silly now, don't they?"

A smile made its way across RJ's face. "Mystery Babylon has fallen. That satanic, man-centered system of politics, religion, and commerce is now gone. No more hatred. No more wicked agendas. No more devastated souls. God *is* good, isn't he?"

They moved swiftly over Indonesia, then over Southeast Asia and up through China. Land masses flashed by in a matter of seconds. Smoke rose from fires and volcanoes. Disaster masked the ground everywhere, and blood saturated the waters.

They covered India and the Middle East and then dashed over the Red Sea into Africa. Activity stood almost still in all of the cities and towns. Erector-set buildings and Hot Wheel cars had more oomph.

As they traveled, Axel's thoughts wandered back to the kicks of the heavenly realm, where he had bolted about void of any abandon or barrier and without any reliance on a supernatural pony. Somewhere over the Serengeti, he shouted, "Abiron, do I still need this horse?"

"Oh, you want to fly?" the angel replied.

"Yeah, can I?"

"No, you will drop like a rock."

"Really? I thought I'd be able to move freely here."

"That only applies in the extra dimensions. Rotate in and rotate out. In these dimensions you are subject to the earth's physical laws."

The Lord then led them out over the Atlantic. They reached the east coast of Brazil and raced across all of South and Central America, finally approaching the United States as darkness fell.

"This isn't going to be easy, seeing our homes devastated," Marie said.

"I don't know," Taj replied. "I'm not looking back. Life is so much better now."

"I don't disagree, but I have memories here, of God's blessings that I'm still thankful for. All that he gave us. Our kids. Our homes. His mercy and grace."

"I'm with you, Marie," Francisco said. "He was very good to me."

They stormed into the US over Texas and turned to the east, through the Southern states and then up the Atlantic coast. The destruction here rivaled that of every other place they'd seen. Atlanta, New York, and Boston had all incurred tremendous damage. They then weaved their way west, covering parts of Canada as well.

Axel recognized familiar sights as they arrived in California. They made their way north along the coast, coming to the cities between San Diego and Los Angeles where he'd made his home. He remembered learning to surf as a young boy at one particular beach and climbing with his friends on the lofty bluffs of another. The grim reality of the carnage gripped him inside.

They continued up the Pacific coast and on into Canada. After passing through Russia, they rapidly canvased all of Europe.

Spain and Portugal zoomed by in a blink, and the Lord made a left turn at Gibraltar. Axel's anticipation of their imminent conflict soared as they entered the home stretch. Over the bloody Mediterranean off the coast of Morocco they charged toward the Holy Land, their final destination, where the forces of evil had assembled seeking to deny Jesus of his rightful claim to the throne as King of Kings and Lord of Lords.

7

Conquering

Jesus moved the heavenly army into the primary time dimension of the earth, making them visible to every man, woman, and child. Eyes snapped to the sky, consumed by the spectacle of divine glory, and those indoors dashed outside to survey the commotion.

The Lord's radiant crowns and scorching eyes enticed the attention of every soul as his stallion charged through the air, leaving no question as to his identity. Right behind, multitudes of pure white heavenly riders followed and eclipsed every slice of the heavens above, streaming forth for a half-hour or more until the last of them rode away over the horizon and out of view.

Terror filled the hearts of those who had rejected Christ, but believers rejoiced with loud cheers and shouting.

✷

Axel looked down on the Mediterranean from high above the surface. Small ships now cruised across the crimson waters, and the sound of the wind rushed into his ears.

"We're back among the living," Holly said. "I'm starting to feel it, aren't you?"

"The breeze?" Axel replied.

"No, the tension . . . the anticipation of what the Lord's going to do. Don't you have a pulse in that chest of yours?"

"Technically, no. But yeah, I am getting pretty fired up."

Axel peered toward the horizon as they surged ahead. The morning sun rose in the east without a single cloud in the sky. Smoke cloaked the coastlines to each side, and long vessels spiked with cannons and artillery came into view out front. His first dance with the enemy stood right before him.

"What kind of ships are those?" Brianna said.

"Some battleships, some destroyers," Derek replied. "Man, that's a lot of firepower."

WHOOSH! Suddenly, a blur whizzed right under Axel's horse. A resounding boom sounded twice. A bright light flashed, and metal and flames scattered everywhere. Smoke smothered him like a blanket, and the smell of sulfur clogged his nose. Seconds later, he emerged into the open air again and turned to survey the area. "What was that?"

"Something hit me really hard!" Holly shouted. "Right on the side of my horse and on the lower part of my leg. It almost knocked me completely off. Like a rhinoceros slammed into me or I don't know what."

"Are you okay?" Derek yelled.

"I think so. Nothing hurts, and everything's still here."

"Surface-to-air missile," Francisco said. "I saw it at the last moment."

Taj grinned from ear to ear. "Mom, you're indestructible!"

"Woo-hoo!" Holly shouted back.

As Axel laughed, Francisco pointed to his right, toward the shores of North Africa. "It must have come from down there. I guess the opposition knows we're here."

Axel raised his eyes to see thousands of jet fighters storming out of the south, dropping down from high altitude, darkening the sky like a swarm of angry bees.

"Abiron, what should we do?" Brianna yelled.

"Hold steady. We must stay the course."

Missiles ejected from the furious swarm. Axel grasped tightly to the reins as countless numbers whistled past on each side, but not a single missile connected. *Can't they do any better than that?* Was this the best the world's finest pilots had to offer?

The planes continued to close in. Axel tracked their path, discerning the markings of many different countries on their wings and tails. He had never dreamed he'd be able to see with such fine detail.

The fighters soared into the airspace directly ahead at an elevation slightly above. "They're heading right for us!" he shouted.

"Brace yourselves!" Derek yelled.

Axel ducked and slapped his hand on top of his head as the lead planes screamed past just yards away with a deafening roar and plunged nose-first into the water. The entire formation followed right behind, and jet after jet crashed into the sea below. The smell of exhaust infected the air. Many burst into flames as they smashed into floating debris, and towering liquid explosions and raging firestorms erupted. Within seconds it was over.

"Awesome!" Taj yelled.

Axel looked back upon the burning wreckage, astounded by the outcome. "What was up with that?"

"The Lord made some *adjustments* to their flight controls," Abiron said.

RJ raised his chin. "Ah yes, the rerouting of a few electrons would certainly do the trick."

They sped onward. Gusts continued to press into Axel's face, disheveling his shaggy hair in every direction.

BOOM! BOOM! BOOM! The air shook with far more force than the previous missile attacks. Jesus bolted ahead without wavering even as the blasts came more and more frequently.

"Must be cruise missiles," Derek said. "But they're exploding before they get to us."

"The Lord's countermeasures again," Abiron replied.

Marie peered intently through an opening in the smoke. "I see the coast of Israel up ahead."

"I see it too," Brianna said. "How far away are we?"

"Probably eighty to a hundred miles," RJ replied. "We'll be there in less than a minute."

Ferocious blasts continued to rattle Axel's teeth. His horse began to descend, and all at once the explosions ceased. He emerged from the smoke and debris to see Israel's shoreline directly ahead. The sound of a soft current of air floated into his ears, but a drum line pounded inside his head. The battle of the ages was about to begin. *Time to turn up the volume.*

His mind wandered into the sense-of-purpose space again. He'd spent his entire existence in heaven awestruck by God's throne and God's glory, but he'd also hoped Jesus would thrust him into a vital role serving with Abiron and the angels who opposed fallen spirits. Jesus had encouraged Axel that a vital calling awaited him, but not necessarily one among the angelic ranks. And it would be a calling that Axel would need to wait patiently for, one that would be given at an appointed time yet future. *Maybe that time has come*, he thought. He was ready for whatever his king would ask him to do.

"There's Tel Aviv!" Marie shouted. "It looks like we'll make landfall just north of the city."

Jesus charged forward over the beach, not far above the ground. Axel looked up and saw foothills directly ahead in the distance. Desecrated fields rushed by below.

His stallion tracked with those in front of him as they made a wide, arcing turn to the north and flew parallel to the coast. The sprawling heavenly force covered the entire width of the plain, miles and miles across. Axel searched the ground for signs of the enemy, but to his surprise, he didn't detect a single soul.

Holly turned and looked back to the west. "Hey, not everyone came ashore with us. Most of them stopped out over the sea."

"Only so many will fit on the battlefield," Abiron replied. "It is not a large area. They will join us later in Jerusalem."

Axel inspected the dreadful damage below, viewing catastrophe even more disastrous than the other places they'd been. A stampede had seemingly run through the fields, the houses appeared to have been gutted and razed, and the fruit trees had all withered or burned. *This earth doesn't hold much appeal as a place to live.* He reminisced about the beauty and grandeur of heaven and lamented about having to leave it. A thousand years was a long time to dwell in a wasteland like this.

Abiron turned to him. "Very grim it is. There is no doubt about that."

"It's worse than I could have ever imagined."

"A few of years ago, armies from the north invaded Israel. With the shortages of food and other resources at the time, this area became very desirable, and they ravaged the countryside. The Lord sent hail, fire, plagues, and earthquakes to defend his people. The invaders all turned on each other, and Israel was delivered. The people stood in awe of God, and it drove them to commit their lives to him."

"I'm truly glad for the people of Israel, but the land is completely devastated."

"I know it looks bad now, but the Lord will bring good out of this also."

"That's got to be Mount Carmel up ahead," RJ shouted.

Jesus continued to surge forward. His bloodstained robe flowed in the wind, and waves of sunlight reflected off his crowns. Within moments he'd ascended Carmel's peak and ridden over it, disappearing from view.

Axel approached the summit, and his horse's pace began to ease. With each stride it trotted slower and slower, now hovering just a few yards above the surface. *What are we doing? Now isn't the time to hit the brakes.* He stood up in the stirrups to get a look ahead, but he only saw other regiments inching forward near the top. "Abiron, what's going on?"

"Enemy forces cover the valley on the other side. There is not enough room for us to land, so the Lord is going to create some space."

Axel squinted. Was Jesus going to add more sand and extend the beaches?

Moments later, he reached the peak and crept slowly over. *Oh, man! Standing room only at this party!* Crashers had forced their way into the seats at the tables and filled every square inch of the floor.

Rival troops and weaponry carpeted the land in every direction for as far as he could see. Countless units stood positioned across the fields to the north and on the entire stretch of the plain to the east.

His stallion came to a halt. Those in front of him had stopped behind the Lord at the base of the mountain, and silence pervaded the ranks.

"I'd be really scared right now if Jesus weren't here," Brianna said.

"I don't think we're the ones who need to be afraid," Taj replied.

Brianna brought her hand to her lips. "They must have heard you. Look, they're fleeing like mice."

Holly pointed at something high in the sky above. "I'd be running too if I were them."

Axel tilted his head back. A massive wall of fire came tumbling down from the heights of the atmosphere, a raging inferno with flames seething out. Axel's mouth flew open at the sight of it. The fire plunged all the way to the ground and settled lengthwise along the entire base of the mountain in front of the Lord, blazing at least two stories high and completely engulfing the landscape in both directions.

"He is so consistent," RJ shouted.

Axel shook his head. "What do you mean?"

"He did the same thing right here a long time ago, during the time of Elijah."

"Whoa, you're right." Derek said. "Priests of Baal and fire from the sky."

Jesus landed his stallion on the ground and galloped to the north with the wall of fire in front of him, consuming everyone and everything in its path. Axel watched in astonishment as soldiers attempted to flee toward the coast, screaming in panic as they went, but the mass of bodies and equipment in front of them thwarted their escape. Many were trampled, but most burned in the flames. Others tried desperately to shove those behind them out of the way, thrusting a throng of humanity backward toward the sea.

"How many miles will the Lord ride?" RJ said.

"About twenty, to the hills of upper Galilee," Abiron replied. "Just far enough for all of us to land."

RJ brought his hand to his chin. "Is that really a big enough area for all these horses? I'm guessing there's probably at least fifty million of us."

"These stallions have completed their mission. We will dismount at the base of the mountain."

"What will happen to them after that?" Marie said.

"They will return to heaven by the way they came. There is plenty of space for them there."

"And we'll continue on foot?"

"Yes, all the way to Jerusalem."

A short time passed, and the ranks stirred again. Axel stood up in his saddle and looked out over the plain. Choruses of cheers escalated around him, and shouts of praise rang out as Jesus rode triumphantly back. The wall of fire no longer stood in front of him and no enemy troops could be seen.

Axel sat amazed. His Lord had leveled the anthills of the world's greatest armies and stamped out all of their pesky inhabitants in a matter of minutes. Megatons of military firepower. Billions of dollars of sophisticated war technology.

No bounds existed to his potency, yet the extent of his ability to express love and kindness also knew no limits. This same invincible force never hesitated to pour out adoration and compassion on his followers, just as he had after Axel passed away from Earth.

Axel thought back to the dazzling colored light that had greeted him upon his entry into the heavenly realm—beams that ribboned around his fingers and up his arms, all in turquoise and indigo and sapphire, and the deluge of warmth and love that had pulsed through them.

He recalled the flash that soon after eclipsed his vision. Rays of gold and white that surged in from all directions and enveloped him in sheer radiance.

His eyes had adjusted as the new, brighter waves of light settled around him. A thundering voice like rushing waters called out,

"Axel!" It shook the air yet rang more personally than any voice he'd ever heard, as if the caller knew him even better than he knew himself. A tempest of love rushed through his being.

"Axel!" the voice roared again. It echoed through the expanse and rumbled sweeter than honey.

He turned and beheld the outline of a glorious figure—a man, but so much more than a man—a figure of majesty and grandeur, dressed in a robe reaching down to his feet with a golden sash around his chest. His hair hung white like wool, purer than the whitest snow, and his eyes blazed like fire. His feet glowed like bronze in a furnace, and his face shone like the sun in all its brilliance. The Holiest of Holies!

Axel immediately dropped to his knees, still hovering in the vast expanse. "Lord Jesus, my King and my God!"

"Rise, Axel my child," Jesus said.

Axel's focus snapped to the Lord's eyes, pools of enchantment, deeper than the most dazzling ocean he could imagine, more loving than a mother's first glance at her newborn child.

"Know my peace, my faithful servant," Jesus said. "I have loved you since before the beginning of time. Now it is time for you to be with me in my kingdom, prepared for you from before the creation of the world."

Axel stood speechless. The Lord's glory overwhelmed his thoughts. After a moment he found the words. "So I'm . . . I'm in heaven?"

Jesus smiled and placed his hand on Axel's shoulder.

It was true.

"Through my resurrection, you now have an inheritance that can never perish. I have kept it safe for you here."

Axel's thoughts rushed incoherently, struggling even to keep up. He felt a strong sense of gratitude, a sense that he didn't *deserve* to be here, yet here he was. "Lord . . . thank you, I don't deserve this . . . I'm just so grateful. I know you made this possible through your suffering for me." Axel looked down at his feet. "And this body you've given me . . . it feels so incredible."

"Yes. Your old body was sown perishable, but your new body has been raised imperishable," Jesus replied. "Your old body was sown in dishonor; your new body has been raised in glory. Your old body was sown in weakness; your new body has been raised in power. Your old body was sown a natural body; your new body has been raised a spiritual one."

The words were all vaguely familiar, but they meant something so much more now. "Imperishable? In power? This is epic! Lord, I didn't get it." All his questions, all his doubts about heaven, sounded like a joke now. "I didn't realize things would really be different and better here. I'm sorry for doubting."

The Lord smiled. "All doubt is now cast away. I have raised you up and seated you with me in the heavenly realm, in order that in the coming ages I might show you the incomparable riches of my grace."

The *incomparable* riches of his grace? Axel tried and tried, but he couldn't grasp the extent of what was happening to him. How much blessing could an infinite, almighty, all-knowing God bestow? Certainly treasures beyond anything he could conceive. The prospects seemed limitless, and he yearned for Jesus to say more.

One old question came to the surface. "Thank you, thank you so much, Lord. And what will you have me do in these coming ages that you speak about?"

"I know the worries you had on Earth, but you have no need for those concerns here. You are my workmanship, created in me to do good works, which I prepared in advance for you to do. That is why you possess an eagerness to serve and a hunger for purpose in my kingdom. I promise you, my son, that hunger will be fulfilled."

Axel felt himself blushing inside. "Please excuse your servant for asking, but you won't be upset with me if I desire to do something more than just singing and dancing around your throne?" The blush deepened as he realized just how thickheaded that sounded. "Don't get me wrong, I'm sure beholding your majesty there will be nothing short of amazing, just like it is now."

Jesus smiled. "I have made you to be a priest to serve my Father for his glory forever and ever. You seek to bring glory to his name because I have given you that desire. You will be able to say to a mountain 'Move from here to there,' and it will move. Nothing will be impossible for you."

Nothing would be impossible? Axel's expectations swirled with wonder. Visions of hoisting the foundations of long-established obstacles to more fitting locales, whatever that meant. Images of skimming on light waves through the oceans of heaven's realm. He had no perception of how far this could go. "Lord, this is all so incredible, but how will I know what you want me to do?"

"The Counselor is with you, as he has been and will be with you forever, the Spirit of Truth. He will bring glory to me by taking what is mine and making it known to you."

"So I'll still have choices?"

"Yes, many, but only in righteousness. You have fought the good fight. You have finished the race and kept the faith. Now you will have your crown of righteousness. Come, walk with me."

They strode together between the colors of light streaming through the expanse. They talked about Axel's life, the pains he had suffered and much of what he had never understood, and then about his future in the Lord's presence.

His heart had burned as they talked, exhilarated beyond anything he'd ever experienced. All of his adrenaline rushes on Earth—the heaviest waves he'd ridden—they had all faded to the back of his memory.

His focus returned to the present as Jesus moved to the right flank of the army at the base of the mountain and motioned for the first row of stallions to descend.

Axel made his way to the bottom of the hill behind Abiron and slid off of his horse. His gallant steed bolted toward the heavenly realm, and he followed it with his eyes until it disappeared from view. He moved to his place in the formation next to Francisco. "It's like going back to the neighborhood you grew up in after a long time away. The sights, the sounds, the smells . . . they're all so familiar, but the houses look different, and the people you knew don't live there anymore."

"You're right about that," Francisco replied. "This is almost surreal."

"I couldn't agree more," Holly said. "I was so caught up in myself the last time I was here. Hurrying everywhere. Worried about stupid things. Rarely trusting the Lord."

"This time it'll be different," Francisco said. "Having seen what we've seen, we're going to live really differently here. There's no doubt in my mind."

Axel watched intently as others came off the mountain, scanning the faces for Arielle, but she never showed up. *She must be with the group that didn't come ashore. I'll have to meet up with her when we get to Jerusalem.* He missed her already.

Jesus turned his stallion to the southeast and initiated his charge. Axel marched fervently, still about thirty rows behind, understanding that his role for now consisted of remaining in formation. His eternal calling still hadn't arrived, and Armageddon had begun. *No time to ponder anything other than the task at hand.*

He quickly traversed all obstacles, swimming rapidly across rivers and streams and effortlessly scaling walls and other barriers in the abandoned towns, feeling like some kind of video-game avatar. But fantasy held no claim here. This was the real deal.

"Look at all these high-tech weapons," Taj said, kicking at a rifle in the dirt as they passed. Other weapons littered the road on all sides. "They just left them here."

"I think they know what they're up against," Derek replied. "Almighty God is right on their heels."

Flocks of soldiers came into view ahead, and Jesus charged on at a blistering pace. Once again, the enormous wall of fire fell from the sky and moved forward in front of him, expanding and contracting with the width of the plain. The searing temperature pressed against Axel's skin, and the heat of the chase burned inside his chest. Within moments, the Lord overcame those at the back of the enemy army and continued to advance, leaving only ashes in his wake.

Axel moved on at a feverish pace near the edge of the heavenly force with glowing embers under his feet. An isolated, pyramid-like peak appeared on his left, and a boomerang-shaped mountain range emerged on his right. Jesus made a right turn into an expansive lowland with a river running down the center and drove directly to the south. *This must be the Jordan Valley.*

More and more enemy troops perished under the wall of fire. Axel's feet dashed steadfastly ahead, and he continued to watch it all unfold, but he felt like little more than a spectator. The battle of the ages hadn't turned out to be much of a "battle" at all. Jesus had asserted his authority and deity with absolute power and dominion, and Axel strode on humbly in awe. He tried not to let disappointment mar the majesty of the moment, but he'd hoped to do more than just march idly behind.

8
Ascending

Jesus halted the army's advance. The wall of fire stood motionless from one side of the valley to the other, and the sun shone high in the midday sky, free from any clouds or haze. He then turned his horse to the west and trotted off toward the hills.

Axel turned to Abiron. "Where's he going?"

"You will find out. He has requested that we join him."

Axel and the rest of Abiron's group broke away with two other regiments and sprinted in behind the Lord. The rest of the army remained in the midst of the valley.

Axel couldn't think of why he and the others had been singled out. Maybe to witness another of the Lord's remarkable triumphs? That would certainly be cool. He would respectfully pull up a chair and observe whatever was about to take place.

Jesus led them to the edge of the wall of fire and around it toward the south, now with uncharred ground beneath them. They dashed along the base of the hills and approached an oasis city brimming with palms. Axel scanned the abandoned buildings. No signs of life crept anywhere, and heaviness and depravity hung thick in the air. A spiritual fog of epic proportions.

Axel figured they would enter the city, but Jesus turned to the west instead and rode up into the hills. Higher and higher in elevation they climbed.

Holly whispered to RJ, "Do you know what city that was?"

"Jericho," he said softly.

"Where the walls fell down?"

"Yes, but that's the modern city. The ancient ruins are about a mile away."

"Do you know what the Lord's searching for?"

"He is not searching," Abiron interrupted. "He knows exactly where he is going."

Holly's eyes widened. "I forgot how good your hearing is. I didn't want to bother you again."

"It is never a bother, daughter of the most high."

"It's like we're on some kind of special forces mission or something," Holly replied. "So serious and secretive. And maybe it's just me, but it's kind of odd: the steps keep getting harder."

Strangely, Axel's drive began to wane as well. The spiritual darkness clasped heavier upon him with each stride, weighing down on his shoulders and projecting a pasty-gray haze in the air.

Jesus turned into a small rift valley. Rocky crags swallowed up the sides of the lowland, blocking any other way in or out.

All at once, six tanks became visible through the mist, with chrome cannon barrels aimed directly at them. Armored transport vehicles loomed right behind. Axel raised his eyebrows and slowed his gait. *Whoa, Nellie!*

The tanks opened fire. BOOM! BOOM! Explosions ignited all around. Blast after blast rumbled the ground, splitting up the landscape as charcoal smoke rose into the air. Unfazed, Jesus rode forward.

Axel marched in formation some distance behind, deafened by the thunderous barrage.

BOOM! Suddenly, a massive thrust detonated into his chest, punching him backward with a brilliant burst of light. The next thing he knew, he lay looking up at the sky.

"Axel!" Holly screamed. "Are you okay?"

RJ, Francisco, and others scrambled over.

Axel shook his head and looked to one side and then the other. Dirt flew around him. Shells burst above him. He moved his hand over his torso and down onto his stomach. No rips. No cuts. No wounds anywhere.

"Thanks, but I'm good," he said.

With smoke still rising off his body, he let out a roaring laugh, jumped back to his feet, and resumed his stride.

Jesus turned his head and looked Axel right in the eyes, his gaze laser-like, pouring love and affirmation into the core of Axel's soul. Axel stopped and stood captivated. The Lord's clear reminder connected like a right hook. Patience still applied, and paths still needed straightening. Reigning with Jesus in his kingdom wouldn't be any spectator sport, and exhilaration *would* present itself at every turn.

Axel marched on with a spring in his step. A tank shell had knocked his body to the ground, but Jesus's cannonball notice had floored him even more. The Lord hadn't given him a specific assignment yet, but he'd blown away all of Axel's concerns about his future calling.

Explosions continued to blast all around, and shrapnel showered each step Axel took. Smoke and dirt enveloped his body, but he pressed on, undeterred.

Jesus raised his hand, and the heavenly contingent came to a halt. The thundering explosions continued for another few seconds and then ceased. Moments later, Axel heard shouting and loud voices cursing blasphemies against the name of God. The silhouettes of angels came into view through the dissipating smoke, pulling two creatures from one of the armored vehicles. A few more seconds and it all became clear.

"Satan's instruments of the last days," Abiron said. "Their time here has come to an end."

The Lord's blazing eyes stared right at the duo, but he didn't utter a sound. Profanity spewed from their mouths as they raged against him with sheer hatred and rebellion. Axel shuddered at the sound. Angels secured the two beasts and hoisted them into the sky, apparently escorting them to their prophesied end.

Axel stood tall and shouted, "My Lord and my God!"

Jesus turned toward his regiments, and Axel fell to his knees along with the rest, again overcome by the Lord's greatness, again overwhelmed by his glory. They spent the next few minutes pouring out praise to him, and Jesus heaped his abundant love right back on them.

Jesus then retraced the way down through the hills, and Axel replayed the entire episode in his mind. "Abiron, what happened to me back there? Holly wasn't knocked off her horse when that missile hit her."

"Simple answer," Holly cut in with a smirk. "You just don't have what it takes."

Axel laughed and shook his head.

"Actually, it wasn't her; it was her horse. Those stallions are affected by gravity in a different way," Abiron said. "Her horse absorbed the impact of the missile, so she was able to ride on without any problems."

They marched back to the north along the foothills. Jesus soon reached the edge of the wall of fire and moved around behind it. Those on the right flank of the army erupted into loud cheers that spread through the entire crowd, and rousing chants of "Our God reigns! Our God reigns!" rang out, sending the sound of their celebration echoing through the valley.

After Axel and the others had returned to their places in the formation, Jesus advanced with the wall of fire in front of him again. All the way down the Jordanian plain he charged, consuming enemy troops and equipment in his path. A short time later, the wall of fire vanished into thin air, and the shore of the Dead Sea came into view.

The Lord brought the army to a halt and turned his stallion to the east. He dashed off, with a number of regiments from the left flank falling in behind. Axel pushed up onto his tiptoes and strained to peer over the crowd. *Must be another commando raid.* This time he would remain content as a spectator, though. An onlooker without any reservation or agenda.

"The Lord has gone to take out the enemy forces that have retreated into the desert," Abiron said. "He will circle the sea and advance upon Jerusalem from the south. On the way, he will pass through ancient Edom, just as Isaiah prophesied. We will approach Jerusalem from the east and meet the Lord there. The enemy have either fled this area or have taken up positions in the Holy City, so we will not see much of them along the way."

The angel paused and turned toward Holly. "Any questions?"

Holly smiled. "You explained everything perfectly."

"For the first time, I guess," he replied, grinning.

The heat of the late afternoon sun warmed Axel's skin as he marched. Upward in elevation he climbed, moving briskly without even an inkling of fatigue. A hike like this would have required plenty of water and numerous breaks during his previous stint on Earth, but those old symptoms of decay wreaked havoc on his body no more.

Eventually, neighborhoods appeared in front of him.

"The outskirts of Jerusalem," Abiron said. "Before us lies the northeast side."

Bloodstains tainted the earth under Axel's feet. The skeletons of houses and buildings stood ransacked and burned. Windows lay shattered, and garbage and debris littered the ground, all reminders of the treacherous souls they were dealing with.

"Enemy troops have built up their strongholds inside the city, and many Israelis remain captive among them," Abiron said. "But the Lord's forces now surround the area. Those who didn't come ashore at Mount Carmel now stand positioned in the central mountains to the north and the west."

Axel continued to advance through the streets on the northeast side, eventually coming to the top of a ridge with thousands of gravestones scattered below. Jerusalem sprawled on the other side of the valley, the sight of it stopping Axel cold, staggered by what lay before him.

He reflected on photographs Arielle had shown him long ago, though he'd never actually visited. Portraits of an ancient city with timeless beauty. Pictures of diverse cultures and alluring artistic venues. Her portrayal had etched a flawless image of this place, but the desolation in front of him now gouged a deep gash in those memories.

The remembrances brought Arielle's voice ringing back in his mind and echoing in his ears. Surely she had arrived in the area, but he had no idea where she might be among the millions surrounding him. And she wouldn't have any idea as to his whereabouts either. Sadly, he would have to continue to wait this out.

"Our next move will be to the north," Abiron said.

Confusion swept across Axel's face. "We're going to march to the north?"

Abiron just smiled and winked at Holly. "No, we are staying right here, but we will be moving to the north."

"Hey, the Lord's up there behind us," Marie shouted.

Axel turned to see Jesus standing near the top of the Mount of Olives, no longer riding his white stallion. His garments gleamed, his crowns shone, and his eyes blazed. *With majesty upon majesty!* Axel thought. *With glory upon glory!*

Jesus raised his hands and fixed his eyes toward heaven. Reverence and awe surged inside Axel again. He began to drop to his knees but hesitated as an enormous jolt shook the ground. The earth quaked like a jackhammer. Upheaval drowned out every other sound.

"Hey, we're moving!" Taj yelled.

Holly pointed to a huge crack opening in front of Jesus from the top of the Mount of Olives all the way to the bottom. "He's making a crater or something!"

The intense rumbling continued, and the crevasse became larger and larger, now burgeoning into a gorge. Axel sprinted to the rim and watched as the widening crack thundered onward into the city, splitting the earth apart just to the north of the Temple Mount.

The shaking came to an end a few minutes later. A perfectly formed valley now ran in both directions as far as he could see, right through the heart of Jerusalem.

A huge commotion broke out just down the hill.

"Look at all those people running out of the city!" Brianna yelled. "They're coming right toward us!"

Axel turned to Abiron. "Is the battle back on?"

Abiron shook his head with a faint smile. "No, they are not the enemy."

A wave of humanity pressed up the Mount of Olives. Within moments, a young man and woman trudged over the rim right in front of Axel, each one gasping for air. They bent over, their bodies frail and thin, their clothes soiled and stained, their hair tangled and matted.

Axel stepped back. *Is there a doctor nearby?*

Marie rushed over, followed closely by the others. "Are you okay?"

The young man sat down on the ground. "You don't know how glad we are to see you. We've been trapped inside the city for months."

"By soldiers?"

"Yes," he said, panting. "It was like a nightmare. The ground started to shake, and they began attacking one another. As we were trying to find shelter, their skin began to rot right off their bodies. They basically disintegrated in front of us. We just ran as fast as we could."

Axel stayed cool as he listened, but his imagination spun out of control. Images of zombie invasions bounced through his mind. Disfigured personages with blood splattered about and skeletal sections revealed. He used to enjoy a good horror flick, but this sounded a little too over the top.

Derek walked up with a jug of water and some bread and handed it to the newcomers.

"Thank you . . . and thanks to the Lord for everything," the young man said.

"We're just happy that you're free now," Marie said. "Would you share your names with us?"

"I'm Hadassa, and this is Maor," replied the young woman.

"I think it's safe to say that your lives will be much better from now on."

Hadassa's eyes shone as she took a sip of water. "We've been praying for your arrival. The Bible told us you were coming with the Lord. You're the Risen Ones, aren't you?"

Marie looked at her curiously. "Risen Ones?"

"Yeah . . . his priests. That's what his Word says, right?"

"I think so. I just hadn't heard it said that way before."

At that moment, an angel strode by and handed Axel a palm branch. Choruses broke out from higher up on the Mount of Olives, and many others moved in around him, fixing their gazes out over the rim and up the hill. Axel leaned forward and saw Jesus riding down the center of the valley on a donkey. He raised his branch high in the air, and a smile swept across his face. The King of Kings was making his way to the throne. He recognized the words of the song and joined in the singing. "Hosanna! Hosanna! Blessed is he who comes in the name of the Lord!"

"Hey, didn't this happen the first time he was here?" Brianna shouted over the din.

"Yes, but who will reject him now?" RJ replied. "I don't think anyone will have a problem welcoming him for keeps this time."

The sun began to set on the horizon, and hues of crimson and lavender and apricot beamed across the sky. Axel waved his palm branch with vigor as Jesus rode past. *All glory be to the King of Kings and Lord of Lords!*

Jesus arrived at the bottom of the hill and rode through the gate into the city. Axel's eyes remained anchored upon him as he proceeded onto the Temple Mount and stepped off his donkey. Crowds danced and sang around him, continuing their profuse worship and celebration as he made his way through the courts and into the temple building itself.

"Some of my angelic colleagues have purified the grounds from the recent abominations," Abiron said. "The temple now brims with holiness, glistening pristine and perfect over every square inch. A large golden throne now stands in the Holy of Holies, and the Lord will take his rightful place upon it. Our God now reigns over all the earth. The kingdom is now established!"

"Praise God!" RJ exclaimed. Axel nodded, overcome by the wonder of the moment.

Suddenly, a massive pillar of fire materialized above the temple, extending high into the night, furious and turbulent. Axel leaned his head back with his mouth open wide. The flames didn't seem to top out anywhere. They extended far beyond the earth's atmosphere, onward into the realm of starry hosts.

After a moment of marveling, the encounter with Jesus that afternoon reeled back into his mind. The God of all creation had taken the time to fill him with personal care and encouragement, even in the midst of something so monumental as the apocalypse, and it meant everything to him.

But what does it mean to serve as a priest in the kingdom? Certainly purpose and exhilaration would saturate all of it. He had finished his bout with impatience, but curiosity wouldn't leave him alone. *Where will this calling take me?* The Lord's reign extended over the entire planet, and quite possibly Axel's duties would land him far away from here. To a role filled with vitality and elation. He couldn't wait to get started.

9

Restoration

Axel spotted a solemn look on Abiron's face as the group stood on the Mount of Olives facing Jerusalem. He'd never seen the warrior angel so pensive. Something must be going on.

"Our mission has come to an end," Abiron said. "It has been my pleasure to serve with each of you. I know you will be tremendously blessed here in the Lord's kingdom."

Alarm blanketed Holly's face. "Wait, you're leaving us?"

"Yes, the Lord requires my presence elsewhere. I am off to other dimensions where agents of evil still remain."

"So it's time to put the adversary away," RJ said.

"Yes," Abiron said with great satisfaction. "We will secure him and his followers in the abyss. That way they will not be able to deceive anyone for many years during the Lord's earthly reign."

"And after that?" Holly said. Axel wondered the same thing.

"I will return to heaven and worship before the throne. From there I will await the Lord's instructions. Whatever the case, we will always be working together."

"That's comforting, but I'll miss having you with us each day."

Axel stepped forward. "So will I, Abiron. I've learned so much from you." He considered asking the angel if he could accompany him on his mission, but the idea quickly faded. It was a different conversation now. He had committed to wait for the Lord's timing, whatever that would turn out to be.

"I will certainly miss all of you," Abiron said. "There is a good chance we will cross paths in the other dimensions. And beyond that, after the Lord brings his earthly reign to an end, heaven and earth will be made new, and he will permanently open extra dimensions of time to us so that we will enjoy each other's company every moment, no matter where we are. We will fellowship together for the rest of eternity."

"Wow . . . that's incredible," Holy replied. "It's amazing to think we have even greater treasures to look forward to."

"Thank you, Abiron. Thank you for everything," Axel said.

The angel smiled and bowed his head. "You are very welcome. Enjoy your time on Earth. You are free to do whatever you wish. Just make sure you are back here at sundown tomorrow, for the Lord has something spectacular planned."

He rotated out of their view, and other lead angels also vanished around them.

Axel spent the next few hours with the others recounting the events of the day, revering everything Jesus had done and beholding his glory as it blazed into the night sky over the temple. But his mind wouldn't rest. Flashbacks to the heavenly realm whirled through his thoughts, memories of when Jesus had given him a view into the battles of angels and fallen spirits. *What was the significance of all that?*

A short time later the sun began to rise in the east, and a loud sizzling resonated from the area above the temple, seizing Axel's attention. An enormous pillar of smoke had replaced the pillar of fire. Colossal volumes of pure marshmallow haze with no source or flame anywhere. "Check that out."

"Amazing," Taj replied. "I don't think anyone will ever question who reigns here again."

"That's for sure," Holly said. "Hey, what do you guys want to do?"

Suddenly, Axel began spinning in utter darkness, with the sound of rushing wind filling his ears. He twirled around and around, trying to gather his bearings. Then, in an instant, he froze.

His eyes began to focus, and a galactic wonderland came into view, teaming with myriads of stars and shining beams cast against the sheer blackness of space. *Where am I? This doesn't make any sense.* It wasn't like the cosmos he had just ridden through on the white stallion. The stars moved at blinding speeds and collided with one another, agitated and violent. Supernova-like explosions scattered across the sky. He strived to move closer, but something hampered him from twitching even a finger.

More glowing objects smashed headlong into each other in the distance, detonating like the falling leaf, chrysanthemum, and dahlia firework formations he'd marveled at in his childhood. Only the faint rumblings of their clashes reached his ears. *What in the world is going on?* The drama enthralled him, but the mystery of it all enticed him even more.

The lights began to fade into the darkness. One by one they would flicker and disappear until all had vanished, and calm permeated the expanse like that of a meandering backwoods stream.

After a few seconds, a speck of light appeared far, far away. It moved rapidly toward him, looming larger and larger, and within moments it closed the gap to where he stood suspended. It came to an abrupt halt, and Axel immediately recognized not what, but who it was.

"No more adversary?" he said.

"Not for a while, anyway," Abiron replied.

Axel's mind whirled. He was glad to be here and glad to see Abiron again so soon, but he had no idea why this was happening. "So . . . I'm kind of puzzled, and kind of . . . frozen, but why am I here?"

"To see how it all unfolds at the highest levels."

"Unfolds? How what unfolds?"

"Justice, Axel . . . justice." Abiron flashed away without uttering another word.

Axel found himself back among his friends on the Mount of Olives. His hands and feet could move again, and the word "justice" flashed through his mind.

A voice bellowed in his ear. "Axel! Axel!" He turned to see Holly staring at him with her arms folded in front of her.

"Are you daydreaming?" she said.

He considered giving her the Abiron explanation but quickly realized he couldn't really even explain it himself. "Uh . . . I don't know . . . I mean, no, sorry."

"What do you want to do then?"

Axel blinked. "Want to do?"

Holly rolled her eyes. "Yeah, where've you been? We've been talking about it for the last few minutes. I thought maybe you'd like to join the conversation."

Axel shook his head, trying to get his focus back. What *did* he want to do? The possibilities seemed endless. He looked around the wasted landscape of Israel and decided that he'd rather go somewhere else for a while. "Oh . . . well, I think . . . I think I've seen enough here for now."

"Maybe we should take a road trip somewhere," Nina said.

"Like where?" Derek asked.

"Not too far, since we need to be back by sundown," Holly replied.

Axel pressed his lips together. The others didn't have the breadth of extradimensional experience he had. "Actually, I think we can probably go as far as we want and still make it back by sundown no problem."

Holly shook her head. "What are you talking about?"

"It's simple. We can cover a lot of distance very quickly in the other dimensions. "

"Like the way angels move?" Brianna said.

"Exactly. We'll use the dimensions that intersect the physical universe, just like we did on the stallions yesterday."

Brianna smiled. "I always thought it would be fun to run on those huge sand dunes in the Sahara Desert."

Brilliant. "Nothing's stopping us," Axel replied.

Holly nodded. "Okay, I guess I'm in then, but how do we get there?"

Axel grinned. "Just follow me, Cuz."

Axel rotated slowly out to the other dimensions and laughed as he watched the others fumbling to find their way. He loved them dearly, but sometimes his family provided more amusement than animals at the zoo. These dimensions required a different rotation than the ones in heaven, and they were obviously a little harder to locate.

Moments later RJ figured it out and joined him, followed by Holly and the rest.

"This is wild, Axel," Brianna said. "It was like you vanished right before our eyes!"

"Sorry, maybe I should have given you a little more direction on how to get here. Are we ready to go?"

"Yeah, but do you actually know how to get to the Sahara Desert?" Holly said. "I'm guessing you've never been there before."

He winked. "Thousands of square miles of sand shouldn't be too hard to find."

Axel leaned toward the south and began moving rapidly through the other dimensions with the others right behind. Streets flew by below. A tall building appeared in front of him, but that didn't matter. The others veered to one side, but Axel passed right through as if it weren't even there.

He led them to the west until he reached the coast and followed it down to the Nile Delta, all in a matter of moments. He made a slight left turn and motioned for everyone to stop a split second later, hovering over miles and miles of sand undulating and rolling through lofty peaks and deep valleys. "How's this for a playground?"

"The view is amazing," Brianna said. "Nothing but dunes and dunes for as far as I can see."

"Let's get our feet on the ground then," Axel replied.

He rotated back into the earth's dimensions on top of a towering ridge, and the others followed.

Derek turned his head from side to side "This one must be at least three hundred feet high."

Axel put on his best John Wayne voice and said, "A man's got to do what a man's got to do, Pilgrim." And he flung himself over the edge, landing far down the slope. Immediately he began rolling, picking up speed with each turn. Faster and faster he tumbled until he reached the base and came to a crashing halt with sand flying everywhere. He picked himself up off the ground, laughing and buzzed, and waved back up the hill.

"Aren't you dizzy?" Marie shouted.

"Not a bit. It was awesome!"

Each one jumped off in turn and reveled all the way to the bottom. Axel spent the next few hours climbing up and plummeting back down with them, hooting and laughing. The temperature had risen to scorching levels, but it was no sweat for him—literally. He felt no fatigue and didn't work up even a hint of a thirst.

Brianna pointed at Axel's steel-white garment. "I can't believe it. The sand doesn't stick to your clothes."

"Cool, no laundry this time around," Holly replied.

"No showers either," Taj said. "I'm still totally clean, even after all of this."

"Hopefully you'll still use deodorant though," Brianna said, wrinkling her nose at him.

"Really? I don't smell, do I?"

Brianna just laughed.

"Relax," Holly cut in. "I guess we haven't totally lost sibling rivalry."

Soon after, they rotated out to the other dimensions and began moving back toward Israel. As they approached Jerusalem from the south, Axel noticed a striking change in the appearance of the land and brought the group to a stop. Barren shades of tan had morphed into luscious hues of green, and grape vines and fruit trees sprawled across the landscape. "Wasn't this just a parched desert when we came through earlier?"

"It certainly was, but it's looking like a cultivated wonderland now," Holly said.

"God said this would happen," RJ replied, looking satisfied.

"Really? When did he tell you?" Taj said.

RJ laughed. "In his Word. In the books of Isaiah, Ezekiel, and Joel. All of them talk about Israel looking like the garden of Eden again."

The miraculous changes elated Axel. A hole in his heart had been filled, and he rejoiced to see it. The Lord had not only reversed the devastation of the last few years but had rewound the earth's botanical clock back much farther, to the artistry of his original creation. Axel laughed for sheer delight. Sculptures evidently could be restored, and when God was the one performing the work, you couldn't tell the difference from the original. *Seeing the oceans blue again will be unreal.*

The crew resumed their trek toward Jerusalem and arrived there almost instantly to find the city buzzing with activity, even more so than when they'd left. Workers had piled loads of gold, silver, bronze, iron, and wood in the streets. Construction had begun on buildings, walls, and gates. Laborers hurried about the temple grounds, expanding, restoring, and beautifying the holy site.

Axel signaled for them to reenter the earth's dimensions near the Temple Mount, where massive crowds of angels, Risen Ones, and survivors of the recent atrocities had gathered. Excitement filled the air as he stood with his family and friends waiting for the Lord's emergence. Then, out of the corner of his eye, he noticed a young woman with long, dark hair and olive skin looking his way—but not just any young woman.

"Arielle?" he said softly.

He moved toward her, but she'd already disappeared into the crowd. He searched frantically, examining face after face. They all blurred together. He nudged people to the side, clearing a path, but he saw no sign of her.

"Axel, where are you going?" Holly shouted.

Continuing his quest seemed pointless, so he turned and made his way back to the group, shaking his head. "I thought for sure I saw her."

"Saw who?" Holly said.

"Arielle. I'm positive it was her."

"Aw, I'm sure she would have joined us if she was nearby. There are so many girls in this city that look like her."

Axel just remained silent. The sting of her absence again pelted his heart like hailstones. Wouldn't she be trying to find him among the crowd as well? It seemed like a one-sided effort at this point, one without a hint as to where to look next.

A short time later, the sun set on the horizon. A bright flash ignited the sky, and the pillar of fire reappeared over the temple. Jesus emerged robed in a high priestly garment with a crown of gold on his head, driving Axel to his knees with head bowed.

A mighty angel flew down from the sky and hovered in front of the temple. With a loud voice echoing throughout the land he cried out, "All glory, honor, and praise belong to our God. He has now become king and high priest over the earth! As it is written, worship will now commence according to the schedule of the holy festivals."

Countless angels appeared in the sky, caroling towering harmonies of praise. Spectacular waves of light in every color imaginable beamed high into the night in all directions, rays of burgundy and sapphire and goldenrod.

Axel joined the celebration as dancing and laughter erupted everywhere. Baskets of freshly baked breads, succulent fruits, and fine meats arrived in the streets. Tantalizing aromas rose, and God's love brimmed over the edges of Axel's heart, encouraging him to partake of the treasures of the kingdom.

10

Purpose

The worship and celebration accelerated on into the early hours of the morning with an open throttle. Axel and the others paraded through Jerusalem shouting and rejoicing with everyone they met.

Soon morning came, and the enormous pillar of coiling smoke burst into position to replace the pillar of fire above the temple. Axel lifted his sights to the sky and watched as angels streaked away to their places of service somewhere in the other dimensions. Local residents passed by on their way back to their lives of purpose, but Axel had no agenda for the day.

Taj tapped him on the shoulder. "Hey man, what do you wanna do today? Another extradimensional journey?"

"How about Mount Everest or somewhere in the Himalayas?" Holly suggested.

"That would definitely be cool, but I'm thinking about something really radical," Axel replied. "Like maybe an active volcano or a visit to another planet or something."

"Make sure you stop by Neptune when you get a chance," said a voice from behind him. "That one is my favorite in this galaxy. But you will need to save universe exploring for another day."

Axel swung around to see a well-groomed, dark-skinned angel with medium build and a slick deep-wave hairstyle clothed in a striking white garment.

"Hananias!" Holly exclaimed, and she embraced him.

The angel grinned widely. "I am delighted to see all of you again."

Axel had appreciated Hananias from his first moments in the afterlife, when the angel had mentored he and his family and friends in the ways of the heavenly realm. Immediately after Axel's initial meeting with Jesus, Hananias had appeared to answer his questions and give him a tour of the territory around the throne. Always cordial and extremely intelligent, Hananias had played an essential role in turning Axel on to the treasures of eternal life.

"Whatcha doin' here in Jerusalem?" Holly said.

"Oh, you know, more fun and games," Hananias replied. "But first, there is someone who would like to talk to all of you."

Holly's face lit up. "Now who could that be?"

A dazzling light flashed, and Axel found himself suspended in a new expanse with Holly, RJ, and the rest floating beside him. Waves of light in gold and honey bronze beamed in every direction, endlessly, as if he'd returned to heaven again.

Suddenly, the Lord appeared with his high-priestly robe cascading down his body in royal purple and crimson. A gold crown rested on his head, and his eyes blazed like fire.

"Greetings, my children," he said, smiling. Jesus's voice didn't sound like rushing waters—it *was* rushing waters. It was the crackle the fire gives off and the deep-bellied roar of the lion. Every powerful and exquisite sound Axel had ever heard on Earth was amplified and perfected in Jesus's voice, the voice of his king.

"You were all made in the image of God," Jesus said. "You became children of God, and you will now be made priests of God and will reign with me on the earth."

Axel rubbed his hands together slowly. Jesus turned and met eyes with him, sending Axel's mouth into a beaming grin. Jesus nodded just once, but it was all Axel needed—like the spark that lights a bonfire or the whisper that launches an avalanche.

"Lord, I . . . I don't know what to say," Marie stuttered. "I don't deserve to . . ."

Jesus smiled at her. "All things have been renewed, my beloved. Now that I sit on my throne, everyone who left houses or brothers or sisters or a father or mother or children or fields for my sake will receive a hundred times as much."

Axel searched for the words, but he couldn't muster even a syllable. "Thank you" just sounded underwhelming when compared with how grateful he felt.

"My desire is that you remain in me, and I will remain in you," Jesus said. "No branch can bear fruit by itself; it must remain in the vine. Neither can you bear fruit unless you remain in me. I am the vine; you are the branches. If you remain in me and I in you, you will bear much fruit; separated from me you can do nothing. My servant Hananias will describe the fruit I have given each of you to bear."

RJ rubbed the back of his neck. "This is so incredible, Lord."

"It is all to my Father's glory that you bear much fruit. You are my beloved disciples, and your fruit marks you as such."

Axel's thoughts spun. *Fruit. Purpose.* He now stood on the threshold of God's destiny for him, and it promised to be more intricate and adventurous than the fantasies of any fairy tale. The future the Lord had prepared for him glimmered like a deep pool with the colors of the sunset reflecting above the waters—and reflecting below it as well, whatever that meant. He had no idea what lay there, but God's plans for him waited above and beneath, as captivating as they were mysterious.

Jesus rotated them back into the earth's dimensions after they'd feasted on his words for a little while longer—down to the streets of Jerusalem, where they quickly crowded around Hananias.

"Fellow servants, each of you proved faithful in the few things the Lord asked you to look after during your lives on Earth," the angel said. "So just as he promised in the parables of the talents and the minas, he will now put you in charge of many things. Your calling in the kingdom is to work together with a group of other Risen Ones to represent the Lord in the area known as San Diego, located in the southern region of the state of California. You will each have responsibilities in the northwest region of the city, which includes the neighborhoods known as Del Mar in the north down to the body of water known as Mission Bay in the south."

"That's not far from where we used to live," Brianna said.

"Yeah, we know that area well," Derek said.

Holly laughed. "I'm thrilled. So what is it that we'll be doing?"

"I was getting to that," Hananias replied. "Axel, Holly, and RJ, you will handle the ministry of justice. The Lord has declared that righteousness prevail in the kingdom."

The word "justice" echoed in Axel's ears. *It's all beginning to make sense. Watching mercenaries' plans thwarted. Witnessing the devil's imprisonment in the abyss.* It all had to do with upholding the Lord's righteousness, and Jesus was calling him to make a stand, a stand for his holiness and a stand for his purity. The possibilities seemed endless—the sense of purpose exhilarating.

"Wow, that's right up my alley," Holly said. "But how will we do that?"

"You will perform surveillance, conduct investigations, and if warranted, apprehend those guilty of criminal acts."

"Okay then. I'm ready to get started."

"Now, moving on," Hananias said. "Marie, Derek, and Nina, you will provide the ministry of compassion and care. You will coordinate activities to assist people in need and will extend the Lord's love through any and all kingdom resources."

Marie nodded eagerly. "I imagine that a tremendous amount of healing needs to take place after the events of the last few years."

"Yes, you will have much to do from the moment you arrive."

"I can't think of a more fulfilling assignment," Derek said.

"Me neither," Nina replied.

"Very good. Let's see . . . Francisco, Taj, and Brianna, you will handle the facilities ministry. With kingdom resources, you will lead the people in rebuilding and maintaining their cities and infrastructure. The last few years have left many with poor living conditions, so you will ensure that facilities exist to deliver the Lord's blessings to all. Housing, water, electricity, and so on.

There will be others on your team in that region who will have responsibilities for worship, teaching, food and clothing distribution, transportation, coordination, and other duties. You will meet up with them when you arrive."

Derek raised his hand. "Hananias, I've been wondering, how will money work in the kingdom?"

"Actually, it does not. There is no need for it. The Lord will provide abundantly for everyone. Food, clothing, housing, transportation, and everything else will be made bountifully available to all."

"Great. Then no one will need to get all worked up about that stuff."

"Mystery Babylon is long gone," Francisco said. "With all its greed and material obsessions."

"Hananias, will you be there to help us?" Brianna said.

"From time to time, but you do not need me. Just depend on Jesus, as he said, and *nothing* will be impossible for you."

11

Arriving

The Mediterranean whizzed by beneath Axel and the others as they began their journey toward California, and angels and other Risen Ones swarmed the heavenly airspace like shooting stars.

Axel perceived everything that entered his senses with much greater clarity than his old body ever could, in what he could see, what he could hear, and what he could smell. Even though the earth dashed by below, he could make out every detail below him. Blood no longer tainted the deep blue hues of the Atlantic. Sharks swam with dolphins, and orcas frolicked with sea lions. All of it a wonderful reminder that the Lord's kingdom had truly arrived.

He raced onward into the United States with the others right behind. Groups of Risen Ones gathered in the expanse above many of the cities.

Moments later, he crossed the Colorado River into California, where the desert bloomed with cactus and wildflowers. Purple, tangerine, and blonde blossoms dotted the ground amidst bright green shrubbery and the small trails of the river. Chocolate and violet peaks towered in the distance to the north, drenched in the light of the sun. Wildlife thrived everywhere, with predator and prey prospering serenely together.

Axel slowed the group's pace as they approached San Diego and pointed to a gathering of Risen Ones assembled in the expanse above the UC San Diego campus. A woman in the crowd caught his eyes as they arrived, and he hastened to move over and embrace her. "What an incredible last few days this has been, Mom! I can't wait to tell you all that's happened."

After a few more had joined their numbers, a man with an athletic build, fair skin, and sandy-blond hair moved out in front of them all and waved his arms. "I hope you've all had a chance to meet. We'll be working closely together in this region. My name is Ryan, and I'm a member of the coordination team. We're here to assist with all of your efforts and to aid with communication between your teams."

He gestured to a cluster of people who had gathered around him. "Kara, Sandy, and Ian, as well as those from the information team, have been spreading word of our arrival in the community today. People have come from all over the region to meet with us in the university's main gym. Chris and Logan have set up stations for each of your teams inside, where the people will be bringing you the immediate needs that they have. We'll establish better ways to communicate with them over the next couple of days, but this will get us going for now."

Ryan answered a few questions and then said, "Please don't hesitate to contact any of us on the coordination team for help. Now, let's seek the Lord's guidance and strength as we begin our service for him."

After praying with the group, Axel entered the earth's dimensions outside the gym and surveyed the face of the building. Cracks canvassed the concrete, paint had chipped away, and the signage was missing many letters. Scars of the previous years' devastation, he had no doubt.

He and the others walked in through the doors, and many muffled, ringing conversations immediately fell silent. An awkward chill came over him as nervous stares beamed down from the blank faces in the chock-full bleachers. Axel had never enjoyed the spotlight. In fact, he'd always tried to keep it from even being plugged in. But in this case he understood. Here he was with an immaculate appearance, a brilliant white garment, and a reputation for having just annihilated the armies of the world.

"I feel like an alien," Brianna whispered.

"To them, you are," Derek replied softly. "It'll be fine in a few minutes."

True to form, Axel gravitated to the edge of the group, just a few yards away from the first row of bleachers, where his superhuman hearing caught the conversation of two women nearby. He blushed as he realized they were talking about him.

"Take a look at that young man, Mary."

"Everything about him is perfect," Mary replied. "Think about it: the proof of everything we've held dear about our faith stands right here before us."

"What a wonderful assurance! One day we'll be resurrected just like he is."

"Praise Jesus, and I hope all the men in heaven are as handsome as this one."

The two women giggled, and Axel turned to give them a smile and a nod. A look of shock came over their faces. "I didn't think you could hear us from there," Mary said.

Axel gave her a slight wave and grinned.

The last few Risen Ones joined the team at the front of the gym, and then Ryan shouted out, "In the name of the Lord Jesus Christ, we've come to share his blessings and love with you."

Someone in the crowd yelled back, "Welcome, Risen Ones!" A hesitant round of scattered applause followed.

"We know you've been through many difficulties," Ryan continued, "and that our presence here may cause concern for some of you, but I want to assure you that we've come in the name of the Lord. We look forward to serving you in our service for him."

Another round of applause ensued, this time more accepting. Axel scanned the faces in the stands, seeing pain in many of the expressions, fueling his eagerness to begin the Lord's work.

"We're here today to address any immediate needs you may have," Ryan said in a strong, confident voice. "Stations have been set up for you to meet with each of our teams. My coordination team will remain here at the front if you need direction or have any general questions."

Voices cluttered the gym again as people walked to the different meeting areas. Many gathered at each station, but the compassion-and-care booth drew the largest number by far.

"Are you ready to show God's love to these people?" Marie said to Nina and Derek.

"Absolutely. Let's get to work," Nina replied, and they scurried toward their post.

Axel, Holly, and RJ headed over to the rectangular brown table and placard that comprised their meeting area. About twenty people stood waiting, eyes glued to their every step. "Hi everyone," Holly said with a smile. "I'm Holly, and this is my cousin Axel and my uncle RJ. We're the justice team for your area."

The group stared back at them, some obviously uncomfortable to be so close, some examining them curiously, and others visibly overwhelmed by the bizarreness of the moment. The atmosphere had dropped from a chill to a full-blown frost. A man in his early forties, wearing a collared golf shirt, spoke up. "I think I speak sincerely for all of us in saying welcome to our city. I'm Reid, and this is my wife Julie. Sorry about the cold reception."

"That's okay," Holly replied. "We understand."

"And I'm Juanita, and this is my husband Alejandro," said a woman in her midtwenties clothed in a flowered dress. "We're very glad you're here."

Holly smiled. "We're very glad to be here, and we'd like to get all of your names before you leave today. It will be a pleasure to get to know each of you. But right now I think you have some security matters to discuss?"

"We certainly do," Alejandro said. "But I have a few questions first."

Axel took a slightly defensive stance, recognizing a challenge in his tone, but Holly just said, "Oh, sure, go right ahead."

"We were very excited when we saw Jesus and the rest of you in the sky a few days ago. But the next day, many people disappeared and haven't returned. Do you know what's happened to them?"

Holly crossed her arms over her chest, but before she could answer, RJ cut in. "I'll take this one, Holly. I'm very sorry to say that those who took the mark of the Beast, demonstrating their rebellion against the Lord . . . well, to put it bluntly, they won't be coming back."

Countenances dropped. Not a word came from the group, and their heartbreak hit Axel in the face like an ice pick.

Alejandro shook his head. "So many have gone away or been lost. It seemed like people were dying every day during the last few years, and just weeks ago, many of our local military men and women, including my own cousin, left for Israel. And . . . well, you know what happened to the military there. You helped decimate them. We know the Bible says that all these things needed to take place, but losing them has been very difficult for us—too difficult."

Holly faced him. "My heart's broken for all that's happened, to your cousin, to the other friends and family you've lost, but I know it wasn't the Lord's will for them to die—he desperately wanted them to turn to him. But if they didn't want to live under his rule, he wasn't going to force them to. Now he's here to comfort you, and I promise, his compassion is great, and we'll do anything in our power to help you."

"I'm sorry," Alejandro replied softly. "I didn't mean to take my feelings out on you."

"What Alejandro says is true," Juanita said. "We mourn for those we've lost, but we also appreciate the changes the Lord has brought about. There are beautiful flowers and trees around us, we have food to eat, and the air and water are clean again. And there is peace. Those who made our lives a living hell—they're all gone now."

Axel stood up straighter. Justice was on the job. "And we're here to make sure it stays that way."

"I apologize for taking us off track," Alejandro said.

"No, no, it's not a problem," Holly replied. "We're here for you. Is there anything else I can answer?"

"No," Alejandro said. "Thank you. Let's talk about the crimes in our area."

"Okay, then, who wants to start?" Holly asked.

"I think we're all here to discuss the same thing," Reid said. Most around him nodded. "There've been a few incidents in the area—and maybe I'm paranoid, but they all seem to be related."

"In what way?" RJ said.

"Well, mobile device robberies, computers being stolen, all kinds of technology gear taken from retail stores and local businesses. God's enemies had some real sophisticated communication and data networks, but they all went down some time ago, and they still don't work, so I don't know why anyone would want that stuff."

Axel gazed off at one of the other meeting areas. Was that it? Cell phones and PCs? Why was this such a big deal?

"And how long has this been going on?" RJ said.

"A few weeks," Julie replied. "Most of the shops around us are rarely open, and some have been completely abandoned. If they do open, it's only to barter for other goods or to provide services out of the goodness of their hearts. We're really concerned that this is all happening right in our neighborhood. Sooner or later someone's bound to get hurt."

"Has anyone actually been in danger of being harmed?" Axel said.

"Yes. A woman was working late at night at her computer repair business when one of the burglaries occurred. She said two people wearing black clothing and ski masks broke in and held a knife to her throat. They threatened to cut her up but fled soon after without taking anything. Thank goodness she wasn't killed."

Axel raised his eyebrows. So maybe there was real treachery out there. Hoodlums with knives definitely needed to be dealt with.

"We'll need to talk with her," Holly said. "Can you provide us with her name and information on where we can find her, and with the addresses where these crimes took place?"

"We sure can."

"Do you have any idea who's behind it?" Axel said.

"Teenagers," Reid replied.

Axel squinted. Was this guy serious? After all these years, hadn't those in his age group escaped the brunt of the blame for every mischievous and devious act? *Even tabloid journalists deserve the benefit of the doubt sometimes.* "Why do you say that?"

"Well, the rest of us are all believers. They're the only ones left who might not be. As children, they never had to identify themselves with the world's evil regime. They never had to buy and sell in that wicked environment. And as RJ said, everyone who took the mark of the Beast has been removed."

"Hmm." It actually sounded like a reasonable explanation. Biases had no place in this line of work anyway, so he would have to consider it as a plausible theory.

"Has anyone actually *seen* a teenager commit one of these robberies?" Holly said.

"No, not that I'm aware of, but they seem to have a real fascination for that stuff."

Axel had heard enough. The time for action had come. "Okay, we'll get right on this."

"Thank you so much for meeting with us today," Holly said. "Please leave us your names and addresses and the locations of the robberies. We'll follow up with you all very soon."

The group dispersed toward the doors, but Axel, Holly, and RJ remained at the meeting area. Holly began scanning the list of crime scenes. "What do you think?"

"Shouldn't take too long to solve this with a little extradimensional detective work," Axel replied.

"I think you're right," RJ said. "Especially if the culprits are underage."

"Excuse me, can we talk with you for a minute?" a voice said from behind. They turned to see a couple waiting nervously for them.

"Of course. You were just here with the group," Holly replied, looking through her list. "You're . . . Stein and Lisa, right?"

"Yes," Stein said. "There's something else we thought you ought to know. We have an eighteen-year-old son, Josh, and he hangs out with many of the other teens in our neighborhood."

"So what do you think about this theory that they're behind the robberies?" RJ said.

"I have to admit, they are very secretive, and Josh won't talk about what he does with his friends. But I can tell you, I think there's more than just teenagers involved here."

Axel was intrigued. "Go on, go on."

"Well, this stranger showed up in the area a few weeks ago—a guy in his midthirties, I'd say. He showed up about the same time the break-ins started. We don't know much about him except that we often see him around Josh and his friends."

"Doing what?" RJ said.

"Couldn't tell ya," Stein replied. "And Josh won't tell us anything either, other than that his name is Elias."

"Can you describe him?"

"Caucasian, short blond hair, probably midthirties like I said."

"And when did you see him last?"

"Just this morning, actually."

Axel ran his fingers through his hair. "So do you know where this guy usually hangs out? Where we might be able to find him?"

"Now that's a mystery in itself. No one seems to have any information on him, but we thought we should bring it to your attention since it wasn't brought up earlier."

"We appreciate that," Holly replied. "And if you come across anything else, the Risen Ones here at the campus can get in touch with us. We'll follow up with you as soon as we know something."

"God bless you," Lisa said. "And thank you for coming."

12

Justice

Axel stepped outside the gym, and Holly and RJ came right behind him. Night blanketed the Southern California coastline. Stars sprinkled the sky like speckles of bullion sparkling on a black felt cloth.

RJ looked at Holly. "I think you know something about investigations."

"Well, I was only an analyst, but I had some training in field work. The first thing we'll want to do is go to the crime scenes and gather evidence. We'll also want to talk to that woman who was threatened during that attempted robbery, but I'm sure morning will be a better time for her."

"Won't gathering evidence require some special equipment? From what the people inside said, there isn't much equipment that works these days."

"I don't think we'll need anything high-tech at all. Axel, maybe you can find us some talcum powder, and maybe a small brush, some ink, and a roll of clear tape. That way we'll be able to lift some fingerprints."

"Shouldn't be a problem, Holl. I'll bet I can get all that at a grocery store."

"You'll need to ask Ryan how that works. It might look funny if you just walk out with it."

"Okay. So what are you guys gonna do?"

"We'll make a quick visit to some of the crime scenes and see which ones we should focus on," Holly said. "Let's meet back at the gym at, say, midnight?"

"Sounds good."

Axel headed back in through the doors and laid out the situation for Ryan.

"The grocery stores and markets have become distribution centers for food and other goods," Ryan said. "And the distribution team is working with a kingdom-wide network to ensure that inventory levels remain plentiful in our area. People can come and take from the Lord's blessings at any time."

"Sweet. I think everyone's going to be stoked with how easy Jesus has made this," Axel said.

"There's a distribution center down in La Jolla that will have what you need. Thankfully that's close. The rebuilding of industries has begun, but many of the centers are still not well stocked."

"Thanks, man. We'll let you know what we find."

Axel rotated out to the other dimensions and moved casually south along Villa La Jolla Drive. *I don't need to hurry. I'll finish way before Holly and RJ will.*

Not a soul strolled the sidewalks, and no cars cruised the streets. The moon could have altered its phase and no one would have known. He approached the La Jolla Village Square Shopping Center and recognized some store names from his days on Earth. Others didn't ring so familiar.

Suddenly, a subtle flash stirred in the corner of his eye, little more than a blink of light. *That was weird.* He stopped and waited to see if there would be another, but there was nothing. Only stillness.

Why would anyone be in a dark, vacant shopping mall at eleven o'clock at night?

Axel floated slowly past a number of shops, peering in through the windows as he went, and eventually came upon a large home-electronics store. Darkness pervaded the interior. The words "all kinds of technology gear" rang in his head. This place would be a prime target for whoever had been breaking in.

Then a beam flared across the back wall—just a momentary trail of light, similar to the one that had caught his attention minutes before. *I knew I wasn't seeing things.*

He moved quickly inside through the walls and paused near the ceiling above the checkout stands, still hearing nothing.

Two figures emerged from the warehouse doors at the rear of the store, each with a flashlight in hand. Both wore dark clothing and gloves, and black ski masks covered their faces. One pushed an empty shopping cart.

Axel tapped his hand rhythmically on his thigh. His purpose in the kingdom beckoned through a megaphone.

The two proceeded to the computer displays in the middle of the floor. Axel raced to a place above them, still invisible in the other dimensions.

He then caught a glimpse of a slender, dark-haired young woman off to one side, hovering in the extra dimensions with him. His eyes snapped quickly toward her, but she was gone in a blur. "Man, that looked like Arielle," he whispered.

He started to slide over. He could probably catch her.

"How many more of these laptops do we need?" said one of the thieves.

"I think we have enough, but this list calls for a few more network routers," replied the other in a female voice.

Axel paused and shook his head. Painfully, his pursuit of Arielle would have to wait. She was right there within his grasp, but duty called and he couldn't neglect that.

He rotated in onto the ground about ten feet in front of them—blocking their escape. With an ice-cold stare and a throaty Eastwood tone, he said, "Didn't you get the memo, punk? Christ now rules with an iron scepter." It sounded a little cliché, but he didn't care. That's what superheroes did, right?

The two thieves jumped back and a laptop fell from the man's hands, cracking open on the linoleum. The woman yanked out her flashlight, turning it on Axel and his blinding white garment. "It's one of the Risen Ones!"

They turned and fled down the aisle in the other direction.

Axel instantly rotated out and then back in onto the ground in front them. Their flight came to a grinding halt, and the man cried out, "Whoa! How did he do that?"

"Simple," Axel replied as he walked toward them. "Extradimensional physics. But your disreputable minds wouldn't know anything about that."

The woman reached into her pocket, pulled out a small canister, and sprayed it directly into Axel's eyes, but Axel just wiped the stuff aside like sweat from his brow.

The man jumped into a martial-arts stance and threw a kick, landing it squarely on Axel's jaw, and then shrieked and fell to the ground grabbing his foot. The woman spun around to run, but Axel clamped onto her wrist before she had taken even a stride.

"You broke my foot!" the man whined.

"So sue me for police brutality." He then turned to the woman. "Sit down next to him. And both of you, take off your masks."

Axel watched as they obeyed. Reid had been right. In front of him sat a young man and a young woman, each no older than nineteen years of age. The young woman pushed her grown-out dyed-black hair away from her eyes and stared at the floor. The young man wouldn't look at him either.

Axel ignored their toxic aura. "I don't suppose I can get names out of you."

The young woman looked up, glaring, but said nothing.

"I didn't think so, but we can do this the hard way if you want. Talk to me or explain it directly to the living God."

Her eyes widened. Concern came over her face. She parted her lips to say something, but then she just looked back at the ground instead.

At that moment, a bright flash lit up the room. Near the end of the aisle stood a daunting angelic figure with two others by his side, and the teen's faces went from pale to sheet-white. The young woman ran her hands through her hair, but they shook so violently that her fingers only tangled in it. Sweat dripped down the young man's face, past his unblinking eyes.

"Abiron!" Axel shouted. "What brings you here?"

"Business as usual. Well done, Axel," the angel replied.

Axel grinned. "Just following your example, my friend. I really just stumbled upon this though."

"Or maybe you should consider that you were led here."

Of course. "I'm sure you're right, as usual."

A wry smile made its way across Abiron's face. "So things were not moving fast enough for you during this return to Earth?"

Was it really that obvious? He didn't think he wore his emotions on his sleeve. But then again, Abiron always seemed to have insider information. "Yeah, well, about that . . . I know I shouldn't have been so impatient. I was ready to fight spiritual battles in heaven with you, and it was hard to stand on the sidelines during the Lord's return. Jesus took the time to help me figure it out."

"You are fighting the Lord's battles now, just on a different battlefield. Remember, your life in Christ will always be an adventure when you trust in him. He knows exactly what will bring you joy and contentment."

"I know that, and truly I did all along, but I guess I let my passion get the best of me. Look at how it all turned out, though! I'm totally into this justice stuff."

"And return to that you must. You will need to escort these two to the university and hand them over to the team responsible for reckoning. This is not a capital offense, but their punishment will make them think twice about trying it again."

Axel nodded, somewhat relieved to hear these two weren't going to lose their lives today. They were so . . . *young.* "Okay. Cool. I need to meet Holly and RJ there anyway. I appreciate your help as always."

"I will see you again soon." Abiron paused and looked Axel in the eye. "Remember to always depend on the Lord." And he rotated back out to the heavenly realm along with his companions.

Axel sat the young man in the shopping cart, throbbing foot and all, and told the young woman to push. They arrived at the UCSD gym a little while later, and a member of the coordination team approached them. Axel's account of the events sent Risen Ones scurrying, and soon reckoning team members appeared to take the teens into custody.

Holly breezed into the gym moments later. "Did you get everything?"

"Nope. I'm really sorry. I took a detour to the beach to check the waves, and time got away from me."

She pegged her hands to her hips. "I thought you left your surfer tendencies behind."

"I don't know what to say. I guess I'm still a bit of a flake." His eyes twinkled.

Steps came toward them from the side. "Axel, we've processed the two you brought in. They'll receive their sentences in the morning."

Holly tilted her head. "Sentences? What two . . . who did you bring in?"

Axel savored the look on his cousin's face. He'd pulled off the ruse perfectly, and the taste of success lingered blissfully on his tongue. "I just thought it'd be better if we had some suspects."

Holly laughed with mock frustration. "Explain, please."

RJ joined them, and Axel recounted the night's events. After some discussion, they agreed they should continue with their plan to gather evidence. They needed to know if these teens had committed the other robberies as well.

"I think our original plan needs some tweaking," Holly said. "Fingerprints aren't going to cut it. I should've known the burglars would be wearing gloves."

"So I guess we'll need to gather things like hair and saliva samples, shoe prints, and clothing fibers from the suspects instead," RJ said.

"Yes, and we'll also need a more sophisticated way to analyze the evidence. Ink and talcum powder won't give us what we need. Let's see if Ryan can arrange for us to work with the laboratory team over at UCSD Medical Center."

Axel followed Holly and RJ to a number of the crime scenes, where they canvassed the premises quickly.

"I can't believe how sharp my eyesight is," Holly said. "I'm finding hair, thread, and stains, much of it really small—even microscopic."

"It's amazing," RJ replied. "I could have definitely used vision like this in my teaching days, but there's so much potential evidence here. How are you distinguishing what to gather?"

"Well, we took black fabric and dark hair samples from the suspects, so I'm just looking for anything similar."

At the lab, the staff ran a number of forensic tests, compiled results, analyzed the data, and drew some conclusions. Holly was the first to scan the report. "There's no question. It was them at every location."

"Let's go with it then," Axel replied. What more proof did they need?

The sun had begun to rise, with clouds high in the sky above. Axel, Holly, and RJ moved quickly to the gym through the other dimensions where they shared their findings with Ryan, who immediately sent the information team out into the community.

By midmorning, many had assembled on the hardwood floor and Holly stood in front of the crowd. "Welcome, everyone. We're pleased to announce that we apprehended a young man and a young woman during an attempted robbery of a home electronics store."

Exclamations filled the air.

"In addition, we have forensic evidence leading us to believe that these same two individuals also committed the other robberies in the area."

"Can you give us their names?" someone shouted.

"Not at this time. We're still trying to contact their families."

"Are they from our neighborhood?"

"No. From what we can tell, they don't live around here."

"So, do you think they were working alone?" Reid asked.

"The evidence seems to indicate that. We haven't found any indication of involvement by other parties."

"This is really great news. Let me just say that we're very relieved."

"Wait, have you determined why they committed the robberies?" asked someone else in the crowd.

Axel hadn't given much thought to that, but it seemed pretty obvious. Bored teenagers get into trouble, just like he did before God got his attention.

Holly paused. "Well, no, they haven't been very cooperative, but we'll continue to press them on that point."

Silence permeated the room. Questioning looks sprouted on more than a few faces. Holly looked over at Axel, and he shook his head. He wanted to bail her out, but an answer eluded him. *Time to run for the hills.*

"If there are no more questions, we'll conclude for now," Holly said. "The coordination team will contact all of you if any other information comes to our attention. Thank you for coming."

"Thank you, Risen Ones," Juanita said. "Your work is much appreciated. We praise God for sending you."

"We certainly do," one of the community leaders said. "And we'll celebrate his goodness by gathering together at Kate Sessions Memorial Park later today. We hope that you and all of our new risen friends will join us."

Holly nodded. "We'll be there, and we'll spread the word among the team."

After the crowd had thinned, Marie, Derek, and Nina entered the gym.

"Hey Axel, we heard about your excitement last night," Nina said. "You've created quite a buzz in the community."

Axel ran his hand through his hair. He wasn't used to being front-page news and hadn't decided whether he liked that part of the assignment or not. *Just one of the occupational hazards, I guess.* "Really? What are they saying?"

"That some kind of superman is protecting them now."

"Did you tell them to tune in again next week for more heroics from the man of steel?" Holly said.

Axel smiled and shook his head. "It was epic. I'm really grateful that the Lord gave me this to do. Abiron was there too."

"Oh, did he help you?"

"No, he showed up after, but I was glad to see him."

"And what about you guys?" RJ said. "I'm sure your team is doing things just as heroic."

"We've seen the Lord work mightily in the lives of these people," Marie replied. "So much hardship has already been relieved. He's answered our prayers in every situation."

"We could tell you some amazing stories about the miracles he's done," Derek said. "But it would take more time than we have right now."

"That's wonderful," Holly replied. "Maybe you can share some of them at the celebration tonight."

"We'll definitely be there. The people could really use something like that."

Later in the afternoon, Axel and RJ made their way over to the park. The crowd began to gather as the savory aromas of grilled beef, chicken, and fish rose into the air. The drummer struck his snare, and the band launched into a swirling chorus of praise.

Not long after, Stein approached them, flanked by a couple looking like they might be in their late fifties. "Malik and Tanisha think there may be more to these crimes than what you uncovered last night."

Axel wondered what they could have missed. "Please, tell us more."

"Well, first I want to thank you for what you've done," Tanisha said. "Our neighborhoods are already safer. I don't want to take anything away from that."

"We appreciate you coming forward," RJ said. "If there's anything else going on, we'd like to know about it."

"I don't know if you'll find this important or not, but there's a wireless tower near our home with lots of antennae on it. Malik and I go by it on our walks each day. There's a box down at the base where little lights used to be on inside. They were very bright and were always on. That was until our mobile phones stopped working just a short time before you all arrived. After that, we couldn't see them anymore."

RJ brought his hand to his chin. "Like the power had been turned off?"

"Yes, exactly," Malik said.

"Isn't that about the time the Lord took those networks down," Axel said, "to cripple the enemy's communications?"

"I think so," Malik replied. "But the thing is, those lights are now on again."

Axel didn't remember any announcements from the technology team. Maybe there was something to this. "You think the tower is operating? Right now?"

"It seems like it, but my phone still doesn't work. And no one else's does either."

"When did the lights come on?"

"Six or seven days ago," Tanisha said.

Axel folded his arms. Suspicious timing to say the least. "Then our team couldn't have done it. We hadn't arrived yet."

"Since mobile devices were being stolen, we thought there might be some connection."

"There may be," RJ said. "Thanks for bringing this to us, and I'd like you to show someone from our technology team where this is so they can check it out. I know they plan to restore the networks soon, but I'm sure they'll be surprised to find a tower powered up already."

Darkness had fallen, and Axel became immersed in the worship. The band played rousing harmonies, and those around him sang, danced, and proclaimed the greatness and goodness of God.

Countless angels appeared above the trees in a circle around the park, lighting the area like a stadium blazing at full power.

Axel bowed his head and tapped his foot in rhythm while Francisco raised his hands toward the sky next to him. The voices of angels, Risen Ones, and people from the community all united in a spirited symphony of joy.

What a contrast, Axel thought. *I didn't feel this much euphoria in all of my earthly worship experiences put together.* But he realized the problem hadn't been with the worship back then; it had been with him. Heaven had dramatically altered his grasp of God's glory, as if he'd been standing over a gopher hole in the yard his entire life and then turned to find himself on a ledge overlooking the immensity of the Grand Canyon. He would never approach devotion in such a casual manner again.

For about half an hour the crowd sang out, then the angels disappeared just as suddenly as they'd arrived.

The celebration came to an end a short time later, and the people of the community left for their homes. Axel and RJ said their good-byes to Marie and the others, and then Holly came running up. "Guys, we've got work to do."

"Why, what's going on?" RJ said. Axel was shocked by the ashen look on Holly's face.

"They found a body. In the neighborhood just south of here."

"And they suspect foul play?"

"They wouldn't have called for us if they didn't."

13

Investigation

Holly, Axel, and RJ arrived at the scene of the crime in Pacific Beach. There at a house on Ingraham Street, not far from the site of the celebration, they found a man seemingly in his late thirties lying stone cold on the living room floor, facedown in a pool of blood. Family members mourned, and a crowd of people gathered on the sidewalk out front. Axel and RJ began to scour the property for clues while Holly approached a grieving woman sitting at the kitchen table.

"Ma'am, my name is Holly," she said softly. "I'm with the justice team. I'm very sorry about your loss. May I sit down?"

"Y-yes," the woman sobbed.

Holly took a seat in the chair across from her. She had never worked this aspect of a case before. It had always consisted of the sterile back-office analysis stuff, far from the personal side where emotions engage. *I hope I can cope with the sorrows.*

She looked forward to the days when the Lord would create the new heaven and the new earth, with no more death or mourning or crying or pain. But until that time, when sin would be completely removed, evil would have its say in the conversation, even during this kingdom age. And she would do everything possible to use her calling from God to see it silenced.

"I don't want to take much of your time, but I need to get some information from you," she said.

"I understand," the woman replied.

"Would you tell me who the man in the other room is?"

"My husband, Mike Antonelli . . . I'm his wife . . . Denise."

"Do you know what happened?"

"I . . . no, I don't," she said through her tears. "He was there . . . I found him when we came home from the park. Thank goodness I was able to keep the kids from seeing, you know . . . seeing him."

Nina entered the room and waited near the doorway. Holly caught her eye and nodded, then turned back to the grieving woman. "Denise, this is Nina from our care team. I know the anguish you're going through. The God of comfort understands. He'll be holding your hand through this. I promise. All of us experienced loss before becoming Risen Ones, and Nina is going to be walking alongside you as well. She's here to help—"

"Don't you think it's a little late for that?" Denise interrupted, crying. "I thought you were here to prevent this kind of thing from happening! Couldn't you have used your powers or something?"

Holly grasped for a consoling response, but the words escaped her. The Lord had allowed this to happen. But why? She trusted him, but how could she explain it? *What answer can I possibly give?*

"I really wish we could have," she replied.

Denise wiped her nose with a tissue. "I'm sorry . . . Holly, was it? I'm sorry I didn't mean to come down on you."

"No, no, I understand." Holly looked at Nina, and then back to Denise. Determination to get to the bottom of this welled up in her. "Could I ask just a couple more questions?"

Denise nodded.

"Is anything missing from your home?"

"I don't think so, but that's the farthest thing from my mind right now."

"I know, but I have to ask. So this probably wasn't an attempted robbery. Did Mike have any enemies, someone who might want to hurt him?"

"Well . . . I'm embarrassed, because we're all believers and everything, but yes, he did." Denise studied the patch of carpeting beneath her feet. "How do I say this? I mean, things were so difficult; just getting food was a challenge each day. All of our dreams . . . we just lost hope, and the two of us drifted apart. Then about eighteen months ago, Mike had an affair."

The tears rolled down Denise's face again, but Holly knew she had to press on. "What did you do when you found out?"

"Like anyone else, at first, I was furious, bitter, humiliated . . . broken. But Mike showed sincere regret, and he totally changed. He even became more devoted in his walk with the Lord, believe it or not. And I forgave him—not at first, but over time—and our marriage grew from there. The last few months . . ." Denise's mouth grew more distorted. "The last few were honestly the best we've ever had."

Nina put her hand on Denise's shoulder.

"So, who is it that may have wanted to hurt him?" Holly said.

"Well like I said, I forgave him, but Nick, he never did."

"Nick?"

"Nick Reilly. His wife Dana had the affair with Mike."

This could definitely be a crime of passion. It had all the elements. "Hmm. And how do you know them?"

"We went to church together until about a year and a half ago. After that there were no more services because all religions had been outlawed."

"Was there anything specific that led you to think Mike was in danger?"

"Nick threatened him. I know Christians aren't supposed to seek revenge, but he was so angry."

Holly tapped her finger on the table. *What else do I need to ask? Have I covered everything?* Crime reports contained lots of other details, but she couldn't recall anything that applied here. "Okay, I think I have enough for now. Denise, if there's anything I can do or any other information you think I should know, please don't hesitate to have someone here get in touch with me. I wish I could tell you why this happened, but even as a Risen One, I don't have the wisdom of our God. He knows. He was there with you when you found your husband's body, and he is here with you now." She hesitated. "When I was here on Earth the first time, I had so much trouble connecting with him, but he was with me all along. And he's here now, Denise. And he is heartbroken with you."

Holly began to walk away and then turned back. "We'll find out who did this, and why. And I apologize for the inconvenience, but we'll need to take some forensics from you and your family."

Holly searched for Axel and RJ and found them on the front porch. "Well, it doesn't look like a burglary. What have you guys found?"

"I don't think these perps could have left any more evidence," RJ said. "We've got blood, hair strands, fabric fibers, even a piece of a fingernail."

"Do you know what killed him?"

"Knife wounds, from the looks of it. Maybe four or five stabs in the abdomen."

Holly's stomach turned. "So there was a struggle?"

"It looks like it. He has some bruises and scrapes. The living room's a mess. Stuff broken, knocked over."

"That probably rules out the wife. She wouldn't have been able to overpower him."

"Unless she was working with someone. Does she have a motive?"

Holly mulled over the conversation. She hated to cast suspicion on Denise, but it *was* a possibility. "Mmm, maybe. She told me he had an affair about a year and a half ago with a woman named Dana Reilly. According to her they resolved it, but she thinks the mistress's husband never really let go. She used the term 'revenge.'"

"Sounds like we need to make a house call on this guy," Axel said.

"I agree," RJ said. "Let's get some genetic samples from him and have the lab team compare them to what we've gathered here."

At that moment, Reid walked up. "Well, I'm glad our league of superheroes is on the case."

"That's what we do," Axel replied.

Holly rolled her eyes. She didn't really need Reid to fan Axel's flame right now. "Actually, we don't have anything conclusive yet."

"Anything I can help with?" Reid said.

Maybe there was. "Did you know the victim?"

Reid didn't hesitate. "Yeah, I knew him, but I'm not terribly surprised that this happened."

"Why do you say that?"

"You may want to talk to Nick Reilly. Mike got involved with his wife, and Nick didn't take it very well."

"We're already working on that, but thanks for the tip."

"Sorry to interrupt," RJ said. "But there's a man down the sidewalk I've been watching for a while. He seems to be sending text messages or something. I didn't think anyone could use their devices yet."

"Mine still doesn't work," Reid said. "Rumor has it, though, that some covert groups have created their own private networks. I think there may be some shady things going on over those airwaves."

Axel tapped his foot. "Covert groups, huh? We can't let that continue."

"Easy, Clark. No need for your cape yet," Holly said.

RJ pointed stealthily in the man's direction. "Do you recognize the one I'm talking about, short with light blond hair? Near the back of the crowd by the fence."

"Oh, yeah," Reid replied. "That's Elias. Kind of a strange guy."

"We've heard that name. What do you know about him?"

"Nothing really. He just showed up in the area a few weeks ago."

"We've been told that he hangs out with teenagers."

"That's true. People have been a little concerned about him. No one's been able to figure out why he's here."

"I think an interrogation is in order then," Axel said, cracking his knuckles.

"Axel, we need to find this Nick Reilly," Holly replied. "We've got a lot more probable cause on him."

"She's right," RJ said. "We can catch up with this Elias later."

Axel folded his arms. "Calm down, guys. Who says we have to stay together? You two check out the lead on Nick, and I'll tail this Elias guy."

Holly shook her head. She admired her cousin's zeal, but his tendency to shoot first and aim later could hurt the investigation. *I definitely need to redirect his gusto right now. A little flattery should do the trick.*

"I'd really like to stay together," she said calmly. "We may need you to take down Nick if things get messy over there."

After a few seconds, Axel nodded. "Okay, Holl. I'll go with you on this one."

✷

Axel followed the directions Reid had given them to the Reilly's home, speeding through the other dimensions with Holly and RJ close behind. Crickets chirped in the yard, and blinds darkened the windows of the house.

RJ knocked on the door, but no one answered. After a few moments Axel rang the doorbell several times, and the porch light came on. *Finally,* he thought.

"Who is it?" said a woman's voice, half-asleep.

"Mrs. Reilly, we're with the justice team," Holly said. "I'm sorry that it's so late, but we need to speak with your husband. Is he here?"

"Can't this wait until morning?"

"I wish it could. Can you please open the door?"

They waited. Axel put the odds at less than fifty-fifty and prepared to slide in through the walls.

"Ughh. Okay. Hold on."

The door opened moments later. A thirtysomething Dana Reilly stood there in her popcorn-yellow pajamas, her almond-pixi hair sticking out in different directions.

"Mrs. Reilly, we have some questions for Nick," RJ said. "May we come in?"

"If you must," she replied, and then turned and yelled, "Nick!"

Axel stepped into the living room behind Holly and RJ and waited in front of a worn black leather sofa. Pillows lay strewn across the beige carpeting, along with a magazine and bowl of grapes.

Dana shouted louder, "Nick, *please*, come here." She turned to RJ. "What is this about?"

"We can talk about that when he gets here, ma'am."

Dana folded her arms as the silence ushered awkwardness into the room—an unwelcome intruder that always set Axel a little on edge. After another few seconds, she walked down the hall. "Let me see what's taking him so long."

Axel studied an *Endless Summer* poster on the kitchen wall. The same one had hung in his bedroom years ago, with shadows of Mike Hynson and Robert August ferrying their longboards across the sand. Suddenly, a soft click sounded from the back of the house. "Did you guys hear that?"

"Hear what?" Holly said.

No time for conversation. He immediately rotated out to the other dimensions to a place above the roof. Footsteps bounded down the alley. *This guy is making it way too easy.*

Axel raced to a place in front of the deserter and rotated back in, instantly planting his head into the man's chest and driving him to the ground. *Ray Lewis would be proud.*

"Nick Reilly?" he said.

The man shook his head and squinted up at Axel, raising his arms in the darkness. "Okay, okay. I did it. Just don't hurt me."

Axel rose to his feet and pulled Nick up with him. "Did you really think you could get away with it?"

"You guys are scary good," Nick replied. "I didn't think anyone would find out."

"It doesn't seem that complicated to me, man. Everyone says you were angry enough to kill him."

Nick's face went instantly pale. "Kill him? What are you talking about?"

"Oh, come on. We know you threatened Mike Antonelli."

If possible, Nick's face went even whiter. "Mike Antonelli? He's dead?"

"Like you didn't know."

Nick pulled away. "No! Oh my gosh. No! I mean the guy was a jerk, but I didn't kill him. I swear I didn't kill him! I didn't kill anybody!"

Axel folded his arms. He wasn't buying it for a minute. "Then why were you running?"

"Oh, man, this looks pretty bad, doesn't it?"

"Digging deeper and deeper," Axel replied.

Nick dusted himself off and didn't meet Axel's eyes. "I was the church treasurer. Some of their money made its way into my account. No one ever found out. I felt guilty and stopped doing it, but we could never afford to pay it back. I thought that's why you were after me."

Sure, Axel thought. *Divert our attention with a crime that doesn't matter anymore.* "Nice try. Let's go back inside."

Axel and Holly interrogated Nick and Dana while RJ collected forensic samples. After they completed their work, RJ said, "Please don't plan on leaving town in the next few days."

"There's no Mexican border anymore," Axel said. "The Lord rules everywhere, and we'll have no trouble finding you."

The three rushed to the lab, where the staff performed DNA analysis. After concluding their tests, they passed the results on to Holly. She scanned the reports and looked up at her team. "Well, if Nick Reilly did it, he didn't leave any evidence."

Axel shook his head. "Wait, seriously? I thought this was gonna be a slam dunk!"

"They found matches for Denise and her children, but that's it."

"So no one else was in that living room?" RJ said.

"I didn't say that," Holly replied. "You guys collected hair strands and bloodstains from a couple of other people they couldn't match. That's our ticket. We need to figure out who they belong to."

"But who else would even have a motive?" Axel blurted.

"It sounds like Antonelli had issues. I'll bet there are others. The sun will be up in an hour or so. Then we can go back and talk to Denise again."

At that moment, a man with red hair and a red beard rotated into the room. "RJ! I knew I'd find you in a laboratory somewhere. You just couldn't stay away from science, could you?"

RJ's face lit up. "Rusty, you old dog, what are you doing here?"

They grabbed each other by the shoulders and shook each other vigorously.

"You really made me think back there in the hospital," Rusty said. "The Lord was definitely working on me, and I put my faith in Christ shortly after that."

"Praise God! Where would we be if he didn't keep after us? I'm elated that you're here, but I would've expected to find you in a lab somewhere as well."

"Oh no, not me. I had enough of that the first time around. I enjoy working with the coordination team. It's much more of a people job."

"So what brings you here to see us?"

"Well, I'm a bit of a late arrival to your group. I started up in North County but was reassigned a few hours ago. And we've got a missing person—you need to come right away. A woman in Hidden Valley says her daughter didn't come home last night."

"So should we split up?" Axel said.

"No, we can all go," Holly replied. "Denise won't be ready for us at this time of the morning anyway." She gave Axel a pointed look. "I think it's best we stick together as much as we can until we've all got the hang of this a little better."

✷

Holly, Axel, and RJ followed Rusty through the other dimensions to a large home on Hidden Valley Road, where they rotated back in onto the ground out front. The sun was just beginning to creep over the nearby hills, but clusters of clouds kept its rays from shining through.

Holly admired the intricately landscaped courtyard with a two-tiered fountain flowing in the middle and the smell of lilacs hanging in the air. A woman with caramel-blonde hair, looking to be in her midforties, answered the door.

"Mrs. Erickson," Rusty said. "This is Holly, Axel, and RJ. They're from our justice team."

"I'm Erin," she replied, reaching out to shake their hands. Her maple eyes, with dark bags underneath, were swollen. "Please come in."

They followed her through a wide entryway with crystal chandeliers above and spiral staircases ahead. Holly's eyes feasted on the charming decor. *I only saw lavish furnishings like this in magazines during my time on Earth.*

They made their way into a spacious living room with an enormous fireplace and crown molding around the vaulted ceiling. Claude Debussy played faintly in the background.

"Please, make yourselves comfortable," Erin said.

Holly took a seat on one of the plush couches. "Erin, we understand your daughter didn't come home last night."

Erin sighed. "That's right. I expected her back by midnight. That's her curfew."

"Do you know what her plans were when she left the house?"

"To see some friends. I don't really know where they were going. She won't tell me anything lately."

"Lately?" Axel said. "Has something changed?"

"Yes . . . yes. I don't know what to do with her anymore. Ever since my husband was taken, she's become more and more distant. Even angry. I can't talk to her about anything."

Holly tilted her head. This drama plunged even deeper than she'd expected. "Your husband? He was taken?"

Erin paused. Her eyes became misty.

"Oh, I'm really sorry," Holly said. "You don't have to say any more about that." She kicked herself mentally. Honestly, she could be as hasty as Axel sometimes.

"No . . . no, it's all right. I think it's probably important that you know." She wiped her eyes and sighed again. "His name was

Peter—Peter Erickson. He got caught up in the persecution of believers." She looked down at the floor. Tears rolled down her cheeks.

Holly moved over, put her arm around Erin, and handed her a tissue. Here she was consoling another heartbroken soul. This job was supposed to be about justice, but imparting the Lord's compassion and love seemed to be a big part of it, and she thanked God for the opportunity. "We're here for you, Erin, and Jesus is as well."

"Thank you. Thank you so much."

"Feel free to share more, if it helps." *Besides, we might need to know more to help us find your daughter.* But she didn't say that out loud.

"Well, he was a successful businessman. I never thought his faith in God was really all that strong, but when the government officers came for him, he stood up for Christ with such courage."

"When did that happen?"

"About six months ago, and I haven't seen him since. I was hoping he'd come back when the Lord returned. That maybe he was still alive, but . . ." She paused, and more tears flowed. "I apologize. I know that's not why you're here."

"It's all right," Holly said. "Take as much time as you need."

Erin cleared her throat. "Well . . . my daughter's name is Nikki. She's seventeen. She's a really good kid. Before the turmoil of the last few years, she was a straight-A student in school, honors on her swim team, loved doing community service. She always enjoyed going to youth group at church, although they haven't been able to meet for a long time. But over the last couple of months, she's been hanging out with this other group of kids. It hasn't been good for her."

RJ leaned forward in his chair. "What do you know about them? Names? Addresses? Physical descriptions?"

"I don't know much. The only thing she's told me is that they're from Pacific Beach. Alex, Vince, and Tia are the names she's mentioned the most."

"And she was with them last night?"

"Yes. She was going to meet them, but I don't know where." Erin's eyes pleaded with Holly. "Please find my daughter. She's all I've got left now."

"Of course," Holly said, resting her hand on Erin's knee. "Our team won't have any problem locating her friends, I promise. We'll start there and get back to you as soon as we can."

A deep longing tugged at Holly's heart. She didn't usually place the urgency of one case above another, but this one had jumped to the top of the heap for some reason. Maybe it was because she was a mother herself.

"Thank you so much, and I appreciate you coming so quickly," Erin said.

Holly lagged behind with Erin as they all walked out. "Hey, can I ask you one more question?" Something else had occurred to her, and she just had to ask.

"Sure," Erin replied.

"It's on a *totally* different topic, but where is your family from?"

"Oh, both my husband and I are from Olympia, Washington. Why do you ask?"

"Well, my maiden name was also Erickson. And the guy on the left is my cousin, Axel Erickson. His father was my dad's brother. And the other one is my Uncle RJ . . . Erickson. Another one of my dad's brothers."

"And where's your family from?"

"Unfortunately, we lost touch with most of them during my first go-around here, but they were also from the Olympia area. Wild, huh?"

14

Intensifying

Axel leaned against a post on the Antonellis' front porch while Holly questioned Denise inside. RJ sat on a redwood bench a few yards away.

Moments later, a man with light blond hair, a medium build and a gold earring in his left ear came walking up the street. Axel looked over at RJ. "Hey, isn't that that Elias guy?"

RJ peered around one of the trees in the yard. "I think you're right. I wonder what he's doing here."

They headed out to the sidewalk and waited until Elias had strolled in front of Denise's property. "May we have a word with you, sir?" RJ said.

"It would be my pleasure, RJ," Elias replied with a British accent.

RJ's jaw became slacked. "You know my name?"

Elias didn't seem fazed. "Why of course, everyone knows *your* names."

"So what brings you here today?" Axel said.

"It's a brilliant morning, Axel, don't you think? I'm just out for a walk."

Axel squinted. Likely story. And was it just coincidence that this street was part of his regular route? "Returning to the scene of the crime, then?"

Elias raised an eyebrow. "That's quite the probing question. Actually, I pass by here all the time."

"I noticed you were typing on a mobile device last night," RJ said. "Were you texting with someone?"

"You're very observant, but no, I was just taking notes for my journal. Digital is easier than pen and paper you know."

"So what's your business with the teens in the neighborhood?" Axel said.

"I'm a teacher, Axel. They're at an age where there's so much to learn, but they don't pay attention for very long. I find that extremely challenging, don't you?"

The olive branch had been offered, but Axel wasn't ready to be buddies just yet. "Not really, but I do find your presence here the day after a murder a bit challenging, Elias."

"I understand you're new to the area," RJ cut in, heading off Axel's aggressive tone. "Where did you live before?"

Elias smiled. "I was hoping this would be a friendly introduction, but it rather seems more like an interrogation. That's okay, though. I know you have a job to do, and I'm happy to answer your questions. Where did I live before? Well, I was in the military for a long time. I moved around."

At that moment, Rusty appeared. "Hey, I've got an address for you, and a map. My team says Nikki's friends are there right now."

"Excellent, Rusty. Nice work," RJ said.

"You guys go on and head over," Rusty said. "I'll let Holly know where you are. Then I need to get back to the gym. We've got a lot going on."

"Sounds good. We'll try to catch them before they take off. Thanks."

Rusty went into the house.

Axel glanced over RJ's shoulder at the map. At least they could put this missing teenage girl thing to bed and get on with the important stuff. Tracking down Nikki captured his ambition about as much as brushing his teeth at the end of the day. Back when that mattered anyway.

He lifted his eyes, sensing something was awry, and then turned his head to one side and then the other. "Hey, where'd Elias go?"

"Hmm," RJ replied. "I didn't see him leave."

"He was just right here. It's almost like he vanished."

"He must have slipped away into one of these yards or something."

"I would think we would have noticed, but I guess you're right." The guy was *definitely* guilty of something. His behavior practically shouted it.

RJ shook his head. "We'll just have to catch up with him later."

They rotated out and dashed to the address Rusty had given them. Axel moved in through the roof of the small house, remaining invisible in the other dimensions. RJ came right behind. There, in the cluttered living room, seven teenagers stared at a wall-size 3-D computer screen projecting the image of a man in a black mask.

Axel wrinkled his forehead. Something here didn't add up. "I thought the Lord took the Internet down weeks ago."

"He did. I don't know where this signal is coming from," RJ replied. "Maybe they're using one of those private networks Reid was talking about."

Axel pointed to one of the girls, and his sense of purpose surged again. "She looks like the pictures of Nikki we saw at Erin's house. I'm going in."

"No!" RJ said. "This is far too intriguing. Let's see what they're up to first."

The teens remained fixated on the screen. Saying nothing. Just listening to the man in the black mask speaking with a synthesized voice. "Drago is pleased. The infiltrator has been eliminated."

"Infiltrator?" Axel said. "Do you think he's talking about Antonelli?"

RJ brought his finger to his lips. "Shhhhh."

"Your training for the uprising may now continue," the voice said. "You'll each receive schedule information via encrypted text message. All future communications must occur digitally over the private networks. Public discussion of our activities is expressly forbidden. With the Risen Ones now present, we must tighten down security even more."

Axel's eyes widened. "Whoa! An uprising? What's this about?"

"I'm not sure," RJ said tersely. His tone clearly said, *Hush. I'm trying to listen.*

"Remember, Drago is watching all of you closely," the voice said. "The success of our mission depends on you."

The screen went dark. Questions flooded Axel's mind. The mire had just deepened considerably, mushrooming from a mud puddle into a lake of quicksand. "Who was that guy in the funky black wrestling mask?"

"Don't know, but we need to find out. Not to mention Drago—I'd say identifying him is top priority. Let's get back with Holly so we can share this with her."

"Wait, what about Nikki?"

"I think she's fine. Let's leave her here for now. I don't want to spook them and ruin the opportunity to learn more about this rebellion. It sounds much bigger than just a case of a runaway teen."

Suddenly, something shifted in Axel's peripheral vision. He turned and caught a slight glimpse of . . . Arielle. "Speaking of runaways, did you just see that?"

"See what?"

Someone was playing a joke on him, a cruel one that never seemed to get to the punch line. He didn't find it amusing and wasn't going to fall for it again. Every ounce of his soul wanted to go after her, and his heart ached to be by her side. But evidently, something wasn't right. Maybe she didn't want to see him. Maybe she'd decided it was time for their relationship to cool. What else was he supposed to think? "That girl, who just moved down the hallway. She was in the other dimensions with us."

"You're kidding, right?"

"No . . . no, I'm not. And it looked like Arielle. I'm not joking. I'm sure I saw her the other night too."

"Arielle, huh? I'm really beginning to worry about you."

They raced back to Denise's house and gave Holly the news of their discovery.

"Well, that fits with what Denise told me this morning," Holly said. "Evidently, Mike had stumbled onto something that troubled him deeply. He wouldn't share anything with her, but she said it kept him up at night. He tried to explain it away, saying he was just concerned about providing for the family, but it sounds like maybe the fear of something sinister had filled his mind."

"This is all beginning to make sense," RJ said. "He'd become aware of the uprising, and it cost him his life."

"Yeah," Axel replied, "and that means more innocent lives are at stake."

"Certainly there's no threat to the Lord or his kingdom from this rebellion," Holly said, "but anyone who shows even the tiniest bit of suspicion toward their activities will be subject to peril at their hands. They've proven they're lethal in that regard."

"More bloodshed seems imminent," RJ said. "Unless we can find a way to stop this quickly."

"A very precarious situation, no doubt," a familiar voice said from the side.

"Hananias!" Holly exclaimed, whirling around to see their old friend.

"It is very good to see you all again," he replied.

Holly pointed a finger at him. "You can probably help us with this case."

"Oh, it is not my help that you need."

"What do you mean? You've always had all the answers."

"Do you remember the conversation we had with the Lord before you left Jerusalem?"

Axel certainly hadn't forgotten. That marked the dawn of this vital afterlife calling. "Yeah, the vine and the branches and all that."

"Right, and have you been relying on him to guide you in your service for him here?"

Axel searched his memory. Abiron had said the Lord led him to the two teenage thieves. At least his answer was a yes.

Holly pressed her lips together. "Well . . . of course. I think so, anyway."

"Okay. Let me just say then that you need to depend on him more than you have been. Seek his counsel, and he will guide you in all matters."

"I was thinking," RJ said, "Maybe we could go back to heaven for just a few moments. That way we could talk directly to Mike Antonelli and find out exactly what he knows."

Hananias shook his head. "No, that will not be possible." He paused, stood up straighter, and said softly, "I think what we really need to do is pray."

"Oh . . . of course," Holly replied.

"Maybe you could lead us, RJ."

"Well, okay," RJ replied. "Let's bow our heads. Lord, we come before you humbly as your servants, seeking your guidance in this situation. We know that you require righteousness in your kingdom, and we want to bring that about in this case. Please guide us to find Mike Antonelli's killer, so that he or she will be brought to justice. In your name we pray. Amen."

"Good," Hananias said. "Keep seeking him in every aspect of your work. I will be in touch."

They bade him farewell, and he flashed away. Holly looked at RJ and then over at Axel. "So what next, guys?"

A notion jumped into Axel's mind, waving to get his attention. "I think we should head back over to the house where RJ and I watched the videoconference."

"Why do you say that?"

"Not sure. Just sounds like a good idea to me."

Holly laughed but said, "Okay. Can't say that I have a better plan."

They arrived there in a split second through the other dimensions and moved in through the walls of the house.

"There's no one here," RJ said.

Just like the first visit, the place reminded Axel of his bedroom during his teenage years on Earth. Food and dirty dishes strewn about. Clothes and trash on the ground.

Holly wrinkled her nose. "What a mess. They must not mind living in a pigsty."

"Let's have a look around," Axel said. He didn't really even know what to look for, but he sensed he was in the right place.

They rotated in onto the ground, and Holly walked over to the wall-size computer screen. "Wow, that's one huge monitor. It looks like they were playing some kind of video game."

Axel studied the graphic combat scene frozen on the display. Soldiers marched in formation with weapons drawn. Bloodstained casualties lay in the dirt. Smoke rose from recently-fired artillery canons. It was almost lifelike. "Technology's really advanced since my time on earth."

"The 3-D resolution's incredible. You really feel like you're a part of it."

"It looks like some kind of war game. A battlefield simulation or something."

Holly shook her head. "I don't think the Lord would like this. He's destroying anything and everything having to do with war." And she walked down the hall.

"This must be why those teens committed the robberies," RJ said.

"To supply computers and networks for the uprising?" Axel said.

"Exactly. We just need to tie some of that stolen equipment to what's going on here."

"Hey guys, come have a look at this," Holly yelled.

Axel rushed to where she stood, and RJ came right behind. A pile of bloodstained clothes lay on the bathroom floor beside the counter. "Whoa!"

"Yeah, it's pretty gruesome," she said. "We should get these to the lab. And I'll bet I know whose blood this is."

"I'm tracking right with you," Axel replied, "but let's keep searching. The more we can find on this uprising, the faster we can take it down."

"Sounds good. I'll bag these up."

For the next few minutes, Axel opened cabinets, closets, and drawers, but found nothing. Holly and RJ came away empty-handed as well.

"There's gotta be more here," RJ said. "Something, anything that might lead us to that guy in the black mask. Let's think."

"What about the garage or the backyard?" Holly replied.

"I guess we should check there too."

"And where are these kids' parents? Who owns this house?"

"I don't know. I don't see any sign of adults here. Maybe they're out of town."

They proceeded to the garage. Holly and RJ searched through boxes and storage bins. Axel slid out a side door and instantly cringed at the pungent aroma rising from three garbage cans. *Maybe I should just casually mosey on past and make my way out to the front yard.* No fence or gate or anything stood in the way, and no one would blame him for skipping this rodeo. But then again, even the Duke did some of the dirty work in his movies.

He reluctantly lifted a trash-can lid and fished around. After a minute or so of rummaging, he bumped into something sharp. It didn't hurt, but he noticed blood on his hand and immediately pulled it back, alarmed by the dark red on his fingers. *How could this happen? Is my resurrected body fallible after all?*

He wiped his hand clean with a paper towel, but found no cuts. If it wasn't his blood, then whose was it? The truth hit him right away, and he reached down to pull the pointed object out of the can. It was a hunting knife, easily twenty-four inches long, with a bloody rag wrapped around the blade. "Hey, check this out."

Holly came through the door first and whistled. "Wow, that's one scary knife. Nice work, Axel."

Without warning, an electric car rolled up the street toward the driveway. All three Risen Ones brought their heads up at once, startled.

"Rotate out!" RJ yelled.

The car came to an abrupt halt, and two dark-haired young men stared in the direction of the trash cans. Seconds later the tires screeched and the car frantically reversed direction.

"They saw us," RJ said.

Axel darted out in front of the car and rotated in onto the ground as it sped down the street. Holly and RJ rotated in right behind him. Axel folded his arms and bolstered his stance. "My name is Gladiator," he said in his best Maximus voice.

The driver slammed on the brakes, stopping just short of Axel's resurrected body barricade. A burnt rubber odor filled the air. The driver jammed the car into reverse, made a quick three-point turn and headed back down the street the other way. Axel looked at Holly. "You're up."

"They're all mine," she replied.

Holly rotated out to the other dimensions and back in onto the pavement in front of the car. This time the driver made a quick turn to the right onto another street, but RJ had already moved there and stood waiting with his hand extended. The driver tried to reverse again, but this time Holly stood behind him.

The car slammed into her and knocked her backwards, but the impact stopped it dead in its tracks.

"Get out of the car!" RJ demanded as he and Axel walked toward the two skinny, acne-faced teens.

The driver opened his door and stood up, holding out a grenade. He sneered and then pulled a round pin out of the top and dropped the grenade on the ground. Smoke billowed out.

"Can you see them?" Axel yelled.

"No, I can't see a thing," RJ shouted back.

"Let's get to a place with a better view then."

They both entered the other dimensions at once and moved above the haze. Holly hovered there already. Axel scanned fervently to the right, to the left, and then behind, but he saw no one. "Did you see which way they went?"

"No, they didn't come my way," she replied. "I thought they went toward you."

Axel slapped his hand on his thigh. "This can't be. We had those guys!"

"Let's split up and do a quick search of the area," RJ said. "Maybe we'll see them before they get too far."

Axel sped through the other dimensions scanning the streets. He shot through bushes and around fences, looking in every possible hiding place, but he found no sign of them. Irritation set in. *How could they have escaped? They were just yards away!* He shook his head and returned to unite with Holly and RJ.

"Any luck?" RJ said.

"Nothing," Axel replied.

Holly rubbed her chin. "Me either, but there was one thing I found that was interesting."

"What's that?"

"Elias. He was at the teens' house when I passed by there."

First the Antonellis and now there. Did this guy show up at the most suspicious places or what? It couldn't be just a coincidence. "You're kidding. What was he doing?"

"Standing out front, typing something on his mobile phone, like he was texting or something."

RJ began moving in that direction. "Let's get over there right away."

15

Opening

Elias was gone. Holly stood bewildered in front of the teens' house. "He was just here no more than five minutes ago!"

Rusty rotated in next to her with a small tablet computer in hand. "Hey, Stein and Lisa want to speak to you. They witnessed something unusual. Something their son was doing."

Rivers of suspicion began to flow in Holly's head—currents of opportunity to take her to deeper insight. "I'll bet he knows the boys who live in this house, and maybe where we can find them."

Rusty's eyebrows narrowed. "RJ, weren't they here when you came earlier?"

"Well, yes, but things got a little complicated."

"So you didn't find Nikki Erickson?"

"Actually we did, but that's another story altogether. The good news is we think we found the murder weapon, and evidence pointing to something much bigger."

"Hold on, hold on," Rusty said. "Are we mixing cases here? I think what I'm hearing you say is that these teens are involved in the Antonelli killing?"

RJ nodded. "Yeah, it's all connected. Can you send someone here to stake out the house, and have them get in touch with us if anyone comes back?"

"I can . . . but I don't quite follow why Nikki's still missing. Why didn't you take her home?"

Holly wondered the same thing. Maybe Axel and RJ should have escorted her out of there. But then again, would Nikki have gone with them? *We don't really know where her mind is yet.*

"We've got this under control, Rusty," RJ said. "So if you could, we'd like to get word out that we're searching for these guys."

Displeasure canvased Rusty's face as he turned his gaze toward the overcast sky above.

Holly knew she had to push through in spite of his dismay. "Do you have any information on the boys who live here?"

Rusty sighed. "Yeah, two brothers. Alex, an eighteen-year-old, and Vince, a sixteen-year-old. Their parents took the mark, so they're not around anymore."

"Erin mentioned those names, and the two in the car looked like brothers."

"Yeah, I think they're the ones we're after," Axel said. "What about their friends?"

Rusty scanned his screen. "There are quite a few, but their constant companion is a sixteen-year-old female by the name of Tia."

"And now Nikki also," Holly said. The words carved deep. She longed to bring joy back to Erin's life. She couldn't imagine how it would have felt to lose Derek the way Erin had lost her husband. Returning her daughter would hopefully soften the sting. And Nikki needed to get away from that troubled crowd. Holly's still-recent uncertainty about Taj's eternity put an exclamation point on that. She'd waited with concern in the heavenly realm after learning that Taj had rejected the Lord's offer of salvation and followed the ways of the world, embracing addictions and outright rebellion instead. Thankfully, Jesus got his attention just in time, but she didn't want to see Erin have to repeat what she'd gone through.

"Okay," Rusty said, "I'll get right to work on looking for them. But what do you want me to do about Stein and Lisa?"

"Have them meet us at the gym this evening around five," Holly answered. "We need the lab to run some tests for us right now."

"You've got it."

Axel, Holly, and RJ traveled to the lab with the bloodstained clothes and the knife. After about an hour of analysis, the staff confirmed that at least some of the blood was Mike Antonelli's.

"We have pretty convincing proof now," Holly said. "Alex and Vince almost certainly played a part in this murder."

They moved quickly to the UCSD gym through the other dimensions as the clock approached five. Rusty met them at the door and shared that no one had seen their suspects.

"Man, these guys are like ghosts," Axel said.

Stein and Lisa walked in shortly after and shook hands with each of them. "Thanks for taking the time to meet with us," Lisa said. "We know you're very busy."

"I think you can really help us," Holly replied. "The pleasure is ours. Something happened with your son Josh?"

Lisa sighed. "Yeah, I walked by his room this morning and heard some very strange things."

"Like what?"

"Well, his door was closed, but it sounded like he was listening to some kind of computer-generated voice on his laptop. We're really worried about the things he's been getting involved in lately. We're just hoping you can help us get him back on the right track."

"It must have been the same video conference we saw," Axel said.

Stein looked at him with head tilted to one side.

Axel hastened to explain. "We witnessed some teens watching a video conference at a house in Pacific Beach."

"That's really interesting," Stein replied, "because when I went into Josh's room later, after he'd left the house, I discovered that his Internet connection was live. I don't know where he's getting it from."

"Did you ask him about it?" Holly said.

"No, we wanted to bring it to your attention first. It won't be a pleasant conversation with him. And I don't know how long this has been going on, but it looks like he's been playing games over the Internet as well. We thought he was just playing locally on his computer."

Holly turned to Lisa. "Does Josh know two brothers named Alex and Vince?"

She frowned. "He does. They grew up together. Why?"

"Oh, so you've known them since they were young?"

"Yes, we have."

Holly's heart sank. She would have to be the bearer of bad news again. But there really wasn't any other option, was there? A train wreck loomed ahead if Axel or RJ tried to venture into this space.

"Well, I'm really sorry to have to share this with you," she said. "But they're our primary suspects in this murder case."

Lisa's hand flung to her mouth. "Oh, my . . . I can't believe they'd do something so horrible."

"I know this is difficult for you, but we think Josh may be able to help us find them."

Stein shook his head. "You can try, but I'd be surprised if he tells you anything."

"I've got an idea," Axel said. "Something that just might open him up. Can you bring him to Tourmaline Beach at around seven tomorrow morning?"

"I don't see why not. It might be tough getting him out of bed though."

✷

Josh yawned as his father pulled into the parking lot at Tourmaline, with the morning light brightening a thin layer of haze over the water. He stepped out of the passenger side of the car and raised his hands above his head to stretch his six-foot frame. A slight breeze blew back his messy, layered brown hair. He walked behind his dad toward the beach and turned the corner of the restrooms to see a blond-haired guy who looked to be about his age standing there in a white garment with three surfboards and a smile on his face. *Surfing? Oh, great. He can't be serious.*

His father laughed and greeted the stranger. "I had a feeling you were up to something."

"You ever surfed before?" the guy asked.

"When I was younger, but that was a long time ago. This is my son, Josh."

The surfer reached out his hand. "What's up, man? I'm Axel."

"Hey," Josh grunted, halfheartedly returning the handshake. He hadn't been this close to a Risen One before. Axel looked human, but eerily different. Intensity filled his eyes unlike anyone he'd ever known. His hand felt smooth and sturdy, with an unfamiliar texture, and his arms and legs were toned and powerful. He definitely had Josh's attention, but Josh wasn't going to let anyone know.

"How much surfing have you done?" Axel said.

"None," Josh replied. Waves weren't his thing.

"Even growing up this close to the beach?"

"Never really wanted to."

"Well, I hope we can change that. I brought some wetsuits. I think they're the right size."

"There's only two," Stein said.

"I don't need one," Axel replied. "It would take a lot for me to get cold."

Josh pulled his suit on, and Axel ran through the basics: how to paddle, how to push up, where to plant his feet. Josh cooperated, but the whole situation stank like rotten eggs. *Why is this guy showing an interest in me?*

He grabbed his board and followed Axel to the water, seeing some chest-high waves breaking offshore. Light fog still hugged the coast, and a green-tea hue brewed on the surface of the sea.

They entered the ocean, and Axel coached him on where to climb aboard and start paddling. Josh struggled to maintain his balance, but he kept stroking until he eventually made it out into the lineup. There, he and his dad sat up on their boards and panted for air. At least they weren't very likely to get chatty out on the waves.

After a minute or so, swells approached on the horizon. Axel moved into position and took off on the first wave of the set.

Josh watched as the Risen One made a few graceful turns across the wave face, building speed as he went. Then, as if shot out of a cannon, Axel came flying out of the top of the wave, six or seven feet above the crest. He soared through the air for a few seconds and landed back on top of the white water, still standing on his board, then continued to ride for a short time and eventually fell off into the shallows.

Stein looked over at Josh. "Looks pretty fun, eh?"

"Now that was cool," Josh replied.

"You probably won't pull off anything like that, but hopefully you'll get a taste of what it's like."

Josh searched the shoreline, scanning the surface. "I don't see Axel."

Stein turned toward the beach. "Hmm, his board's there, but I don't see him either. He should've come up by now."

"Maybe we should go see if he's all right."

"Yeah," Stein replied, and started to paddle.

Josh stroked as quickly as he could. The shore break had washed Axel's board up on the sand. Josh arrived at the place where the Risen One had fallen off, but he saw no sign of him, so he slid off into the water and prepared to dive under. Then, without warning, his dad's board began moving quickly back out to sea, tail first, with Stein still on it.

"Whooa!" Stein shouted as he reached out and clutched onto the board's rails. He continued to accelerate, his mouth wide open. Water splashed up his back and over his head, and his wake rippled across the surface. He bounced over a few small waves and then suddenly came to an abrupt halt. Axel popped up next to him, howling hysterically.

Stein looked at Axel wide-eyed and panting, and then bent over and laughed with him.

Josh paddled back out and pulled up next to them. His carefully-chosen defensiveness had melted away. "I've never seen my dad look so scared. That was hilarious! How did you stay under like that?"

"I don't need oxygen," Axel said. "I could've stayed down a lot longer. Hey, what do you think of this? Since you're learning, how about if I swim underneath your board to help you get into a wave? Kind of like what I just did to your dad. That is, until you figure out the timing on your own."

Josh's pulse hammered inside his chest. "Yeah . . . why not? After seeing you ride, I'd love to get up on my feet today."

"Cool, here comes a set."

A shoulder-high wave approached. Axel swam behind Josh's board and pushed him into position. "Start paddling," he said and then moved underneath.

Josh gave it a few strokes and jumped to his feet. It was probably too early, but he knew Axel would get him to the right place. The wave started to break, and Josh felt one last shove from below, sending him racing downline with a rush of speed. He crouched low to keep his balance and roared, "Yeeeah!"

The crest fluttered above his head, and the surface of the water flew by beneath. The swell quickened its pace even more as he reached the inside section, and his eyes widened as the pocket curled around him. Suddenly, he hit a bump on the face of the wave and went airborne, separated from his board, and came crashing down. His hip slammed against the bottom, and he tumbled over and over, eventually stopping in a heap. Wooziness set in, but he bounced quickly to his feet and pumped his fist in the air.

Stein clapped and nodded with a big smile on his face. "Yeah, son! Yeah, son!"

Josh paddled back out, beaming. It felt good to hear his dad cheer him on. "That was unreal! I was flying on that wave!"

"Way to go, brah," Axel said. "I think maybe you're a natural. Ready to go again?"

Axel pushed Josh into a few more swells, each one giving him the same thrill as the first.

At the end of their session, they left the water laughing and recounting their rides. They arrived at the parking lot, and Axel sat down on a stone bench while Josh and his dad changed out of their wetsuits.

"So Josh, I need to know, what's going on with these guys Alex and Vince?" Axel said.

The question was totally unexpected. Josh flinched and his jaw tightened. The real reason for this outing had just come to the surface. "I really can't talk about that," he said softly.

"They're in some serious trouble."

Josh pulled his T-shirt on over his head.

"We know they're mixed up in the uprising," Axel continued.

A shiver ran up Josh's spine. *How does he know about that? We've been so careful in everything we've done.*

"I just don't want to see you go down with it. The Lord *will* bring about his justice. You've gotta know that."

Josh's doubts about his own involvement with the uprising came storming back. He'd mulled it over for days. The whole thing had become a little too intense. "I know, I know," he said, his voice breaking despite him. "I've been thinking about getting out, but I can't. If they knew I was talking to you, I'd be toast."

"You can still walk away. We can protect you."

"Listen to him son," Stein said sternly.

Josh swallowed hard. "I wish I could, but all my friends are in really deep. Vince got me involved. At first we were just playing this cool multiplayer war game. He showed me how to get my computer connected. Before I knew it, we were going to all these online meetings. It was real exciting at first, but it's gotten way out of hand."

Axel ran his fingers through his hair. "So tell me about Drago."

Josh shook his head. Axel seemed to have this all figured out. Like a vice clamping down around him. "Man . . . you're good."

He looked out to sea, and then back at Axel. "There isn't much to tell. We've never seen him, but supposedly he's watching us. Maybe even right now." He shivered at the thought. Was he going to die for this conversation? *Too late now.*

"And what about the guy in the black mask?"

"I don't know who he is either . . . How'd you find out about all this?"

"I'll let you in on it sometime. We're also looking for a girl named Nikki Erickson. We know she's been hanging out with Alex, Vince, and Tia. Do you have any idea where she is?"

A warm, trembling sensation swirled in Josh's chest. Desires he couldn't suppress. "I don't know where she is, but she wasn't involved."

"In the murder?"

"Yeah. Trust me. She wasn't involved."

"You sound pretty confident. How can you be so sure?"

Josh knew he was going to have to 'fess up, but it was okay. He had feelings for her, and he didn't care if anyone knew it. He couldn't keep it to himself any longer anyway. "Because," he said, and then paused. He glanced at his dad and then back at Axel. "She was with me."

Stein crossed his arms. "And can you explain to us what exactly you were doing?"

"Just walking . . . talking." A slight smile crept across Josh's face. "She's a really great girl."

Axel grinned. "Ah, I get it."

Stein sighed. "Okay. Okay."

"I really can't tell you anymore, though," Josh said. "I've already said way too much."

"It would really help me if I could ask you just one more thing," Axel replied. "What do you know about Elias?"

Josh hesitated, but his conscience prodded him. One more answer wasn't going to get him further in over his head than he already was. "Not much, but it's kind of freaky. He seems to know where we are all the time. He just shows up, even when we think we're meeting in secret."

Axel nodded slowly. "Interesting." He tapped his foot a few times. Then did it again. "You have to get away from this uprising thing. It won't be good when it all comes down."

He made it sound so easy, but serious consequences awaited all betrayers. Panic threatened to take hold, but Josh fought it down. "I don't know how I can."

"Well, I'm not giving up on you. I need to get back now. If there's anything more you can tell me, your dad knows how to find me."

"Thanks for the surf lesson," Josh said.

"Yeah Axel, I appreciate it a lot," Stein said.

"I'll be in touch," Axel replied, and he shook hands with both of them.

✷

Axel returned the surf gear to its owner and moved through the other dimensions to find Holly, RJ, and Rusty at Alex and Vince's house, searching for anything that might lead them to the brothers or the man in the black mask.

"How'd it go?" Holly said.

"He's a casual dude. I have hope for him."

"Did you learn anything?"

"Yeah. The good news is, according to him, Nikki wasn't with Alex, Vince, and Tia the night Antonelli was killed." He chuckled. "It seems there's a little romance stirring between Josh and Nikki."

Holly's face lit up. "Aw, that's sweet."

"Yeah, whatever," Axel said. He had more important things to disclose. "And it sounds like the leaders of the uprising are luring their recruits in through the multiplayer war game. That's what happened with Josh. All his friends were doing it."

"They must be using it to train them after that," RJ said. "The question I have is: when do they plan for this uprising to occur?"

"Couldn't tell ya, but I also found out that Elias seems to know where Josh and his friends are all the time."

"How can he do that?" Rusty said.

"The global positioning satellites must still be up and running," RJ replied. "All of the teenagers' phones are probably GPS capable, so it wouldn't be hard to pinpoint their location at any time. Once he's got them all using the stolen mobile devices, it shouldn't be hard to track them."

"I'll bet that's what Elias is doing with his device," Holly said. "Running some kind of app to keep an eye on where they are."

RJ clasped his hands behind his head. "Do you see how this is all adding up? The masked man on the videoconference said Drago was watching all of them closely. I think we just figured out who that is."

Axel had put it all together as well. As if the musicians had finally finished tuning their instruments and begun playing from the same sheet of music. "I'm tracking right with you."

Holly's eyebrows rose. "You mean . . . you think . . . Elias is Drago?"

"Think about it," RJ said. "It all fits."

"Hmm, it does seem to make some logical sense."

"We need to talk to him again, like now," Axel said.

Rusty raised his hand. "I'll check with my team to see if anyone's figured out how to find him. It hasn't been easy so far."

It shouldn't be all that hard. Axel knew exactly where to look. "We just need another crime scene. He seems to show up at those all the time."

"Let's hope we get to him sooner than that, before someone else gets hurt, or worse," RJ replied.

"I'll ask the technology team to see what we can do about these private networks," Rusty said.

"Sounds good," Axel said, "but don't let anyone take them down until you've talked to us first."

"You've got it," Rusty said, and he rotated out.

16

Collapsing

Drago loomed somewhere in the vicinity—somewhere within Axel's reach. Whack the head of the snake and the whole menace becomes harmless. Priorities had shifted, and now Alex and Vince were only spots on the serpent. "I think this house has given us all the evidence that it's going to, and Drago isn't going to just drop by for small talk. We need to take this search somewhere else."

"I know we need to find Elias right away," Holly said. "But we can't forget about Nikki. We promised Erin we'd do everything we could."

"I know," RJ replied. "I think I may have blown it. I should have let Axel go in after her when we had the chance."

Axel agreed, but held his tongue rather than saying so. He wouldn't let that happen again. You always buy Monopoly property when you land on it. Who knows if a better one will come along later? If he'd followed his instincts, Nikki's case would be closed. She'd be safe, and they would probably have Alex and Vince in custody right now as well.

Rusty rotated in onto the ground next to them. From his expression, he had news.

"Wow, that was fast," Holly said. "It's only been what, a few minutes?"

"My team's already got a lead on Alex and Vince. We received an anonymous tip from someone who saw them about an hour ago, and evidently that girl Tia was with them."

"And Nikki?" Holly inquired.

"Not as far as we can tell. They were seen going into a hangar at the Miramar Air Station."

RJ's eyebrows came together. "Aren't they tearing those hangars down?"

"Absolutely, just like everything else used for war. The Prince of Peace has no use for them."

"Sounds like a sketchy place to be right now," Axel said.

"It's probably a good place to hide," RJ replied. "And they're sketchy guys. It doesn't surprise me a bit."

Axel, Holly, and RJ hurried over to MCAS Miramar in the other dimensions as clouds obscured the late morning sky. They located the hangar and rotated back in onto the ground outside. The wind rushed against their faces. Large concrete blocks and grave warning signs stood between them and the structure and not a soul could be seen.

"I would think these barriers would keep even fools away," RJ said. "I'm not sure what part of 'Demolition Area' they don't understand."

Large sections of the building had been torn away. Beams and girders had been sawn through.

Axel walked up to one of the openings in the wall and slipped inside. Chaos greeted him, a vast salvage worker's wonderland. Debris covered the concrete floor, and wiring and strips of metal hung from the ceiling. The sound of his footsteps echoed, and the wind whistled through the cracks in the structure. Aromas of dust and jet fuel saturated the air. *I would have loved a place like this during my days on Earth.*

RJ poked his head in. "How's it look?"

"Awesome," Axel replied. "I mean, this place is thrashed."

Holly entered and stepped over a pile of oily rags. "Does it look like anyone's here? It's really creepy."

"Let's try the other end," RJ said. "It looks like there might be a light on in one of those offices."

They walked slowly, scanning for any sign of Tia and the brothers. The building creaked eerily as the wind blew against it, and the walls and ceiling teetered gently back and forth.

Axel laughed under his breath. "Man, this place could come down at any moment."

"You wouldn't have gotten me in here in my mortal body for anything," Holly said.

"Unless you had a death wish."

"Like you did, Ax?"

They reached the other end and approached one of the offices. "There's definitely a light on in there," RJ whispered.

Holly tiptoed up close to the door and pressed her ear against it. Seconds later, she shook her head. RJ crept over next to a small window but stayed behind the wall to one side, then slowly leaned over and peered in. Eventually, he made a fist and extended his thumb toward the ground.

Holly reached for the knob and pushed the door open. Axel stepped inside. His gaze snapped instantly to a small picture frame on the desk of the otherwise empty office. *Boy, was this a sucker's move.* The image was none other than that of the man in the black mask.

A deafening explosion suddenly shook the floor beneath him. The walls began to collapse, squeaking and screeching as they fell. Metal twisted and glass shattered. Debris rushed past his face.

The crumbling mass thrust Axel to the floor and slammed his body against the concrete. Mayhem filled his ears, and a torrent of dust rushed into his nose. The weight of the entire structure piled down upon his head, back, and legs, increasing in magnitude with each second that passed, clamping down like an enormous hydraulic press. Inklings of concern whispered in his ear in the midst of the havoc.

Within moments, the commotion ceased. Sounds of settling wreckage creaked around him as he lay pinned to the foundation in utter darkness. No one would have questioned a claustrophobic reaction, and any attempt to move would have been futile.

"Axel? Holly?" RJ yelled from somewhere in the wreckage.

Axel had no idea how far away he was. "I'm fine," he shouted back. "But I don't think we're walking out of here."

He rotated out to the other dimensions and then in onto the ground at the front of the collapsed hangar, where Holly already waited in clouds of dust and smoke. "You didn't want to stay for the encore?" he said.

She raised her chin. "I rotated out before it all came down. Guess I'm just quicker than you boys."

RJ joined them. "It looks like someone thought they could remove us from the equation."

"I think that tells us something . . . like maybe we're getting close," Holly replied.

"And like maybe they don't know much about Risen Ones," RJ answered.

"Hey, check this out," Axel said. A man was riding toward them on a racing bike, wearing a team jersey and racing shorts. A helmet and goggles obscured his face.

"Is everyone all right?" the man yelled with a British accent.

"We're okay," Holly shouted back.

The newcomer got off his bike, removed his helmet and goggles, and approached them.

Axel looked at him with an icy glare. What were the odds of this being just a coincidence? "Elias, what a surprise to see you at a crime scene."

Elias smirked. "What could you possibly mean by that, Axel?"

Was this guy for real? How obvious could it be? "Aren't you a little shocked to see us still standing?"

"I'm at a loss to answer your question," he replied calmly. "I saw the building come down while on my afternoon ride and simply came over to make sure no one was injured. I'm glad to see you were all outside and not in *there* when the hangar collapsed."

"Or was that to make sure that someone *was* injured?" Holly said.

"Well, I see she's just as welcoming as you two are."

Axel continued to stare him down. "We're not here to sip tea with you, Elias. We have reason to believe you're leading an uprising against the kingdom."

He raised his eyebrows but didn't look offended. "Wherever did you get an idea like that?"

"Maybe because someone just tried to bury us under this jet hangar, and you're the only one around."

"I didn't know Risen Ones could be so delusional."

"Why do you insist on hanging out with teenagers?" Holly demanded.

"I've been through that with your two friends here, Miss. I'm an educator, and there's a lot these young people can learn from me."

Axel folded his arms. It was time to turn up the flame and smoke out the rat. "So Drago, how do you know where they are all the time?"

At that, a hint of irritation flashed across his face. "Drago? Is that some kind of brutish insult?"

A vehement denial, exactly what Axel was looking for. *How much longer are we going to have to play this game? It's time to bring you in.* "I think you know what I'm talking about," he said, and then turned to Holly. "We've got enough evidence. Let's get this felon into headquarters."

"Hold on, Axel," she replied. "There are still holes we need to fill in his story."

"Tell us about your private computer and wireless networks," RJ said.

"It seems you've mistaken me for someone else," Elias replied. "I've heard that some chaps are using them . . . illegally. I imagine it would take some kind of computer genius to get that kind of thing working. A computer genius I am not."

"Let me see your mobile device then," Holly said.

"I'm sorry, I don't have it with me. As you can see, my current attire won't allow me to carry one."

Holly shook her head. "This is going nowhere. Elias, you're a prime suspect in a serious case, and one man's already lost his life. We *will* need to talk to you again later today after we follow up on some other leads. Where can we contact you?"

"I really hope it will be under more hospitable circumstances. You all seem to have missed out on the joy of the Lord."

Axel tapped his foot. *Can't this guy give a straight answer just once?* Talking to him just bred frustration, like trying to corral a dog darting about the yard with your shoe in his mouth. "Where can we find you? Don't you have an address, man?"

"I've been staying with friends, but if you need to talk to me after supper, I'll be taking in the sunset up on Mount Soledad. I'm there on many evenings."

"I don't think we're going to get anything else out of him," RJ said. "Let's head back to the gym. Rusty should have something for us by now."

"Okay," Holly replied, turning slowly. "Elias, we're counting on you being at Mount Soledad tonight. Don't make us come looking for you."

"The pleasure will be all mine."

They moved through the other dimensions to the gym and rotated in onto the ground outside the front doors. Holly gazed up at the overcast sky above, grimacing. "Do you think he was surprised to see us standing there without even a scratch?"

"Definitely," Axel replied. "You rotated out of that hangar within milliseconds of the explosion. Did you see anyone else around?"

"Not a soul. He had to have triggered it."

RJ didn't look so sure. "Unless maybe there was a motion sensor in the office or something."

"Nah, he's our man," Axel said. "I'm more convinced than ever now."

"You know, though, he said something that made me think," Holly said. "He mentioned that getting those private networks up and running would require the skills of some pretty talented people. If we can find *them,* I think we can tie it all back to him."

RJ nodded. "That's a good idea. Let's hope Rusty and the tech team can give us some insight into that. If they can access the networks, we should be able to determine who built them."

Axel still didn't see the need for all of this, but they were a team, and he respected Holly's experience and RJ's intellect. It was just hard to see another opportunity for justice go to waste.

At that moment, Reid came out through the gymnasium doors with his wife Julie by his side. "Axel, Holly, RJ! You're looking a little down today."

"Everything's fine," Holly replied. "Sometimes it just feels like the walls are crashing in on you."

"Believe me, I know the feeling. Is there anything I can help with?"

RJ scratched his chin. "Actually, maybe. You mentioned that there might be some illegal computer and wireless networks out there. Do you have any idea who might be running them? Or who might be capable of setting that stuff up?"

"Let me think . . . Now that you mention it, do you remember Alejandro from the first meeting we had, the guy who was so upset with you?"

"Yes, yes," RJ said.

"Well, I seem to recall that he's very knowledgeable in all kinds of computer stuff. It wasn't his main source of income, but he set up a lot of local networks for the small businesses in the area as a side job."

"What was his primary line of work?" Holly asked.

"He ran an online costume business," Julie replied. "He obviously hasn't been able to do much with that lately."

"Online costume business?" RJ said, glancing at Axel. "He must still have an inventory of things he wasn't able to move."

Axel leaned toward him. "Like black wrestling masks, maybe?" All of a sudden, Holly and RJ's desire to dig a little deeper didn't seem so bad. Their shovels had unearthed a very promising clue.

"He *was* really upset that day," Holly said. "Maybe that means more than we thought. Do you know where he is right now?"

"No, I haven't seen him since the meeting," Reid replied.

"Okay, thanks. You've been a tremendous help again."

"No problem. Let me know if there's anything else I can do." And he and his wife walked away.

Holly smacked her hands together. "Unbelievable. Such deception. He was standing right there in front of us, pouring out his soul about those who've been lost. Yet behind the scenes he was building networks for this uprising!"

"I guess we need to get better at reading people," Axel replied.

"Let's head inside and get his address from the coordination team," RJ said. "And while we're here, we can check in with Rusty."

17

Spiraling

Holly entered the gym alongside Axel and RJ. Rusty stood talking with some others by the far wall, but before they could make their way over to him, Marie, Derek, and Nina rotated in onto the ground just a few yards away.

"Hey, we haven't seen you since the celebration," Derek said.

Holly gave him a big hug, her heart warming at the sight of him. "Yeah, I've missed you guys, especially you."

RJ and Marie also embraced. "How've you been?" she asked.

"Not bad. It's really good to see you."

"So, what are you guys up to?" Nina said.

"Oh boy, where to begin?" Holly replied. "We're onto something big, but there's a lot of moving parts. It's been a little frustrating."

Derek tilted his head to one side. "In what way?"

"We just can't seem to nail any of our suspects. They've been so elusive. And now we need to find this guy Alejandro, who we met here in the gym on the day we arrived. We think he's one of the leaders of an uprising against the kingdom."

"An uprising? Does he have a wife named Juanita?" Marie asked.

Holly jerked back. She didn't remember any episodes of Aunt Marie reading minds before. "Yeah, how'd you know that?"

"I know where he is."

RJ shook his head. "Really? Where?"

"I'll show you. Follow me."

They all rotated out to the other dimensions, and Marie led them eastward to a large church in the Clairemont area. There, they rotated back in onto the ground beside crowds of people at the entrance of the auditorium.

Holly scanned the area, finding joy and elation on every face. She had only seen heartbreak and treachery thus far—this felt like the door of an air-conditioned house stood open in front of her after working in the yard on a sweltering, humid day. "What's going on here?"

"This is one of our main care centers," Marie replied. "People from the community can come at any time to receive assistance with the problems they have. We share the Lord's love in ways that bring healing for their needs."

Holly's eyes glazed with tears. She could almost envy their position. "That's wonderful. What an exciting ministry."

"It's been really rewarding to see the Lord work through us like this," Derek said. "We've been constantly in prayer, and he's provided miraculous answers."

"Well, I'm excited to see more of what's going on." She meant it, too. Even if this visit wouldn't get them to Alejandro, she was eager to see what else the Lord's servants were doing in this world.

"Come on in then," Marie said.

The auditorium bustled with activity inside. Smiling faces conversed in both small and large groups. A lump sprouted in Holly's throat. *This is how life is supposed to be in the kingdom . . . people helping each other and sharing Christ's love. It's here in every corner.*

Marie pointed to a table down near the stage. There, Alejandro and Juanita sat talking to a woman with three young children playing on the floor next to her. "Alejandro and Juanita are two of our leaders here," she said. "They lost many friends and family during the last few years, but instead of dwelling on it, they just wanted to help others going through the same challenges they were. They've been a tremendous blessing to us."

Holly's face crinkled even as her heart fell. Leaders? A tremendous blessing? Something wasn't lining up. She glanced over at RJ and then at Axel, who looked as confused as she felt.

Marie led them down to the stage, and Alejandro stood up. "Holly, it's good to see you!" he called out. His greeting sounded enthusiastic—and genuine. "And I think I remember, Axel . . . and RJ, right?"

"That's right," Holly replied. Juanita stood beside her husband, her face beaming. Holly cleared her throat. "It's a pleasure to see you both again. Marie tells us you've been a big help here."

"I hope so," Alejandro said. "I want to say again: I'm sorry I was so upset when you arrived. Our lives have been so difficult for so long, and my emotions flare a little hot."

"No need to apologize."

"We thank God for giving us this opportunity to work with others so his love can heal them too," Juanita said.

"It definitely sounds like you're bringing glory to his name," Holly said. She looked at the woman sitting with them. "We're sorry to interrupt. We know you have important things to talk about. Alejandro, if we could have just a minute with you when you're done, we'd appreciate it."

"We were just finishing up. Juanita can take care of it from here. What is it you want to talk about?"

They walked outside, and Marie, Derek, and Nina joined them. RJ looked Alejandro in the eye. Gratitude and relief flooded Holly as her uncle took the bull by the horns. "Alejandro, this is really great work you're doing here, but your name was brought up as part of an investigation we're conducting. I hope you won't mind if we ask just a few questions."

Alejandro looked concerned but not afraid. "Go right ahead."

"We understand you have some expertise with computers and networks."

Their suspect laughed. "I'm flattered, but I find that very amusing."

"Oh, why do you say that?"

"Well, I set up my online business, like you probably heard, and I helped a few other people with their computers, but I stumbled through it. I really don't know much at all. I think most teenagers can probably configure a network faster than I can."

"Really?" RJ responded. "Hmm . . . Can you tell us where you were yesterday morning?"

"I was here. I was here all day. Both Juanita and I."

"You weren't involved in any videoconferences?" Axel said.

"He was here," Marie replied.

Holly's ambition crashed like china hitting a tile floor. She didn't know whether to feel disappointment or intense relief. The guy had a solid alibi. Unless he had only engineered the stuff and wasn't part of the rebellion. He seemed so sincere, though. *I really thought we were onto something here.*

RJ turned his eyes up to the sky and then back to Alejandro. "So, you wouldn't know anything about private broadband or wireless networks operating right now?"

"Sorry, but that's way beyond anything I would have any knowledge of." Alejandro shrugged sheepishly.

Holly brought her hand to her cheek. *What else can I ask?* This train had covered all of its track and there was no reason to keep it running.

RJ seemed to come to the same conclusion. "Alejandro, it was nice to see you again," he said, and he reached out to shake his hand. "Sorry to take you away from the great ministry you have here."

"It's not a problem. Is there anything else I can answer for you?"

"No, I think we've got everything we need. God bless you and your wife."

The six Risen Ones all shared hugs as they bade each other farewell. "We'll have to get together at the beach in a couple days," Holly said. "And get the rest of the gang there as well. Just like old times."

"Definitely," Marie replied. "It's been way too long."

Marie, Derek, and Nina headed back inside.

"I'm really happy for them," Holly said.

"Yeah, they seem to be really fulfilled in their work here," RJ replied.

Holly shook her head. "But us on the other hand, we seem to be at a standstill. I hate to say it, guys, but we're out of leads."

✷

Axel stood silently musing over Holly's words. This wasn't turning out the way he'd thought it would. He definitely had a calling here, but what was he missing? The creamy filling at the center of the Oreo had mysteriously eluded him. *It shouldn't be this hard.*

Suddenly, a slender young woman with long dark hair and an olive complexion rotated in onto the ground in front of him. Axel's eyes widened and his jaw became slack.

Arielle shut her eyes, and her chin fell to her chest. "Axel, I'm so sorry. I only have a minute. The angels said I could talk to you—try to explain a little. I've wanted to visit you since we left the heavenly realm. Please know that my love for you has caused me to keep my distance. I know you don't understand right now, but this has all been necessary . . . for you."

He blinked a few times, but the words escaped him. Nothing that came to mind could express the depth of his chagrin. *Am I angry? Am I disappointed? Am I disillusioned?* Probably all of the above, but he hadn't really sorted any of that out. And now, there she stood, right in front of him.

He held out his hands, palms up. "Arielle, why would you ever have to stay away? Now that we've returned to Earth together, and especially for this long."

She raised her head and looked into his eyes. "Believe me, it's been really hard for me too, but it's to keep you on the path to becoming the defender of justice that you're going to become, performing mighty works in the service of the Lord, both now and in the ages to come. He has incredible plans for you."

Axel squinted. "Defender of justice? Seriously? I'm not really feeling it right now."

She stepped forward and grabbed hold of his hands. "You're learning important lessons right now. Think back to when you watched

Abiron thwart that mercenary attack on that small town. Do you remember what he said to you?"

"Yeah . . . sure . . . but . . . wait a second. How did you know about that?"

"Axel, I am so proud of you, and I'm really sorry, but I have to go right now. I *will* see you again very soon." And she began moving away.

"Wait!" he cried.

"We absolutely will spend a lot more time together when the time is right, and I'm *so* looking forward to it."

She rotated out to the other dimensions. Axel followed close behind, unwilling to let her go so soon, but she was gone. Seeing her again had brought back all his feelings for her—the care he'd had for her during their days on Earth and the times they'd enjoyed in heaven. He stood staring toward the horizon, dismayed. Moments later, he reentered the earth's dimensions near the front of the church, shoulders sagging.

Holly frowned. "I'm so sorry, Axel."

Frustration or confusion, he didn't know which was worse. He didn't want to have to deal with either one: the disappointment of the floundering uprising case on the one hand or the mystery of Arielle on the other. *Isn't the afterlife supposed to be filled with abundance?* Maybe he was looking at things the wrong way, but it all seemed pretty empty right now.

The three of them then moved back to the gym through the other dimensions. Maybe Rusty had something . . . anything . . . to put them on the right track.

18

Breakthrough

Axel stepped through the doors onto the gymnasium floor and followed Holly and RJ to where Rusty stood conversing with members of his team near the far wall.

"Great timing," Rusty said. "The tech team is hacking into that private network right now. We can watch them over at their data center here on campus."

Axel followed Rusty, Holly, and RJ through the other dimensions to the technology team's control room and rotated back in. A flurry of activity hit him with gale force as he entered. Risen Ones sat at workstations across the floor, and large 3-D monitors lined the walls, each one packed with images, numbers, and network maps. Fingers tapped briskly against heads-up displays and virtual keyboards.

A digital signboard above the door counted down the time: "12 Hours 36 Minutes to Launch."

Holly scrunched her eyebrows. "What's happening in twelve—"

"The kingdom networks," Rusty said before she'd finished speaking. "People will soon be able to use their computers and wireless devices again. The infrastructure was in shambles both morally and technically when we found it. You wouldn't believe the pornographic filth the evil regime put out there to enslave people. Most of the servers needed to be gutted, and many of the routing protocols needed to be reworked. They've done a complete overhaul. Let's walk over toward the wall. I want you to meet somebody."

Rusty led them to a workstation where a young woman sat typing torridly. Her almond-brown eyes stared intently from beneath screaming-pink glasses as windows rapidly popped up and vanished on the 3-D screen.

Axel grappled with an urge to burst out laughing. If the woman had looked in a mirror—or even just at her reflection on the computer screen—she would have noticed the tangles that made her straight black hair something like a bird's nest.

"Varsha?" Rusty said.

No response.

"Varsha . . . Varsha!"

She jerked back in her chair. "Oh wow, I'm sorry. I didn't see you there."

"Our apologies. We didn't mean to surprise you," Holly said.

Varsha grinned with bright white teeth and giggled, "It's okay. Everyone tells me I get a little, shall we say, *pre-oc-cu-pied.*"

Holly cracked up. "Praise God for that."

"This is Holly, Axel, and RJ from the justice team," Rusty said. "They're the ones interested in those private networks."

Varsha bounced up from her chair. "It's so good to meet you!"

She shook Holly's hand vigorously, and then RJ's, and then Axel's. Axel didn't expect such a vise-like grip from a woman so petite.

"We're truly grateful for your help," Holly replied. "We'd never be able to figure this tech stuff out on our own."

"I'm curious," RJ said. "Do you really need those eyeglasses?"

Varsha grinned. "Oh, no, I see great without them. I just wore some like this for so many years on Earth, and I like the way they look."

"Oh gosh, they're so cute," Holly said. "Do you have them in other colors besides pink?"

"Let's see, there's—"

"Maybe we can talk accessories later," Rusty cut in.

"Right. Well, I just got into that private network a few minutes ago. We definitely didn't set it up, but it is running over some of our cell towers and some of our fiber. And my favorites are yellow and orange."

RJ tilted his head. "Wait, what? Yellow and orange?"

"Sorry, I couldn't resist. I just had to answer Holly's question."

RJ laughed. "Gotcha. So can you tell us who's using these systems?"

"I can't tell you names, but I can see network addresses."

"Is there one particular server they're hitting more than the others?"

She sat back down. "Let's see." Windows flew around as she alternated her hands between the touch display and the virtual keyboard. Axel stared in disbelief at how swiftly she navigated. *I couldn't work that fast even if my brain was attached to the computer.*

Moments later she announced, "That's it!"

Axel smiled. "Um . . . that's what?"

"There's one server that all the other computers have been accessing. Its address is 2007:0db8:81a3:0000:0000:8a2e:0320:7334."

"Excuse me?" Axel replied. Computers had addresses? Did they have backyards and swimming pools too?

Varsha laughed. "Oh, sorry. That's where it lives on the network."

"Excellent. Can you get into it?" RJ said.

"Mmm, gimme a second."

She typed and moved objects rapidly around the display again. About a minute later she exclaimed, "I'm in!"

"Man, you're scary good at this," Axel said.

Varsha giggled and pointed toward the ceiling. "Glory."

RJ looked over her shoulder. "What do you see?"

She navigated the screen again. "It looks like a gaming server of some kind. I can't tell what kind of game, but it's definitely broken up into modules."

"What does that mean?" Holly said.

"With some multiplayer games, the participants progress through a sequence of episodes. It looks like all of them for this game have been played except for . . . hold on a second." She continued to move through different screens and then said, "One."

RJ's brow furrowed. "There's only one game module left to play?"

"Yeah, just one left. Why, what are you thinking?"

Alarms were going off in Axel's head. Fast-forward to the end of the song. Skip the rest of the verses and choruses. The crescendo of the last measure was about to sound. "Their training is almost complete."

"Training? Whose training?" Varsha said.

"We don't have much time," Holly exclaimed. "Their activities will become visible to many more people once they mobilize, and then a throng of lives will be in danger. Anyone who tries to get in their way stands a good chance of ending up like Mike Antonelli."

Axel quivered. Images of the bloody hunting knife and crimson-stained clothing reentered his mind. How many more would stand to perish at the hands of these butchers once they set their nightmare in motion? "Can you see when that last module is scheduled to run?"

"Training? Oh wait, yeah, module. Hold on," Varsha stammered. "It looks like . . . it's supposed to launch at ten o'clock tonight."

RJ glanced at Holly and then at Axel. "So the uprising could be commencing only hours from now."

Holly raised her hand to her mouth. "We need to work fast."

"Hey," Varsha said. "I can take this server down right now with a couple of keystrokes and—"

"No, please no," RJ interrupted. "We don't want to tip them off yet."

Axel wholeheartedly agreed. Justice would tarry no longer. He would finally get his chance to apprehend the notorious Drago. "We've gotta get to Elias before he triggers it."

RJ nodded. "Well, we know where he'll be at sunset, and that's only about an hour and a half away."

"Hold on a minute," Varsha said. "Someone's logged in to this server."

"Right now? Can you tell who it is?"

"Checking . . . it looks like . . . it's . . . oh, so sorry. It's just me. I saw my stealth user ID and thought—"

Axel rolled his eyes. "Well, maybe you can monitor it for us, and if someone does—"

"Wait!" she nearly jumped out of her seat. "Someone just signed in, for real this time."

"Are you sure?"

"Yes! Yes! I'm positive. Here it is. The user name is m-s-k-l-d-r."

RJ brought his hand to his chin. "Musklidder? Or maybe, muskleader? No that can't be it. Think. Think. Wait, it's gotta be maskleader!"

"Like . . . the guy from the videoconference?" Axel said.

"I would bet a tangible beam of light on it."

"No way. Where's he logged in from?"

"Found it," Varsha replied. "The network address is 2073:1ce5:00—"

"Hold on, hold on. We don't speak hexadecimal," RJ replied.

Varsha smiled. "Right. Let me see if I can do a reverse lookup on the domain name server." She typed and moved windows around at a mind-boggling pace. "Yeeeess! Here it is. It belongs to a domain owned by Tandem Associates."

Holly shook her head. "Not ringing a bell."

"It says here that they're a consulting company over in Sorrento Valley, specializing in fiber and wireless networks, and it's showing me a map with their location."

"Interesting," Holly replied. "They must not have had much business lately."

"Except for getting involved in an uprising," Axel replied.

"We'll definitely need to split up this time," RJ said. "Axel, how about if you go over to Mount Soledad and keep an eye on Elias when he arrives? Just make sure he doesn't go anywhere until Holly and I can get there. We'll head to this Tandem Associates to apprehend the masked man and then join you at Mount Soledad as soon as we can."

Axel had been waiting far too long already. The stew was boiling and splattering up out of the pot. It was extremely unlikely he would wait to take Elias down beyond a few seconds after his arrival. "Sure, sure. But I have to warn you, I might get impatient if he's standing right there in front of me."

RJ nodded. "In all seriousness, do it if you have to, but I'd like to be there if you can wait."

Axel thanked Varsha and then flashed through the other dimensions to Mount Soledad in the center of La Jolla. At its peak stood a bright white Latin cross about three stories tall, with seven sets of stairs and terraces leading up to it. He had visited the prominent memorial during his childhood but was too young to understand its significance. Now, the honor it cast upon the men and women who'd fought for freedom and justice hit home like a tidal wave. *Tonight I hope I can uphold that same honor.*

He turned his gaze out upon the Pacific to the west with the entire coastline before him. A familiar sight, but one he never grew tired of. The salty ocean air he'd once known now tasted warmer and sweeter.

The sun crawled toward the horizon behind a curtain of clouds, so he hung back in the other dimensions and waited, but he saw no sign of Elias.

✷

Holly, RJ, and Rusty moved across town to the address Varsha had given them. There, they rotated back in onto the ground in the empty parking lot of a multistory office building off of Mira Mesa Boulevard.

"I don't see any signs that say Tandem Associates," Holly said. She looked right through the unveiled windows, seeing no furniture or commercial fanfare inside. The company must have ceased operations some time ago. "In fact it doesn't seem like there's a business here at all."

"It just looks like vacant space to me," RJ replied.

Holly walked up to the door and pushed it open. Weird that it wasn't locked.

They made their way in slowly, finding mirrors clustered in the center of the reception area and covering the walls as well.

"Very odd," she said under her breath.

Suddenly, the sounds of explosions and gunfire roared from behind three mirrored doors on the side of the room. Holly's eyes snapped in that direction, and hundreds of images of her likeness reflected back in a maze-like effect. She wasn't really in the mood for a funhouse, but the circus seemed to be just beginning.

"I'll take the left side," RJ whispered.

Holly nodded and then rotated out to the other dimensions. She slid through the door on the right and found a very short man in a black wrestling mask at a desk, working a handheld device in front of a battlefield simulation game on a large 3-D screen. Wasting no time, she rotated back in onto the ground and demanded, "Stop what you're doing right now!"

The man turned in his chair and said in a child's voice, "Why? This is fun."

Holly's chin dropped. Before her sat a young boy no more than ten years of age.

"Am I doing something wrong?" the boy said.

"Well . . . let's talk about that."

"This is so cool. I haven't been able to play against my friends like this for a long time."

She didn't remember anything about babysitting in the job description. Things had really bottomed out, but she didn't want to burst this kid's bubble either, so she gave him a fabricated smile. "Can you please take your mask off for me?"

The boy pulled the mask over his head, revealing a chubby face and muddled red hair. Holly led him out to the reception area and found the other two office doors open and RJ and Rusty standing with another young boy and a young girl. Each of them held a black mask in hand.

"How did you get in here?" Holly said.

"A lady let us in," the little girl said, looking nervously at them. "Are we in trouble?"

"No honey, you're not," Holly replied gently. "But we'd like to know more about the lady. Can you tell us what she looked like?"

The girl shook her head. "She just looked like someone's mommy."

"How about her hair? What color was it?"

"I think," she paused for a moment, then said, "black."

"It was fake!" blurted out the other boy.

"So? It was still pretty!"

Holly turned to the boy. "Hold on. You said it was fake. You mean like a wig?"

"Yeah, and she had these big ugly sunglasses on."

"She was still nice though," the girl argued.

Holly raised her hand. "Okay, okay. How did you get these masks?"

"She gave them to us," the girl replied. "She said we had to wear them or we couldn't play the game."

"Holly, I think someone's messing with us again," RJ said. "And now there's a mystery woman in the picture."

"It's a really great game," the red-haired boy said. "Can we keep playing?"

"I'm sorry," Holly replied. "But you can't stay here any longer. I need you to go home and tell your parents about this, and I don't want you to come back here again." It made her sick to think of the uprising using children as bait.

"I'll take them home," Rusty said. "The sun's setting, and I know you need to be somewhere."

"Thanks, Rusty. Maybe you can find out more about this Tandem Associates for us. That may give us another lead."

"Sure thing. I look forward to hearing about your encounter with the notorious Drago."

✷

Axel reclined in the other dimensions at Mount Soledad. The sun peeked through the clouds and inched over the horizon as Holly and RJ came gliding up.

"Any sign of him?" RJ said.

"Nothing. Nice sunset, though," Axel replied. "What about you? I'm dying to know, who is the masked man?"

RJ shook his head. "We didn't get him. It was a setup."

"Are you kidding?" Axel buried his face in his hands. *When are we going to catch a break?* "Unfortunately it's starting to look like this is too. I'm really tired of these people getting the best of us. It's not supposed to be this way."

"I thought this would be our big breakthrough," Holly said. "But we're here without even a clue as to what to do next."

"I don't get it either," RJ grumbled. "Shouldn't justice come much easier in the kingdom?"

The concrete cross at the pinnacle of Mount Soledad towered into the sky in front of them. The light of the sunset shone upon it, illuminating it like a spotlight in a dark room. Brilliant rays of scarlet, coral, and orange spread out across the sky, and the cross glowed a dazzling hue of pure white against it.

At that moment, a man walked up the street toward them. "Elias," Axel said, and he immediately rotated in onto the ground at the foot of the cross. Holly and RJ followed right behind.

Elias stopped near the bottom of the seven sets of stairs and terraces below and shouted, "Brilliant! I'm so glad you decided to join me for this immaculate sunset."

"The only thing you'll be watching tonight is a demonstration of the Lord's justice," Axel replied.

"Whatever do you mean, Axel? It's such a lovely evening."

"We know you'll be mobilizing the uprising soon Elias, possibly even tonight," Holly said.

Elias seemed unfazed, as usual. "Well, Miss, you must have stolen a peek at someone else's calendar. I have no idea what you're talking about."

"We're here to take you in," Axel said. "And you can make it easy on yourself, or you can go the hard way. The choice is yours, man."

"Fancy that," Elias replied, and he quickly dashed to his left in front of the wall of the first terrace, disappearing from sight.

Axel rotated out to the other dimensions and then back in onto the ground in front of the wall. Holly and RJ came right with him.

"He's not here," Holly yelled.

"He's gotta be!" RJ replied. "We just saw him."

"Not true. You went the wrong way, chaps," Elias shouted from behind another wall to the right, four terraces above them.

"Are you kidding me? How did he do that?" Axel said, and then rotated out and quickly back in on the fourth terrace . . . but again only Holly and RJ stood next to him.

Holly raised her hand to her forehead. "Something really strange is going on."

"You don't see me because you're not looking in the right place," Elias yelled, now standing above them in front of the illuminated cross.

Once more they rotated out to the other dimensions, but only Axel rotated back in at the base of the cross. Holly and RJ each rotated back in on other terraces, anticipating his next move.

"Gone again!" Axel shouted.

"No sign of him here," Holly yelled.

Axel's vexation had reached a melting point. "*What* is going on?"

"I don't know, but I think he's completely vanished this time."

19

Correction

Axel stood at the top of Mount Soledad with his hands on his hips. Elias had completely eluded him. Slipped through his fingers at a critical moment. His efforts to stop the uprising teetered on the brink of failure, and his sense of purpose had faded into a far-off memory.

"This isn't working," RJ muttered.

"I can't believe he got away," Holly replied. "We're Risen Ones, aren't we? Why can't we catch him?"

Axel looked up at the cross. Its light soaked him and reminded him of the throne in heaven where the Lord had consumed his every intention and the idea of defeat had never even crossed his mind.

His thoughts wandered to remembrances of the first time he'd beheld that awesome locale. He'd just concluded his initial meeting with Jesus after passing away on Earth, and Hananias had appeared to lead him to his new home.

His vision had whirled into a blur and then quickly cleared. A new expanse stood before him. Lightning crackled on the horizon, and dashes of gold and yellow and bronze zigzagged through the air. Thunder's roar rippled out with no boundary to echo off of. Brilliant light soaked everything, with horizons stretching father than he could see.

His jaw dropped, and he stood rigid. Astonished.

Luminous waves drew fiercely toward the throne, as if magnetized to the heart of the expanse. The throne towered up infinitely in a dazzling mosaic of sapphire hues, its stature ten times Himalayan at least.

Braided flames ascended from the base of the throne. Rays radiated out from it on all sides—more intense than any earthly light, more pure and pulsing and vibrant than any earthly color. What could be more enthralling?

Axel perceived no ceiling or floor or border anywhere in the expanse. Only boundless existence in light. Only the throne at the center. With vastness upon vastness!

The notion of *forever* raced through his mind, and boredom was left for some other existence. Fear couldn't manage even a whisper, and not a twinge of hopelessness lingered.

Citrus and flora swept through the air, twisting on a breeze as thick as nectar. An emerald rainbow wrapped around the throne like a ribbon, and an endless sea of glass lay below, reflecting absolute purity and projecting golden-caramel waves in a symphony of rays.

Axel tilted his head back. Drenching, dazzling light engulfed the one seated on the enormous throne, veiling his appearance. Axel couldn't comprehend anything more majestic or glorious, nothing purer or richer or greater. Nothing more enticing. His lips came together and slowly formed the words "Father . . . God."

A multitude of beings surrounded the Creator. His hair flowed down like silk through the rays of light onto royal garments gleaming as white as snow. His body glistened like jasper and carnelian gemstones. With holiness upon holiness!

Hananias moved in next to Axel. "He has chosen to present his breathtaking image in the dimensions of this heavenly palace, yet he abides eternally outside of it as well, where no dimensional space or time exists. For he *is* Spirit."

"Awesome . . . completely awesome," Axel replied.

A glorious figure stood at the Father's right hand, one like a Son of Man, blazing from head to toe: eyes of fire, feet like heated bronze, and a face as piercing as the midday sun. White robes and a golden sash draped his body. "Jesus . . . my Lord," Axel stuttered.

Jesus cast his glance Axel's way, locking eyes as if they stood alone in the expanse, adoring and affirming.

Hananias pointed to seven golden lamps flaring before the throne, with flames climbing high into the extents above. "The Holy Spirit also makes his presence known. His righteousness and the sevenfold perfection of his being shine for all to soak in and worship."

Axel marveled as the light waves from the Spirit's lamps joined seamlessly with the light of the Father and the Risen Son, waves of crimsons and tangerines and turquoises and cyans and topazes and violets, all blended with fire and dusted with gold. Waves of perfect unity and equality, declaring their bond in infinite love.

A colossal assembly of angels and resurrected believers filled the heavenly amphitheater surrounding the throne, each one reveling in the presence of their God. They burst out songs of gratitude and worship, shouted his praises, twirled, bowed, and danced in the light of the Great I AM.

Axel raised his hand to his forehead. "This is all so incredible. I don't know what was I thinking on Earth, but if I'd have known what I know now, I would have lived my life *so much differently.*"

The words "so much differently" echoed through his mind as his focus returned back to the present on Mount Soledad. *Wow. In heaven, God captivated my every thought. I didn't let anything else get in the way.*

And then it hit him. "Guys, we've been totally off."

Suddenly a bright light flashed, inflating and swelling around him. It twisted about like a breeze, trilled in his ears, and warmed his arms and legs. Blinded, he felt his body become weightless, suspended in space and time.

The bright light softened, and Axel beheld Jesus standing before him, robed in the splendor of his white priestly garments and exalted with a crown of gold on his head and a scepter in his hand. With majesty upon majesty! With holiness upon holiness!

Dazzling hues of gold and white light surrounded his king, projecting far out into a boundless expanse.

"Lord!" Holly cried, and she fell at Jesus's feet.

Axel followed, prostrating himself beside her. Jesus's love poured into his heart and tingled his skin, like walking from a parched desert into a fresh cool stream. Without question, he was home.

At the Lord's command, Axel rose up. Three figures had moved in beside Jesus. Axel immediately recognized Hananias as one and Abiron as the second, but alarms went off at the sight of the third. *This must be some kind of bizarre dream.* "Elias?" he gasped.

"That's right, Axel," Elias replied, British accent still intact.

Axel paused and looked at Holly and then back at Elias. "But . . . how did you get here?"

"I don't know why you're so surprised to see me."

"Surprised? After all you've done?" RJ said.

"It's quite simple, actually. I serve the Lord just like you do."

The birds in Axel's mind flew north for the winter. This was a complete one-eighty. "You're . . . you're a Risen One?"

"Not exactly. My affiliation has been with the angelic realm ever since I can remember."

"But, but . . . what about all your ties to the uprising? Working to train those teens and all that? How could you possibly be on our side?"

"My friends, you came to that conclusion on your own."

"Seriously? So you're not Drago at all," Holly said.

"No, no," Elias laughed. "I was counseling the teenagers—trying to protect them from getting involved in that evil movement."

"But you said you were a teacher," RJ replied. "And that you'd been in the military for a long time."

"I certainly was in the military," he said, looking over at Jesus. "The Lord's, that is. I fought many battles against fallen spirits, but now that they're imprisoned, I've been given a new role."

Allies work together. At least that's how Axel remembered it. With allies like Elias, who needed enemies? "I'm stunned. You should have let us in on all of this."

Elias smiled. "Being confrontational doesn't necessarily get you the right answers. The three of you chose to investigate based on your own hunches and intuition. I didn't want to interfere with your methods of instilling justice—at least for now—so I thought it best to conduct your training this way."

Axel squinted. "Our training?"

"Yes. I told you I was a teacher. That's the new role the Lord has given me: to instruct believers about life in the kingdom, both humans and Risen Ones. You just didn't realize that *you* were my students."

RJ shook his head. "I'm not following. What are you teaching us?"

"The thing you lack," he replied calmly.

"But aren't we Risen Ones?" Holly said. "I didn't think we lacked anything."

"*That*, my fellow servants, is exactly the issue." With a nod from Jesus, Elias stepped forward. "Let's walk through your progress thus far. You've been frustrated. You've been challenged to bring in two teenage fugitives. A runaway girl is missing. The uprising is still moving forward, and you've reached a dead end in the case. Wouldn't you agree that something has been lacking?"

They stood in silence. Axel knew he was right.

"And the reason is quite simple," Elias continued. "You have everything you need to bring glory to God in this service, but you just haven't *depended on him*."

"You will remember that I spoke to you about this a few days ago," Hananias said. "But you continued to rely completely on your intellects, your new bodies, and your access to other dimensions."

Axel hung his head. His retrospect on the throne had brought him to that same realization moments before this little get-together, and the light of the truth had now brought his blunder into even broader daylight. "I don't know what to say."

"I'm so sorry," Holly said.

Hananias smiled. "No need to be sorry. We are all learning. That is why Elias has been specifically appointed as a teacher, and I think you will agree that he chose a very effective training method. You relied on your own strength, and he allowed you to experience the failure that goes along with that. It will serve as a very strong reminder going forward."

Holly turned to Jesus, and he held out his scarred hands to her. She took them, bowing her head. "My Lord, it's like I reverted back to some of my old ways of thinking—I've tried to control everything. How did I get so far from following you after we returned to Earth? How can I serve you in this ministry to the people of San Diego and yet be with you as I am now?"

"As I said to you before, dear one, remain in me and I will remain in you," Jesus replied.

"Maybe if I'd learned to depend on you more during my first life on Earth, I wouldn't be needing to learn this now."

Axel gazed out into the heights of the expanse. *How did I drift so far off course?* It was just so obvious now, like a bulldozer hitting him head-on. The Lord had blessed him with this incredible gift, yet he'd fixated only on *the gift* and forgotten about the fuel that made it go.

"Axel, my son," Jesus said.

Axel turned back. "Yes, my King." The Lord's affirming eyes drew him in like a magnet.

"I know your deeds, your hard work, and your perseverance. However, you must realize that it is I who work in you to will and to act according to my good purpose. You must rely on me for your will and your actions if you are ever to find fulfillment in the calling I have given you."

Axel's heart burned with a longing to please his Lord, and he hungered for more of Jesus's words. "I see that now, Lord. I understand why I've failed so miserably."

"My love never fails," Jesus said. "Remember, I am the Good Shepherd. I will make you to rest in green pastures. I will lead you beside still waters, but you must pray in the Spirit on all occasions with every request you have."

Axel nodded vigorously. "Thank you, Lord. I totally get it. I'll be totally focused on you every moment going forward . . . totally."

Jesus smiled. "Pray, Axel, that you may bear fruit in every good work, growing in the knowledge of God, being strengthened with all power according to my glorious might, joyfully giving thanks to my Father, who has qualified you to share in the inheritance of the saints in the kingdom of light!"

The brilliance melted away, bringing Axel, Holly, and RJ back to Mount Soledad in the extra dimensions. Hananias, Abiron, and Elias remained with them.

"I am the Vine, my beloved." Jesus's voice fell among them like mist, tangible and fresh, and faded away as he said, "If you remain in me and I in you, you will bear much fruit; apart from me you can do nothing."

The sun sank beneath the horizon with its final burst of rays, leaving the clouds in creamy lavenders and blushes amidst the darkening backdrop.

"Thank you, my King," Axel said softly, and then looked to the three angels still with them.

"I think it's quite comical that you thought I was Drago," Elias said with a grin.

A smile made its way across Axel's face. "No need to rub it in."

"Believe me, we've learned our lesson," RJ said. "At least I hope so. God's patience is so beyond my comprehension! I know we are perfected in Christ, but wow, I never stop proving how deficient I am when compared to him. He calls the shots, and I do not."

"So why keep us in suspense any longer?" Holly said. "Who is the mysterious Drago?"

"Do I really need to spell it out for you?" Elias replied.

"Well, we only heard the masked man talk about him," Axel said. "We haven't been able to uncover another shred of evidence. I'm beginning to doubt whether he really even exists at all."

"Bullseye," Elias replied.

Axel's face twisted. "I'm glad we're on the same side, Elias, but I'm still having a hard time understanding you."

"It's just as you said. He doesn't exist—on Earth anyway."

"Uh, still not following."

"I'm guessing you've never been to Rome. If you had, you might have learned that *Drago* is Italian for *dragon.* However, this dragon is locked away in the abyss."

Axel pondered Elias's words. This case had gone from strange to stranger since day one, but this had to be the height of the insanity.

RJ shook his head. "How can he be involved in the rebellion then?"

"The teenagers do not know it is the Evil One," Abiron replied. "But the adult leaders of the uprising do. Years ago, he gave them instructions to prepare for a revolt against the Lord during his kingdom on Earth."

"The devil still has followers here?" Holly said with a shudder.

"Not many, but yes. They masqueraded as Christians for many years and infiltrated the church. They did not publically reject the Lord by taking the mark during the recent atrocities, making their deception even more believable."

"Didn't you know about them?"

"Oh yes, we knew, but the Lord has waited until now to take them down. This will constitute the final phase of the earth's cleansing at the start of his reign."

The scope of this insurrection loomed much larger than Axel had ever perceived. Its treachery seemingly threatened regions far beyond the boundaries of San Diego. "So this uprising is taking place all over the kingdom then?"

"You are correct," Abiron replied. "But they shall receive a major setback now."

A worldwide insurgence—Axel stood staggered by the magnitude. Pockets of defiance lurked in every corner of the globe. The possibilities to enact justice seemed endless, but before he got too far ahead of himself, he knew he needed to clean up the mess that lingered right here at home.

"How many innocent lives will be in danger as these renegades leave the area for Israel?" Holly said. "I don't know how we'll be able to protect them all. We can't be everywhere at once."

"Your assessment of the numbers is correct, daughter of the most high," Abiron replied. "Legions of angels stand ready to engage at my order, but let's see how our commander decides to deal with it."

"Isn't this revolt supposed to happen much later?" RJ said. "Like at the end of the thousand years?"

"Your scholarship never seems to fail you, RJ."

"So why are they preparing for it now?"

"They are very deceived, mistakenly thinking they can fast-forward the very Word of God."

"Wow, and I thought you were impatient, Ax," Holly said.

Axel just smiled. He couldn't disagree with her, at least based on his track record, but that was all going to change.

"Okay, so Drago is locked up for now, but I'm still dying to know who this masked man is," RJ said.

"We'll need to take a little road trip for that," Elias replied.

Suddenly, Arielle flashed up directly in front of Axel and gave him a sheepish little grin. A smile made its way slowly across his face, and he tapped his fingers on his thigh. The curtain was peeling back, and the matinee was about to begin. "So this was it, wasn't it? For some reason that is still not entirely clear to me, my dependence issues have kept us apart, right?"

Her grin became broader and her eyes opened wider. "Uh-huh. You were always a little slow, but I think I can overlook that."

He reached out, grabbed her by the hand, and gently pulled her into his arms. They embraced as if no one else was around, just like when they were young. Barriers had fallen. He had waited far too long, but none of that mattered now.

"This is so neat," Holly said. "I'm really happy for you guys."

After a few moments, Axel stepped back, still holding her hands. "So I get the dependence thing now, but like I said, I'm not really tracking with what that has to do with you?"

"Axel, it goes so far into our past," she replied. "So intricately meshed into the fabric of our lives, to places I didn't share with you when we were in heaven because of the plans the Lord had for you. But now the time has come for you to know."

"I've been so confused about you since we returned to Earth—"

"I know, and I'm sorry, but I hope it will all make sense to you now. You see, the roots of this uprising actually began many years ago—in Israel, when certain evil factions actually began to believe God's Word where it says that the armies of the world would be defeated when the Lord returned. So they figured they needed a contingency plan."

"Abiron told us about that, but again, where do you fit into all of it?"

She looked at the ground and paused, then said solemnly, "That's . . . that's how I was taken away from you."

Axel stood silently. It still wasn't adding up. He reached out and softly lifted her chin, expressing the question with his eyes as their gazes met.

"When my family and I took that that vacation to Israel, many years ago, when you and I were in high school . . . I somehow crossed paths with them."

He shook his head. During their time in heaven, she had shared very little about her murder, so he just assumed she didn't want to find out. Understandable when you've been through such a traumatic experience. "So you *do* know who your killers were."

"Yes, I do. They thought I was someone else, someone they were after, but it didn't matter. They weren't interested in the truth."

Axel looked up at the sky and then back at her. His temperature vaulted inside, and his nostrils flared. Long suppressed emotions sprang to the surface. "So they took your life . . . and a big part of mine with it."

He was intimately tied to this uprising in ways he had never known. His calling to uphold righteousness had deep roots, dating all the way back to his relationship with Arielle. The scattered pieces of his picture were coming together, infuriating as it all was.

But lashing out in revenge wasn't the answer. He'd been down the road of taking matters into his own hands and had failed dreadfully.

Following the Lord's lead is the only way it will work. Jesus owned this battle. Assurance flooded Axel's heart—justice would prevail if he went about it the Lord's way. *I can definitely count on that.*

"Axel, we have every reason to be upset," Arielle said. "But I know now that Jesus allowed it to happen, and he took me according to his perfect timing. I'm hoping we can just move on together into the treasures of his eternity."

Axel's brow relaxed, and he nodded. "You're right. We definitely need to seek him on this." And he hugged her again. "So, like you said, I'm a little slow, but why couldn't you tell me any of this before?"

Her face lit up. "Oh, this is the fun part. My calling, in the kingdom . . . I work out of Jerusalem, cataloguing evidence against all those involved in this rebellion, worldwide, so their justice will be swift. I couldn't talk to you because of the things I knew—things that would have allowed you to bypass the lessons Elias had prescribed for you. You see, you and I," she tilted her head to one side and smiled, "we've actually been working together. You just didn't know it."

"Ahhh!" he shouted. "So that was you! I knew you were there, with me in the extra dimensions, but no one would believe me."

He looked over at the others, and Holly said, "Sorry I doubted, Ax. I'm just so glad this all worked out for you."

"As am I," Elias said. "But I think we need to get going."

Axel stared at Arielle. How could he leave her now? He didn't want to risk losing her again for another who knew how many days, weeks, or even years.

"Go," she said. "Go do what the Lord called you to do. This is your time. I'll be waiting for you when it's over."

He smiled from ear to ear and nodded. "Okay, but you'd better not disappear on me like that again."

"You'll never have to worry. That's all behind us now."

"Very well then, let's move along," Elias said.

"Okay, but we need to pray first," Axel replied.

Elias grinned back at him. "Well said."

Axel bowed his head and began. "Father, we come before you, humbled by your glory. We know that we're nothing without you and that nothing can be accomplished for the kingdom outside of your wisdom, knowledge, and strength. Father, we empty ourselves now, seeking that your power will work in us and through us. Lead us to apprehend those who've led this rebellion against you and those who've taken the life of an innocent man so that your justice will be upheld. May you be exalted in all that we do. We are your servants. In Jesus's name we pray. Amen."

Axel raised his head, and his eyes met with Abiron's. For the first time in days they stood on common ground. On a Rock not formed of Axel's own devices. On the Stone the builders rejected, who reigned as the Capstone over all creation.

20

Chariots

Axel looked up at Mount Soledad's glistening white cross, and reliance saturated his heart. *Thank you, Lord.*

"I can't stand the suspense any longer," Holly said. "Who is the masked man?"

"Follow me," Elias replied. He led them back into the earth's dimensions on the top terrace. Darkness had now completely fallen, and fluorescent beams danced up the cross, setting it apart from the shadows of the night.

"He is not far," Hananias said.

Elias walked down the steps to the street. "I had intended to lead you to him earlier this evening, but you were so focused on arresting me that you missed out on it."

Holly looked at Axel, but he just shook his head and followed the angels. His darts had missed the board completely. After the surprises of the last few minutes, it was clear that he needed to adjust his aim before throwing again.

They marched down the street past a few houses, then up the driveway of a large luxury home with a few lights on inside. A radio antenna atop a four-story metal tower stood out back with wires going into the house.

"What an eyesore," RJ said. "How did we not see this from up at the cross? These things aren't usually connected to people's homes."

Elias just smiled at him with an "I told you so" look.

"So who exactly lives here?" Holly said.

"Why don't you move in through the walls and have a gander?" Elias replied.

"Aren't you coming with us?"

"No, we'll tarry right here. The Lord chose *you* for this job, not us."

Axel rotated out to the other dimensions and then back in onto the floor of the front room of the house. Holly and RJ came right behind. Luxury furnishings congested the space, expertly arranged beneath a silver chandelier and surrounded by original impressionist artwork on the walls. No expense had been spared on the decor. A Bible rested on the center glass coffee table, and a small decorative cross hung on the wall of the entryway.

"It looks like believers live here," Holly whispered. "They're putting on a good act."

Light jazz played faintly in the back of the house. RJ motioned in that direction, and they stepped gently down the hallway with Holly leading the way. She stopped to examine some photographs on the wall, and her jaw fell. "Whoa," she said softly. "You're not going to believe whose house this is."

Axel looked over her shoulder. *Are you kidding me? Impressions can be so deceiving. The loudest kid on the block probably isn't the most honest.* He'd been burned by that as a boy and should have learned his lesson then. "Reid and Julie?"

"Oh my word," RJ grumbled.

"If we'd only asked the Lord for guidance the first day we met them," Holly said. "I completely trusted them!"

"Elias said they were here," Axel whispered. "Let's keep moving."

At the end of the hall, they found a kitchen and a large family room with a state-of-the-art theater system. The music played from a speaker near the stove.

Holly and RJ surveyed the backyard through a window while Axel slipped toward the home theater screen and around a corner, then down another hallway where he heard muffled voices beneath the floor. He expected to find a stairway leading down but saw only a closet containing coats and jackets. No rooms, no stairway, only solid walls and a closet. *Peculiar design.*

Holly and RJ joined him moments later, and Axel pointed to the ground.

"That doesn't sound human," Holly breathed.

"It's not," Axel replied. "It sounds exactly like the computer-synthesized voice from the videoconference. I can't make out any of the words, though."

"I can't either, but it's definitely coming from below us. Lord, please give us your wisdom!"

"I don't know how there could be a room down there. We're on the first floor, aren't we? It must be underground. Not very typical here in SoCal."

"I'm sure there's a hidden entrance somewhere," RJ replied. "And fortunately we don't have to find it."

They rotated out to the other dimensions and moved through the floor, taking up positions near the ceiling of the secret hideaway. There, Axel looked down upon a man in a black mask sitting in front of a large command console with multiple computer screens, cameras, and virtual keyboards. A red light shone from the video unit directly in front of him, and one of the displays read "ON AIR." Off to the side at another workstation, Julie sat working to adjust the quality of the broadcast. A black wig hung from a hook on the wall in front of her.

"Training will commence in ten minutes," said the masked man into the microphone. "Remember to work as a team. When the real conflict occurs, you'll be fighting against those with more firepower than you have, but Drago has ensured us that the victory will be ours."

RJ shook his head. "Why are these kids buying into this garbage?"

"I'm heartbroken," Holly replied. "God is making everything new, and they're holding fast to old lies. It's like continuing to bang on trash cans outside when your father has a grand piano waiting for you indoors."

"Well said," RJ answered. "Let's put an end to this clamor."

Axel nodded. A rush of energy shot through his limbs. "Reid's mine. First things first, though."

They each bowed, and Axel prayed, "Lord Jesus, you're the center of our lives. We find purpose and fulfillment in you. Thank you for bringing us here and for bringing about justice in your kingdom. Please strengthen and guide us now as we perform your work. In your name we pray. Amen."

They raised their heads, and Axel rotated in onto the floor of the room.

Reid jerked back in his chair the moment he saw him, but he quickly composed himself and began typing feverishly on the virtual keyboard.

Holly came in next to Julie, who froze in her seat, flushed with terror.

Axel put on his best Doc Holiday voice and said, "I'm your huckleberry."

Profanity spewed from Reid's mouth as he rose up to throw a punch, but Axel seized him by the top of his mask and threw him to the ground, twirling him around and rolling him over. "That bogus disguise isn't going to help you now, man."

Reid groaned and tried to jump to his feet, but Axel sent his foot down into the middle of Reid's back and drove him to the floor again.

"Are you ready to confess to Antonelli's murder?"

"You're . . . all . . . *going down!*" Reid yelled into the tile beneath him.

"He didn't kill Antonelli," Julie pleaded. "Some teenagers did that."

"Yeah, but we're quite sure he ordered it," Holly said. "And you're through soliciting children to do your dirty work. That stunt you pulled over in Sorrento Valley is gonna cost you."

RJ walked quickly over to the command console. Words and images ribboned their way across the large center screen. He reached for the virtual keyboard and banged frantically on the enter key.

"It's no use," Reid said defiantly. "The system is locked. There's no stopping it now."

"So you thought you would trigger your little rebellion anyway, even though you won't be a part of it," RJ said.

"Thought? Ha! It's moving forward, you idiots. The young people of this area will carry out their orders and perform the tasks they've been prepared for, becoming players in a real-life war game, only this will not be a simulation."

Holly sported a smug smile. "Good luck, masked man. We'll marshal angels to protect those who incidentally wander into the path of your recruits once they show up in the streets. And seriously, what harm could a band of teenagers bring to the Lord Almighty?"

Reid's eyes glinted from his position on the floor. "Oh, you've greatly underestimated us. They are very well trained, and they will join with others, but before they leave, they'll shed the blood of friends and family here in San Diego, right in their own homes and neighborhoods, well before you ever get them on your radar."

Holly and RJ looked at each other. Her eyebrows rose and his forehead wrinkled.

Axel dropped his knee into Reid's back. "What are you talking about, man?"

"Aaaaagh," Reid cried out, then gasped sharply. "And that blood will all be on your hands, *Risen Ones*. I hope you mourn deeply when you hear all the wailing."

Holly looked back at RJ again. "Do you believe him?"

"He's a liar," RJ replied. "But I don't think we can take this lightly."

"We may not have much time then, and I don't have any idea as to where to start."

"Gotcha, losers," Reid groaned.

Axel grabbed Reid's mask again and tightened his grip. But then he paused. His first impulse was to drive Reid's face into the tile. Flatten that ego out a little bit. Tenderize the meat so it cooked to perfection. But he didn't. The guy deserved it, but justice was coming the Lord's way. No need for anything beyond restraining the offender, so he released the mask.

At that moment, reckoning team members appeared in the room and took Reid and Julie into custody. Axel, Holly, and RJ immediately rotated out to the other dimensions above the house.

"Do you really think those teens will hurt the ones they love?" Holly said.

"You mean those they *used* to love. I believe some will and some won't," RJ replied. "We just don't know who or where."

"I think we know who can solve that for us," Axel said, and they bowed. "Lord, mountains stand before us right now. We don't know who might be in danger or where they might be, but you certainly do, and we look to you to lead us. We know nothing is impossible for you, so please use us to move these mountains so that your justice will prevail."

A streak appeared high above. It instantly closed the gap to where they stood and came to a stop right next to Holly.

Axel smiled as he recognized their visitor. "Are you here as our answer, old friend?"

"Not exactly," Abiron replied. "But they are." He pointed up at three shimmering points of light that grew larger and larger as they approached. Within seconds they flashed past with a loud WHOOSH! Flames seethed out from around them, sending Holly's hair flying into a tizzy from the gust.

The lights reversed course and sped back to where Axel and the others hovered in the expanse.

"Unbelievable!" Axel shouted. Three spectacular chariots of fire drawn by flaming stallions stood before him. The numbers seemed to add up: three chariots and three of them. He was no math professor, but it looked like he would be taking a wild ride.

"What are you waiting for?" Abiron said. "Climb aboard."

"No way. Really?"

"You need to get moving. Lives are at stake here."

Axel stepped into one of the chariots, and Holly and RJ each did the same. He peered right through the burning orange and yellow bodies of his escorts and the glowing floor beneath him. The supernatural had come into play once again. It was a world unbridled by the laws of the physical universe, and he yearned to see where it would take him this time.

He looked to Abiron for his next command, but the angel just raised his eyes to heaven, held his hands above his head, and prayed to God. At once, Axel's fiery steeds jolted forward, accelerating his chariot to blinding speed with a deafening rumble. Blazing embers spewed out around and behind him.

He looked back over his shoulder to see RJ's chariot veering to the north and Holly's heading due east while his raced directly to the south.

Sparks discharged off the whirling wheels. Galloping fury filled his ears, and the heat of the flames warmed his skin. He stood slightly crouched on the flaring floor, grasping the reins with his arms extended, staring straight ahead. The waters of Mission Bay flew by beneath him. *Hopefully, these guys know where they're going.*

Suddenly, the stallions descended to within a few yards of the water at the south end of the bay and drastically slowed their pace, then made their way overland and rotated into the earth's dimensions above a park lined with athletic fields. Sets of headlights loomed directly ahead in one of the parking lots, with one set of beams shining much larger and brighter than the others.

Not more than a second later, Axel's chariot flashed right over them. A delivery truck stocked with partially rusted propane tanks sat parked in the center of the lot, and a group of teens, both boys and girls, unloaded tanks into their cars.

Must be homemade bombs or maybe carbon monoxide dispensers. He would definitely need to stop this—but his horses kept dashing away from the athletic complex toward the south.

"Hey, turn around," he yelled, but the fiery steeds continued racing on, leaving the scene far behind.

"Guys, we need to be back there!"

Still, they didn't respond.

He looked up to the heavens. *Lord, how do I get their attention?* A scan of the cockpit yielded no answers. Axel leaned backward and turned to search the rear, unintentionally jerking one of the reins. The horses instantly veered to the left. *Interesting.* He pulled on it again, and they responded once more.

I get it. I'm flying this baby now. He whipped the chariot around and accelerated back toward the fields. Within moments he'd retraced his path.

His stallions raged down onto the parking lot. One of the teens dropped her tanks and pointed as Axel approached. Others scattered, and some tried to duck under the truck or under their cars.

"Eeee-ya!" he screeched as his chariot ripped right through the middle of their operation just inches off the ground, flames casting out in every direction.

Vehicles lifted off the ground and turned over in his wake. Propane ignited inside the tanks, exploding with vermilion and sulfur hues bursting high into the air.

Axel turned and surveyed the mass chaos behind. A vicious whirlwind, swirling and untamed, touched down on the ground seconds later and lifted each of the teens high into the sky above. Elijah could relate . . . but then this whirlwind probably wasn't headed for heaven.

Axel faced forward with satisfaction. One sinister plot foiled, and who knew how many more to go. He rushed onward out over the bay again without a clue as to where the remaining treacheries lay. Time to pray and trust autopilot again. *Thank you Lord. Please lead me.*

Denise Antonelli awoke abruptly to the sound of children crying. Sirens went off inside as her thoughts became more lucid; the wailing voices came from her own son and daughter.

She bolted out of bed and down the hall, but found the bedrooms empty.

The backyard! she thought, and scurried out the sliding glass door.

"What took you so long, Aunt Denise?" said a teenage girl with spiked black hair and tattoos on her arms.

The children sobbed as several teenage boys and girls pressed them against the wall with sharpened billiard cues.

"Tia, what do you think you're doing!" Denise screamed.

"Finishing the job that Alex and Vince didn't," her niece replied. "Uncle Mike was going to expose the new order, so his family needs to pay, like he did."

"Are you out of your mind!"

Tia's face twisted in a sadistic smile. "Oh, come on. Haven't you known that for a long time?"

Suddenly, a raging fireball shot through their midst, knocking Denise and her assailants to the ground. A whirlwind taller than the house followed immediately behind and snatched up the teenagers, launching them into the sky.

Denise scampered to huddle over her little ones, each one now bawling even louder than before.

Seconds later, the blazing mass came hurtling back and stood motionless at the back of the yard, hovering inches above the ground. A young man in a stunning white garment came out from the midst of the flames and walked toward her as the outlines of a chariot and fiery horses became apparent behind him.

Denise closed her eyes and drew her children even closer.

"Denise," the young man said. "There's nothing more to fear."

She raised her head and stuttered, "I . . . I remember you. You were with Holly."

"Yeah, I was," he replied with the light of his chariot cast upon him. "My name is Axel, and the Lord is cleaning all of this mess up. For you and your children, and for all of his people in the kingdom."

✷

Axel drove his chariot through the area for another hour or so, scrubbing the filth from those neighborhoods and diffusing every evil scheme. He short-circuited electrocutions, doused drownings, negated knife attacks, and snuffed out explosions. The teenagers who'd acted on Reid's orders to execute friends and family were swept away in the whirlwind. The Lord had completely disarmed the uprising in that part of San Diego, and justice felt really good again.

At the end of his campaign, Axel rode the chariot back to Mount Soledad, where he found RJ and Holly standing at the foot of the terraces in the glow of the cross, having completed their rescue missions as well.

"What took you so long?" Holly yelled, smiling.

"Parks and fields," Axel replied.

"What? Parks and . . . ?"

Axel stepped down onto the ground, trying not to laugh at the confusion on her face. "Yeah, it was really annoying. These boys stopped to graze every time we flew over even the smallest patch of grass, but the place would always go up in flames before they could eat a blade of it."

"Nice try," she replied, folding her arms in front.

As he watched, Axel's stallions burst toward the sky and disappeared into the other dimensions.

"That was quite a ride," RJ said.

"I'll say," Holly replied. "I showed up just in time to pull Alejandro and Juanita out of a close one."

Moments later, Abiron, Elias, and Hananias rotated in right next to them.

"Good show!" Elias said.

"We did it the Lord's way this time," Holly replied. "He led us through the whole thing."

"Mountains can certainly be moved when he has the lead."

Axel grinned and nodded. "So I've heard. So I've heard."

"I am curious though," RJ said. "All that technology we saw at Reid's place, and the uprising's computers and wireless devices—how were they able to put it all together?"

"Oh, you will find this very interesting," Elias replied. "Reid's one of the owners of Tandem Associates. He always used an alias on corporate documents."

"So he's been deceiving people for a long time."

"Yes, indeed. And he has a master's degree in electrical engineering. He's been working on the fiber and wireless infrastructure in this area for years, so he had all the knowledge he needed to create the uprising's private networks."

"Then he must have been behind all those computer equipment robberies too. I can't believe we didn't see this earlier."

"Me either," Axel said. "But we're dependent now, and we won't get fooled again."

21

Uncovering

A cool ocean breeze whisked across Axel's face, and stars stood frozen high in the sky above Mount Soledad as he reflected on the chill they'd just applied to the rebellion's diabolical scheme.

Abiron placed his heavy hand on Axel's shoulder. "You are the first justice team to give this uprising a setback—anywhere."

"Even with all of our delays and mistakes?" Axel said, surprised.

"Yes. The rebellion is not quite as far along in other areas, but they will all be taken down soon. There is also a central command that needs to be dealt with, and the Lord would like the three of you to assist with that."

Axel's eyes widened and his thoughts quickened, but then his recent reliance failures forged their way back into his head. Illustrious assignments like this usually went to the top dogs. *How did this one come to us?* They deserved a bowl of store-bought kibble, but a plate with a juicy top sirloin and all the fixings sat in front of them. "We're all over it, Abiron. Where does he need us to be?"

"Hold on, hold on," Holly replied. "We have a little unfinished business to attend to first."

"I was just about to point that out," Hananias said. "And you have some time before the central command mission gets underway."

"Will you pray with us?" Holly said.

They all bowed, and Holly began. "Lord Jesus, thank you for your love for us. Thank you that you never give up on us, that you're always there, and that all we have to do is reach out to you. Help us, Lord, to remember our weaknesses and to trust in your strength. We look to you now in dependence. Please lead us, as you already have done so magnificently today. In your name we pray. Amen."

"Amen," they all agreed.

"We'll catch up with you soon," Axel said to the angels.

"It will actually be the other way around," Hananias replied, smiling. "But I look forward to seeing you all again. May the Lord be with you and guide you." And the angels departed.

"Anyone have any ideas on where to start?" RJ said.

"Not really," Holly replied. "I know we're dependent now, but it kind of seems like we're back to square one on some of this stuff."

All of a sudden, a large bird flew up and roosted on Axel's shoulder. Axel flinched, but he collected himself and tilted his head to the other side, eyeballing his new, almost eagle-like companion.

"Axel, who's your friend?" Holly said.

"Not sure, must be a hawk or something. Very cool looking." He slid his hand up next to its talons, and the bird stepped on to his wrist.

"Has anyone checked in with Erin lately to see if she's heard anything from Nikki?" RJ said. "Maybe she's returned home already."

Axel ran his fingers over the bird's feathers and studied its features. Broad wings with pointed combs at each end and a fanned red tail. A body of chocolate brown on top and speckled white below. Eyes like lasers. A natural-born hunter, noble to its core, declaring God's creative genius over every square inch of its being.

"I'm sure Rusty would have let us know if that were the case," Holly replied. "But that's not a bad idea. We should see if Erin has any new developments to share with us."

"Okay Axel, I think we have the plan," RJ said. "Looks like it's time for you and your new associate to part ways."

"Too bad," Axel replied. "This is the kind of bird I could enjoy hanging out with." He raised his arm and the hawk fluttered upward, then made a couple of powerful downward sweeps with its wings and began circling over them. Faster and faster it flew, whistling each time it passed.

"That's weird. What do you think he's up to?" Holly said.

The hawk continued to race just yards above their heads, and its shrieks became louder and shriller.

"I know this sounds ridiculous," Axel said. "But I'm getting the feeling that he wants us to follow him."

"Yeah, that would be way too magical," Holly replied.

"I don't disagree," RJ said. "But we did just pray, and God's not going to grab us by the ear and just take us to where we need to be."

"You have a point," she replied. "And I sure don't have any better ideas."

The three rotated out, and the hawk burst away toward the northeast. Axel, Holly, and RJ took up the pursuit and passed over a number of towns. They continued on into the hills, and shortly thereafter, their feathered friend landed at the base of a cliff. Axel, Holly, and RJ rotated back in onto the ground as the bright morning sun rose in the east without a cloud in the sky.

Holly surveyed the area. "I guess there's something here we're supposed see?"

Axel walked over to a bed-size opening in the side of the hill. "Looks pretty desolate to me. I'd be totally up for exploring this cave, though."

RJ peered in from behind him. "It's actually a mine shaft. I believe this used to be known as the Pala mining district."

"No way. Is there gold down there?"

"Sorry, only small gemstones. Mainly tourmaline and different types of quartz."

"Oh, you've been here before, RJ?" Holly said.

"No, but the earth sciences teacher at the high school used to take field trips here. The guy was passionate about stones."

Holly angled her head to one side. "I'm getting the feeling we need to take a look inside, but before we do, we should probably thank our escort for getting us here."

"You don't really mean that, do you?"

"Yeah, that's how they do it in the Disney movies. You know, talk to the animals and stuff."

RJ laughed. "I think the thanks belong to the Lord in this case, but Mr. Hawk, we appreciate your assistance." He saluted, and the hawk seemed to dip a wing in response.

Axel entered the shaft first and quickly became smothered in darkness as black as the surface of the sea on a moonless night. He felt his way along the wall and shuffled his feet. Not even a flicker of light made its way into his eyes. If the Lord had truly led them here, he was going to have to navigate their path one step at a time, but Axel had no problem with that.

"Do you think we should keep going?" Holly said. "I can't see a thing."

"We walk by faith, not by sight, right?" RJ replied.

Holly laughed. "Okay, okay. Very cliché, but I can't argue with that. I was referring to maybe rotating out though."

"We still wouldn't be able to see. Either way, we're going to have to slug it out."

The shaft grew cooler and cooler as Axel made his way down. Each brush on the wall felt like touching window glass on a damp winter morning. The trail turned to the left, then to the right, then back to the left again, forging deeper and deeper. "I still have no idea where we're headed. Do you guys think we're in the right place?"

A soft clanging entered Axel's ears, and he stopped. "Hold on . . . do you hear that?"

RJ bumped into his back. "Yeah, I do. It sounds like someone hammering a spike into the ground or something."

Axel continued to shuffle forward in the darkness, and the noise became more and more distinct. Moments later, his hand met with something solid. "End of the road." He ran his fingers across it. A barrier of dirt and rock stood in front of him, and the banging rang out from behind it. "I guess we're going through."

He rotated out to the other dimensions and moved through the obstruction. A flashlight beam instantly met his eyes as he emerged on the other side, revealing a lethargic Nikki Erickson, straining to strike a metal rod against some old mining equipment. On the ground just a few yards away sat Josh, with dried blood saturating his pant leg and a piece of cloth wrapped around his head.

Dirt and dust covered their skin and clothing, and they each labored to breathe. Axel wasted no time and rotated in onto the floor of the mineshaft. Holly and RJ came right alongside him.

"Axel!" Josh exclaimed, gasping heavily. "Thank God you're here!"

"Thank God is right. He led us right to you."

Josh looked curiously at the other two.

"This is Holly and RJ," Axel said. "We work together."

Holly smiled at Nikki. "We're gonna get you out of here."

Nikki sighed and smiled back, looking very much like her mother, with long caramel-blonde hair, blue eyes, and a lean build.

Axel examined Josh's leg. "That looks pretty brutal."

"I'll be fine. There's no way I'm gonna miss our next surf session."

"Spoken like a true waterman. Can you move toward the back wall? I'm gonna need some room to dig us out."

"Not a problem." Josh attempted to get up but instantly collapsed back to the ground. "Whoa! That does hurt a little."

"Let me help," RJ said.

Axel began to dismantle the mound of debris.

"I've heard of taking a girl's breath away," Holly said, "But this isn't exactly the most romantic place for a date. How'd you get in there?"

"It was a trap," Josh replied. "We decided we didn't want to be part of the uprising anymore."

"We both came to realize it was a big mistake," Nikki said. "Together we agreed that we really want to follow the Lord."

"I tried to set up a meeting with Alex and Vince to tell them we were through," Josh said. "They told us to meet them here at five o'clock today. Everything they do is so secretive, so we didn't really suspect anything. When we got here, we found a flashlight and a note telling us to meet them inside the mine. After we'd walked down the shaft for a while, we heard an explosion behind us, and the walls caved in."

Nikki smiled. "Josh shielded me from the falling rocks. He was so brave."

Axel sensed that this romance had turned the page to the next chapter. He hid a knowing smirk even as thoughts of Arielle flooded his mind.

"Before we knew it, we were stuck down there, running out of air," Josh said. "You guys are the answer to our prayers."

Axel's hands worked like a circular saw cutting into a stack of twigs, rapidly slicing through pieces of rock, clay, and wood while RJ and Holly cleared the debris to the sides. Within minutes they'd bored an opening large enough to fit through.

Holly and Nikki slithered out first, then Axel and RJ supported Josh on each side to help him through. After slowly making their way up the mineshaft, they surfaced into the open again. Josh sat down on a rock next to Nikki as the two gasped in air.

At that moment, Rusty appeared. "Nice work, guys."

"Right on cue, as usual," RJ said. "Can you get a truck up here to take them home? He isn't going very far on that leg."

Rusty's forehead wrinkled. "Why don't you just take them through the other dimensions?"

Axel laughed. "You're kidding, right?"

"No. No, I'm not."

"How would we get them there?" Holly said.

Rusty looked surprised. "Really? You guys don't know this?"

"News to me."

"Okay, okay. I guess I shouldn't have assumed. It works like this: the Spirit has to take them, and they need to be holding onto you . . . but RJ, I'm really surprised. You're the one who told me about Philip in the book of Acts."

RJ laughed. "Sorry, Rusty. Another casualty of our independence I guess."

"Well, after you get them home, come see me at the gym. We think we know where Alex and Vince are."

"You found them?" Holly replied. "No one's seen those guys for days."

"You'll kick yourself when you find out where they've been hiding."

Axel had already kicked himself enough, but things had really come together now that they'd begun seeking the Lord. It was just like Jesus said—green pastures and still waters. The Good Shepherd would definitely lead them right to Alex and Vince.

"That obvious, huh? Is it somewhere near their house?"

"Not gonna tell," Rusty replied. "You'll have to come see me first."

"Okay, we'll play along." Holly turned to Axel. "Maybe you can take Josh back. I'm sure his parents have been worried."

"I'll meet you there with the medical team," Rusty said.

"Sounds good," Axel replied.

"I want to go with them." Nikki said.

"That's sweet," Holly replied. "But your mom's been really worried about you. RJ and I will take you home."

"My team's already been in touch with Erin," Rusty said. "She knows you're on your way. They've also spoken with Stein and Lisa."

They helped Josh to his feet, and he grabbed Axel's shoulder.

Nikki put her arms around Holly's neck. "I'm not choking you, am I?"

"Oh, you don't have to worry about that." Without another word, she and RJ rotated out to the other dimensions, taking Nikki with them.

Axel raised his chin. "Are you ready for the ride of your life?"

"Seriously?" Josh replied. "I thought I had it the other day in the water."

Axel felt his brotherly bond with Josh growing. Not only had he become hooked on surfing, but he'd also chosen to follow God's direction for his life—something Axel had struggled to do during his first stint on Earth. "Not even. This goes way beyond that."

"Hard to imagine."

Axel rotated them out and leaned in the direction of Pacific Beach. They sped across the expanse, and Josh shouted out a rousing "Woo-hoo!"

Within moments they arrived at Stein and Lisa's doorstep and rotated back in onto the ground. Axel helped Josh brace himself against a post, where he suspended his injured leg a few inches above the ground. "Man, that was unreal!" he shouted.

Axel grinned. "We'll have to take a longer journey sometime."

"Definitely. How much time would it take to get to, say . . . London? An hour?"

"More like a split second."

Lisa burst through the door and immediately brought her hands to her mouth. "Oh my, what happened to your leg?"

"It's just a flesh wound, Mom," Josh replied. "I'll be fine. I'm just glad to be home."

Lisa paused for a moment, and tears came to her eyes. "You haven't said that for a very long time."

Emotion played on Josh's face as well. "I know, Mom, and I'm sorry. I know I need to make some changes."

Stein joined them on the porch. "We've always had confidence in you, son. We knew you would do the right thing." He turned to Axel. "Thanks so much, Axel. You've blessed our family again."

If they only knew the whole story. With Axel driving the bus, he would probably have ended up somewhere south of Mexicali, and Josh would still be in that mineshaft. "I've got to give all the glory to God. He led us right to them."

"I know, but thanks for your part in it anyway. It means a lot to us . . . all you've done for Josh."

Axel just smiled. Jesus's plans for him were already turning out better than he could have imagined. "Truly, it's been my pleasure. And you definitely haven't seen the last of me. I think maybe Josh and I will be hanging out more often."

"That would be awesome," Josh replied.

Members of the medical team rotated in onto the ground. Stein and Axel helped Josh to his bedroom, where the doctor immediately went to work on his leg.

✷

Holly, RJ, and Nikki returned to the earth's dimensions at Erin's front door in Hidden Valley. Birds chirped from the aviary in the courtyard, and drops of water pattered in the fountain.

"Wait," Nikki said. "Can you let me tell her what happened?"

"Sure," Holly replied. She understood. This wasn't likely to be an easy conversation for Nikki.

"I don't want her to know everything. I've already disappointed her so much."

"I think she'll just be happy to have you home and to know that you'll be following the Lord again."

"I've definitely learned my lesson."

RJ knocked on the door, and Erin opened it moments later. Without a word she embraced Nikki, squeezing her as if she would never let go.

"I'm so sorry, Mom," Nikki said, and she began to cry.

"I know, baby, but you're home now."

"I don't know what I was thinking. It's just been really hard since we lost Dad."

"You don't have to try to be so strong. Jesus is there for us."

Joy swarmed through Holly's heart. The Lord had used her to reunite mother and daughter. The crowd in her imagination stood to their feet and erupted with cheers and shouting. Horn blasts sounded, applause rang out, and the jubilee persisted for the next few seconds. "God bless you, Erin," she said. "We'll get going so the two of you can talk."

"Wait." Erin hastily wiped tears from her eyes. "Holly, RJ, what can I do to show my appreciation? You've given me such a precious gift today."

Holly already counted herself blessed. She felt that she had received a precious gift as well. Seeing the glee on Erin's face rated better than any bouquet of flowers or shiny piece of jewelry. "Just keep loving this amazing daughter of yours."

"Oh, that won't be a problem."

Holly and RJ turned to leave, but then Erin spoke up again. "Oh, I almost forgot. I know you're busy, but can you come in for a few minutes? Real quick?"

Holly smiled, curious. "Sure. What's up?"

"Come take a look."

Erin led them inside and into the living room. Diagrams, photos and printouts stood in piles on the coffee table. Holly stared at the clutter. "Wow, you've been busy."

"I had to do something to keep from having a nervous breakdown."

Nikki pointed to one of the pictures. "Isn't that Grandpa Jens? He looks so young."

"Uh-huh. He was probably still in his late twenties then."

RJ moved closer. He stared at the picture, and his jaw dropped open slowly. "Is this your father?"

Erin shook her head. "No, he was my husband Peter's father."

He picked up the photo and drew it within a few inches of his face. "I don't know what to say. This is truly remarkable . . . you see, the man in the picture, he was also my cousin."

"I had a feeling," Erin said, smiling. "I can see the likeness."

"His dad and my dad were brothers. The two of them had a falling out when I was a teenager, and I never saw Jens again after that."

Erin ran her finger over one of the diagrams. "So your father was . . . Anders Erickson?"

"Yes. Yes, Anders Erickson."

No wonder Holly had felt such a deep bond with them! Certainly their tragic situation warranted it, but this had gone far beyond her normal sense of compassion. Bloodlines ran thick, even after she'd been raised from the dead. "That must mean we're all second or third cousins or something."

Nikki scrunched her forehead. "So I'm related to you?"

Holly grinned. "Yeah, isn't that incredible?"

"I guess you look like you could be my aunt."

"I'm good with that. You call me Aunt Holly from now on." And she walked over and gave Nikki a hug. It felt good to have more family.

Erin turned her eyes to the ground. "I wish Peter could be here to meet you. Looking through these pictures has brought back a lot of memories."

Holly didn't reply. Erin needed time to process, and more time to grieve.

"Can you find out . . . what happened to him?" Erin asked. "I . . . I think it would be better if I had some closure . . . and didn't keep hoping he'd come walking through the door again someday."

Holly moved over next to her. She had decided on the answer before Erin even finished asking the question. "We will, Erin. We *will* find out what happened to him."

22

Reckoning

Axel stood with Rusty on the gymnasium floor as they waited for Holly and RJ. He replayed the first episode with Alex and Vince in his mind and cringed at his performance. What had he been thinking? He had muscled his way around like he was playing some kind of Superman, but it turned out more like a portrayal of Wile E. Coyote. Fortunately, this movie had a sequel, and it promised to draw to a close with a far different ending. This time he would read straight from a divinely inspired script, and no improvising would find its way into the plot.

Holly and RJ rotated in next to him.

"So, Rusty, what's the big secret you have for us?" Holly said.

"I'll let Varsha tell you," Rusty replied. "The Lord has led her to some pretty wild discoveries. She's really been looking forward to sharing them with you."

They headed to the technology lab and walked up behind Varsha at her workstation. She spun around to greet them with a huge grin. "Saw you coming in the monitor's reflection this time."

"It sounds like the Lord's been doing some incredible things through you," Holly replied.

"Isn't it incredible? I never dreamed this would be so fun!"

"Rusty tells us you've got a lead on our teenage fugitives," RJ said.

"Oh, is that ever right. It seems we didn't go far enough the last time you were here."

"What do you mean?"

Varsha looked triumphant. "Well, I did more investigation into that Tandem Associates company. It turns out they own a number of buildings in that same complex."

"They all looked vacant when we were there," Holly said.

"Exactly! And they've been that way for years. Tandem never even tried to lease them to anyone. It seemed a little suspicious to me, so after researching a few different angles and coming up empty, I decided to look at some subsurface satellite images of the area."

Varsha's love for her calling struck Axel again. Subsurface satellite images? How much nerdier could it get? But her infectious enthusiasm drew him in. "And what did that tell you?"

"A lot of those buildings are connected to each other."

He was still struggling to process. "Subsurface? You mean under the ground?"

"Yes. We're talking full-out underground tunnels. And strangely, it doesn't show up on any of the architectural drawings. Take a look at this." She turned back to the computer display and moved some windows around. "See, there's a tunnel system running between these four buildings."

"That doesn't surprise me," Holly said as she and Axel leaned closer for a better view. "Reid had an underground room in his house too."

"Reid? What's a Reid? Something I should know?"

"Oh, sorry. He's one of the owners of the company. Turns out he was the one who set up the private networks."

"Got it . . . I think. Anyway, the thing I can't figure out is why the spectral readings show a high concentration of glass in these tunnels and under the buildings. Last time I checked, there wasn't much of a need for windows below the first floor."

RJ rubbed his chin. "Mirrors, maybe?"

"Ha! That's funny."

"No, really. There were a bunch of them in the reception area on the first floor of the office building we went into."

Varsha tilted her head. "Oh, that is interesting."

Axel had heard enough science. It was time to get down to business. "So what does this have to do with Alex and Vince?"

Varsha's face lit up. "Oh, yeah. That's why you're here."

"I wish I could impress you with hyperspectral imaging evidence too," Rusty said. "But quite simply, Reid told us they're hiding out there. And he's still claiming innocence on the murder rap. Trying to pin it all on the boys."

"So why would they be in his buildings if he wasn't involved?" RJ said. "Harboring fugitives isn't exactly the best way to prove your innocence."

"I don't know. His story keeps changing, but he insists they threatened him and forced him to give them a place to disappear after the crime."

Axel had the trump card in his hand, and now was the perfect time to play it. "The infiltrator has been eliminated!" he said with his best monotone, man-in-the-black-mask voice. "RJ and I heard him say it. Let's see if he can wiggle out of that one."

"We definitely need to seek the Lord on this," Holly said quietly. "These guys have gotten away from us before."

RJ nodded, and they bowed. "Lord Jesus, we've seen your power at work in us and through us as we've sought you. You've led us to bring about justice in your kingdom, and we ask now that you'll do so again. Please guide us in apprehending these young men. Thank you for the knowledge you've given us through Varsha. You know all things, and we ask that you'll direct us according to your wisdom. In your name we pray. Amen."

The three rotated out to the other dimensions and jetted over to the business complex in Sorrento Valley with the warm afternoon sun shining down. Axel followed Holly and RJ into the building where they'd found the children playing the day before. They plunged down through the carpet and rotated in onto the floor of a cavernous underground room where Axel gazed out upon hundreds and hundreds of reflections of himself echoing back from a myriad of mirrors. *Boy, I think I gave Reid too much credit. His mental state is even more suspect than I thought.* "This explains all that glass that Varsha saw, but why would anyone want to build such a thing?"

"Treachery," RJ replied. "Reid's a deceiver just like his boss. He's obviously got something to hide, and he evidently likes to conduct his covert affairs below ground. This whole mirror business would make it almost impossible for someone to find him if they got down here."

"And it probably made for an effective way to escape if he needed it," Holly said. "I'm sure he and his people are the only ones who know their way through here."

Axel couldn't let a venture like this pass him by. "I'm ready to give it a go."

"Some other time, Ax," Holly said. "We've got higher priorities right now."

He sighed, but he knew she was right. Solving puzzles with twists and turns could wait for another day. So he moved out to the other dimensions and slid through the mirrors to the other side of the floor, still beneath the first building. Holly and RJ came right behind. They rotated in onto the ground in front of a row of eight computer workstations with e-mail printouts scattered on the desks.

Axel walked over to an opening in the wall and peered in. "Here's an entrance to one of those tunnels, with more mirrors all the way to the end."

"Not surprising," RJ replied.

Holly's brows bumped together in a scowl as she leafed through the papers. "This is gruesome. I can't believe some of these memos."

"They seem to be persecution orders," RJ said, picking up a few and scanning them after Holly. "Lists of believers to be tortured or killed. They date back to . . . looks like a little over eighteen months ago. I hate to say it, but it all points to this place as the San Diego headquarters for the regime of the Beast. Reid is one wicked individual."

"I think you're right," Holly said, still flipping through the printouts. Her eyes scanned them quickly, her gaze intense. "But some of these e-mails are more recent, like from the last few months, and most of them from someone named Mundaka."

Axel stood tapping his foot. Conversation wasn't going to rid the world of its felons. "Justice is calling, guys. Let's get moving so we can nail these dudes."

"I see some of those here too," RJ said. "But they seem to be related to this current uprising. It's almost as if this Mundaka has something to do with the central command Abiron mentioned."

Holly brushed her bangs back. "Maybe this is bigger than we thought. We'll have to ask the angels when we see them."

"Holl, Uncle RJ, we need to go," Axel said. "Alex and Vince are here somewhere."

Holly and RJ agreed and fell in behind Axel as he slipped through the tunnel in the other dimensions. Another large room furnished with a maze of mirrors stood waiting at the end.

"More of the same," Holly said.

They traversed their way through and rotated back in on the far side of the floor where more workstations lined the wall. Half-eaten sandwiches, scraps of doughnuts, slabs of moldy cheese, and piles of dirty clothes littered the ground. Steam rose from a half-full coffee cup, and the entrance to another tunnel stood just yards away.

"Eeeew!" Holly said. "Smells like a garbage can! It's totally gross."

RJ walked over to one of the monitors and scanned the display. "Well, look at this. I think they know we're here."

Axel came up behind him. A live black-and-white camera shot of the room he, Holly, and RJ had just left played on the screen. "Yep, they must have bolted the moment they saw us."

Again Axel rotated out and moved through the tunnel in front of him. He returned to the earth's dimensions at the entrance of yet a third underground chamber. Holly and RJ trailed him by only a moment. Vince's likeness reflected from hundreds of mirrors across the room. The word "Infidel" was silk-screened on his shirt. He stood with his hands on his hips and let out a sordid laugh that echoed off the walls.

"It's all over, Vince!" Holly yelled.

"Yeah, right. You losers will never catch us. Just try to figure out which one is the real me." And he disappeared.

Axel immediately rotated out and raced to the other side of the floor, but Vince had vanished. Footsteps and snickers came from inside another tunnel a few yards away, inciting Axel to dart in behind the two outlaws as they entered a fourth large room, but he paused in the other dimensions, allowing them to flee into another maze. *What fun will it be if I don't give them at least a sporting chance?*

Holly and RJ joined him. Likenesses of Alex filled half the mirrors while likenesses of Vince filled the others.

"Aren't you coming?" Alex yelled defiantly. "Or have you given up just like last time?"

Axel, Holly, and RJ stayed quiet, watching.

"They're probably lost in the maze somewhere," Vince said, laughing.

"So much for the heroics of the *Risen Ones*."

"Come on, let's go. We'll be here all day if we have to wait for them."

At that very moment, RJ rotated in onto the ground and sauntered toward them, sending the two teens scampering. An urge prompted Axel to retreat back through the tunnel into the third room of mirrors. It didn't really make any sense, but he was dependent now, so he hustled that way as fast as he could. Once there, he rotated in onto the ground and leaned against the wall near the tunnel opening. Moments later, Alex came bounding through.

"Is that you, or just your reflection, Pilgrim?" Axel said in his best John Wayne voice.

Alex stopped dead in his tracks and turned around, his face flushed pale as a ghost.

"Why are you so surprised?" Axel said. "You asked if I was coming, didn't you?"

"How . . . how'd you do that? You weren't supposed to be able to see—"

"Don't trouble yourself. The Lord sees everything. He *is* light, and the days of getting away with deeds of darkness are over, man—for you and every other social deviant."

Axel led him back through the tunnel to find Vince facedown on the floor with Holly twisting his arm behind his back. She looked up at Axel with a grin and nod.

Together, they escorted the two felons to the gym through the other dimensions and handed them over to the reckoning team. Soon after, Abiron, Elias, and Hananias appeared next to them as they stood conversing near the bleachers.

"Nice work," Elias said. "You've truly learned your lessons well."

"Things definitely work out better that way," Holly replied.

"Are you ready to put that faith to work one more time?"

RJ nodded. "I think we're ready to do it for the rest of eternity."

Axel straightened his posture. "The uprising's central command, then?"

"Yes, the time has come," Abiron replied.

"And does it have anything to do with someone named Mundaka?"

"Yes, it does," Hananias said. He focused his knowing gaze on Axel. "And he is a big part of the reason why the Lord has called *you* to be involved."

23

Conquest

Axel stood electrified on the gymnasium floor. The Lord's power working in him and through him had already charged his day, but this dynamo was only just beginning to heat up.

"Follow me," Abiron said.

Axel entered the other dimensions right behind the angel, along with Holly, RJ, Hananias, and Elias. They flashed over the entire United States instantly and the Atlantic passed by in a breath, pushing them into the beginning moments of Spain's golden-ember sunrise. A split second later, Abiron brought them to a stop over a grassy valley enveloped by steep blue mountainsides. A campus of buildings stood a short distance away.

"Where are we?" Holly said, turning about.

"This is Switzerland, near the French border," Hananias replied.

RJ's face lit up. "I know this place. We're just outside Geneva, at the European Organization for Nuclear Research."

"Or CERN, as they like to call it."

"But I don't remember the complex being this big," RJ said. "It must have really grown since I was here last."

"I'll bet you know a little bit about the LHC then."

"Precisely. Studied it and its experiments extensively."

Axel wasn't enjoying the taste of the acronym soup. "Guys, not following here."

RJ wrinkled his forehead. "The Large Hadron Collider—the most powerful particle accelerator of my time. A loop seventeen miles long and almost six hundred feet underground in places, built to generate particle collisions producing temperatures as high as those present at the formation of the universe, some one hundred thousand times hotter than the center of the sun."

"That's some serious heat," Axel replied.

"Your specifications are a bit dated, though, if I may say," Elias said. "It's actually over twenty-one miles long now, and they've upgraded its power capabilities several times through the years. With all the breakthrough discoveries here, this place became even more the zenith of human science. Everyone wanted a piece of the action. They came from all over the world, but those with evil intent seized control of its operations so they could create scientific propaganda to blind the hearts and minds of mankind."

It struck Axel that RJ had been a victim of that same kind of propaganda, persecuted when he refused to follow the party line. Axel had seen it played out during his uncle's last days at the high school, the idea that humanity had all the answers apart from God, that man stood as the most intelligent being in the universe, and that those lines of thinking couldn't be challenged.

But the Lord had now brought RJ to CERN, to the ivory tower of mankind's godless thinking, where he would deploy RJ to help remove the last remnants of humanity's intellectual assault on the divine. Axel patted his uncle on the back, and RJ returned a wink and a smile.

Others congregated near them in the expanse, seemingly about forty Risen Ones in all, arriving from other places around the globe with their angelic escorts.

Another mighty angel approached and captured Axel's attention. The angel's body radiated hues of chrysolite green. His eyes flamed like torches, and his arms and legs glimmered like polished bronze.

"For our king and for our God!" Abiron shouted.

The chrysolite angel came to a stop in front of them, thrust his fist in the air, and acknowledged Abiron with a nod and a fierce countenance.

"Thank you all for coming," he said. "You've been chosen for a very important mission. The Lord has the utmost confidence in each one of you, for in him we have our strength. One final task remains to eliminate the earthly evil that existed before the Lord's reign. There will certainly be more unrighteousness to deal with, but this marks a significant milestone in the establishment of the kingdom. As you know, the adversary planted the seeds for an uprising before he was removed. The central command for that rebellion resides right here at CERN. In a few moments, you will be carrying out the Lord's will to bring this revolt to an end."

Axel considered his previous observations of angelic strategic offensives. He turned to RJ and whispered, "This is awesome. I've seen stuff like this before, but now we're going to be a part of it!"

"I'd never have imagined this even in my wildest dreams," RJ replied softly.

The chrysolite angel pointed to the buildings below. "The leaders of the uprising occupy a number of areas within this complex. We'll be dispatching you to apprehend targeted individuals according to a finely synchronized plan. Some of my officers are here to brief you on the specifics of the operation. Go now in the strength and power of our Lord Jesus Christ."

A few angels and Risen Ones gathered around the chrysolite angel, and Axel, Holly, and RJ glued their eyes to Abiron.

"So you wanted to know more about Mundaka?" Abiron said.

"Is he here?" Holly replied.

"In living color, and your assignment is to take him out, both him and his staff."

"So he's one of the leaders then, isn't he?"

"Actually, he is *the* leader," Hananias replied. "For the whole uprising, handpicked by the Evil One himself."

Axel knew this couldn't be just a coincidence. The Lord had deliberately led them to those e-mails with a view to this task. It was all part of the chase through the mirrors, but God's mastery at working every event together to bring about his purposes hadn't escaped Axel's attention, and it sent his sense of reverence and awe soaring to alpine heights again.

"Wow, I'm kind of overwhelmed," Holly said. "This is a *big* responsibility."

Axel shook his head. He'd seen the Lord rattle so many "unshakable" foundations recently that the magnitude of this task didn't really seem to matter. "Just another mountain to move."

"But how will we know who he is?" RJ said. "We've only seen his name on some printouts."

"The Lord will direct you. Just follow his lead as you have been doing."

"We should probably spend some time talking to *him*, then," Holly said.

"Exactly," Axel replied. "Let's bow. Lord Jesus, again we come before you in faith, knowing that in your strength nothing is impossible for us. You've blessed us with another opportunity to do your work, and it's blowing my mind that you would ever choose to use us. You could just wipe out this uprising yourself, Lord, but instead you've given us the privilege of serving you. Please show your power through us again. Thank you for the lives you've given us in your kingdom. May your name be lifted high. Amen."

Axel continued to pray silently for a moment, then the three of them prepared to leave.

"Before you go, there is something you need to know," Hananias said.

"This doesn't have anything to do with our dependence again, does it?" Axel replied.

"No, I think you've crossed that hurdle. This is really more for your understanding than anything else. The reason you three are tasked with this specific mission is that the Lord wanted you to witness Mundaka's fate."

Axel frowned. "Wait, like, why us specifically?"

Hananias made eye contact with each of them in turn. "Because . . . you are related to him. From an earthly perspective, that is. Each one of you. And you made a promise to someone."

Holly scrunched her forehead. "Promise? Do you guys have any idea what he's talking about?"

Axel scoured his mind, but all his promises had been fulfilled and cleaned out some time ago. "Not I."

"Holly, think about it," RJ said. "Just hours ago."

"Hold on . . . you don't mean Erin, do you?"

Hananias nodded and slowly circled his hand, like in a game of charades.

She moved her finger to her chin. "No . . . it can't be . . . Mundaka is Peter . . . Mundaka is Peter Erickson?"

Hananias didn't say a word.

Axel angled his head to one side. Something wasn't adding up. "Wait, I thought he stood up for his faith when they persecuted him?"

"Yeah, we figured he'd been executed," RJ said.

"That was all staged by the factions of evil," Elias replied. "A deception to extract him for this purpose and to make everyone think he was dead."

"So he was never a believer?"

"No," Elias said sadly. "It was all a skillfully choreographed act."

Holly looked down and shook her head. "I can't believe it. I don't know whether to be angry or . . . I mean . . . how could he just leave them like that? In the middle of such desperate times!"

Axel burned inside. Peter Erickson wasn't just a revolting blasphemer against his Lord, but also a heartless home wrecker, inflicting so much pain on Erin and Nikki, Axel's newly discovered family.

"He craved power in his heart," Hananias said. "And without the influence of the Holy Spirit, he became easy prey for the devil, who came knocking with a deal he couldn't refuse."

Holly slapped her hands on top of her head and groaned, "Oh, poor Erin." RJ put a hand on her shoulder and drew her in tight. After a few moments she sighed. "Okay, okay. We know what we need to do."

"Without question," Axel said.

"Here is the intelligence we have," Abiron said. "We know that Mundaka conducts his staff meeting at this time every week in the council chamber of the main building at the Meyrin site. You will enter the earth's dimensions at the place where the Lord leads you. You should be able to take out Mundaka's entire leadership team with one strike. The other Risen Ones will be conducting their raids simultaneously with yours, all coordinated from above."

"We're ready," Axel said. Holly and RJ nodded in agreement.

Abiron raised his hands. "The Lord be with you."

The three then moved to the front of CERN's main building and rotated in onto the ground. But Axel's thoughts wouldn't settle, as if his plane had just landed for a brief stopover. His final destination seemed to lie not here, but at some as-yet undisclosed location. But where could that be?

"This doesn't feel right. I don't think I'm supposed to be here."

Holly's brow furrowed. "Huh?"

"I think I'm supposed to be somewhere else," he replied.

"What are you talking about? Abiron just told us to go—"

"Actually, he told us to go where the Lord leads," RJ said. "I'm definitely supposed to be here, and it sounds like you are too, Holly."

"I don't know where I'm supposed to be, but I should probably go find out," Axel replied. "I'm going to stay back and seek the Lord's guidance for a minute."

"Axel, really?" Holly said.

"All right, all right," RJ cut in. "If the Lord wants you somewhere else, then that's where you need to be. We'll just have to catch up with each other later."

Axel wasted no time and rotated back out to the other dimensions.

✷

Holly's fire to bring down Mundaka flared as she and RJ made their way into the main building where another Risen One had already taken the guards into custody. They moved on past and crept down a long corridor, finding an unmarked chamber at the end. Tempers flared behind the doors.

"It's all unraveling!" yelled a man from inside the room. "We've lost control."

"This would have been avoided had you taken the appropriate *measures!"* barked another.

"Vat did Drago say to do in tis situation?" a woman with a strong Eastern European accent said.

Holly pointed forward with her index finger, and RJ nodded. They kicked down the doors, splintering the wood, and took up defensive stances as they vaulted inside. Five women and four men sat startled around a low, circular table, and the room reeked of darkness.

"Mundaka, reveal yourself!" Holly said.

Silent faces stared back at them.

"Absent," one of the women finally snickered.

"This is his staff meeting, is it not?" RJ said.

The woman grinned. "He's attending to another matter."

Holly's face fell. It was a swing and a miss. A *big* one. Apprehending Mundaka's staff was of some importance, but she'd missed out on the chance to drive home the winning run.

With no one talking, Holly and RJ forced the staff out of their seats and into custody. None of them put up a fight.

They escorted them to CERN's main auditorium at Meyrin, now set up as a collection station, where a number of Risen Ones had already brought in other leaders of the uprising.

✷

A few miles to the northwest of the Main Building, Axel rotated in onto the floor of a structure resembling a jet hangar. The walls stood roughly five stories high, and massive steel beams supported the roof. Through the center, an enormous metal cylinder lay on its side lengthwise across the floor, almost as high as the ceiling above and covered with electronic circuitry. A silver tube, about the diameter of a sewer drain, extended out from the middle of the cylinder on each end and continued outdoors through the walls of the building. The cylinder's massive doors stood open on one end, allowing him a view inside. He peered in cautiously. *Things kind of collapsed on me the last time I was in a place like this.*

All at once, two women and a man dressed in white lab coats entered and made their way toward the center of the room, sending Axel dashing swiftly around a corner and out of sight. There on the wall next to him hung a sign with the words "A Large Ion Collider Experiment (ALICE)." He read further to find descriptions of violent particle collisions taking place inside the ALICE cylinder. *This is the place where they simulate those super-high temperatures. Interesting.*

He knew the Lord had him hot on the trail of something, but what? Were these people members of Mundaka's staff? Was he supposed to disarm this mammoth electronic Coca-Cola can?

Before he'd finished reading, a loud humming filled the air, and he peered around the corner to see the cylinder's doors closing. *Time to make something happen.*

He walked out into view. The male scientist stared right at him and then shouted in French, a language Axel had struggled to learn in high school, "It's one of the Risen Ones! Let's get out of here!" And they fled.

Evidently they had reason to run, so Axel moved quickly to block their escape. One of the women veered and scrambled up a ladder, while the man and the other woman dashed back into the ALICE cylinder itself.

Axel scampered up the steps and grabbed the woman by the bottom of her lab coat, then turned to see the cylinder's doors completely shut behind her colleagues.

"Are there other ways to exit further down in those tubes?" he said. "Is that how they're trying to escape?"

Her eyes enlarged like a frightened doe's. "Oui, oui."

He escorted her to the ground, directed her into the nearest office and jammed the door shut, then quickly rotated out to the other dimensions and moved in through the walls of the cylinder. There, he rotated back in onto the floor and heard shuffling down in one of the tubes. "You're not moving fast enough," a woman's voice said.

Axel rapidly closed in behind them. He found them crawling on all fours, and he accepted their peaceful surrender. He led them back into the cylinder, where the woman pointed to some kind of maintenance hatch three stories above, but he knew that a route through the other dimensions would prove less taxing. So with his best French, he instructed them to grasp onto his arms. They just huddled together and looked at him wide-eyed.

At that moment, a piercing whine shrieked through the cylinder, and the scientists let out bloodcurdling screams. Laser-like beams entered from the tubes on each side and met right in the center, bursting out a brilliant flash and a vibrating orb of fire no larger than a soccer ball. A tiny nuclear explosion had detonated right in their midst.

Searing heat crawled across Axel's skin. He turned his head feverishly to one side and then to the other, but the scientists were gone.

Waves of energy shot out from the fireball in every direction, toasting his body hotter and hotter. He gritted his teeth and clenched his fists. Pressure mounted inside his head and his legs shook, but he wasn't going to blink. Vibrations jolted up his torso, shaking everything into a blur. The swelter became unbearable, the heat beyond anything he could have imagined.

Suddenly, the fireball and laser-like beams dissipated, just as quickly as they had appeared.

Axel stood alone. The scientists had apparently perished instantly.

Seconds later, the loud mechanical humming began again, and the cylinder's hulking doors swung slowly open. A platform two stories above came into view. Upon it stood a blond man in a black suit, looking distinguished and proud, with two others looming right behind him.

"Very impressive," said the man in the suit. "Risen Ones are immune to the hottest temperatures ever known. I underestimated you."

"Mundaka, I presume," Axel replied in his best Jack Nicholson tone. "Or should I say . . . Peter Erickson?"

"Ah, resourceful as well I see."

Axel gave him a wry smile. "You must be shaking underneath that arrogant demeanor of yours."

"Do you really think you can scare me?" Mundaka replied. "Deception is far more powerful than weapons of force."

This guy obviously hadn't been keeping score. By Axel's count, it was something like God: trillions, deceivers: zero. "Clearly, you're not familiar with Psalm 2."

Mundaka let out a roaring laugh. "I really don't have time for sermons."

"Let me summarize it for you, man. The Lord will smash you like a piece of old pottery. We'll see how far that expensive suit gets you then."

Even from where Axel stood, he could see the dangerous look in Mundaka's eyes. "Oh, you're greatly mistaken. I don't think you're seeing the big picture."

"Maybe not, but I'm following the lead of someone who does."

Mundaka and the two others dashed from view. Axel rotated out to the other dimensions and headed up toward the platform in pursuit, but he immediately felt an impulse to reverse course. He debated for a moment but then complied and dropped down through the floor. A split second later, he emerged into an underground bunker to see Mundaka and his accomplices arriving on a hydraulic elevator. They stepped off and walked briskly through an opening into a dark corridor.

Without hesitation, Axel moved to a position out in front of them, remaining unseen in the extra dimensions.

One of the accomplices laughed. "That was way too easy. You'd think those Risen Ones would be smarter."

"Just keep moving," Mundaka replied. "I wouldn't be surprised to see him coming right behind us."

Axel rotated in onto the ground and glared right at them. "Actually, it'll be from out in front of you." He began ambling forward. Mundaka and his men stopped in their tracks and quickly sprinted off the other way.

"Maybe you'd like to hear the end of that sermon," Axel shouted. "So we can slam the book closed on this little uprising of yours!"

He ran his fingers through his hair and watched as the evil cohort approached the end of the corridor. *I still have way too much of an advantage.* He paused. They turned the corner out of sight, and then the game was on.

Axel burst forward and closed the gap instantly, driving all three of them to the ground at the same time. They writhed in pain as he held them down, bruised and scraped from the fall. He put Mundaka in a headlock under his arm, grabbed the other two by their shirt collars, and escorted them all to the main auditorium through the other dimensions.

✷

Holly's thoughts shifted from a brisk walk to an agitated gallop as Axel rotated in onto the ground next to her with three men in his grasp. One of them had to be public enemy number one. "Mundaka?"

Axel leaned his head toward a blond man in a suit. "In the flesh."

"Have you told him anything?"

"Not really. We only talked a little bit about our favorite psalms," Axel replied. And he released the three fugitives.

Holly pressed her lips together. Favorite psalms? Now wasn't the time to get caught up in another one of Axel's antics.

Peter Erickson looked up at the ceiling. "Can we get on with this? I don't have time for chitchat."

"You really don't get it, do you?" she replied. "Your selfish escapades are over. Yeah, we'll hand you over to face justice in a minute, but first you need to dig deep down inside and tell me if you have even a trace of a conscience in that depraved soul of yours."

"I don't regret any of my actions," he said, now looking her straight in the eye.

The challenge had been issued, and backing down wasn't an option. The full extent of his atrocities needed to be declared. She closed to within an inch of his face. "How can you say that? What about the wife and daughter who loved you, and who have grieved deeply since you left them?"

"They were expendable," he fired back. "They only hindered my pursuit of the important things in life. I was so tired of that charade."

His arrogance reeked like burning refuse, but she didn't need to fan the flame any further. She had completed her task, and the rest was up to the Lord. She pulled back and surveyed him. "I'm heartbroken for you then. Because charades are common in the place where you're probably going. There are plenty of imposters there. I sincerely hope you will recognize your need for salvation and turn to follow Christ." And she walked away.

"Who do you think you are?" he yelled. "You have no right to judge me!"

Holly froze, hesitated for a moment, and then turned back to him. "Who do I think I am? Let me tell you, Peter. We're Ericksons. We're your family. But the fact of the matter is, we're not expendable. The Lord has assured us of that, and he's assured Erin and Nikki of that also."

A couple of Risen Ones walked up and ushered Peter and his men away.

After wrapping up some final details at the auditorium, Axel, Holly, and RJ rotated out to the other dimensions and reunited with the angels in the expanse above CERN.

Holly recounted the entire blow-by-blow exchange with Peter in her mind. Was it fitting for a Risen One to lash out like she had? Maybe expressing her displeasure in that way was out of line. "Sorry guys. I guess I kind of lost it back there."

"He needed to hear it," RJ said.

"Yeah, everything you said was true," Axel replied.

Hananias tilted his head back. "I believe the Lord himself has expressed his righteous anger a few times."

"Thanks, I appreciate it," she said. "It's a good thing I can only act righteously! It would've been really hard to resist the temptation to drive him into the floor back there."

Axel grinned. "Actually, I've got you covered on that one. But in my defense, he was running away at the time."

"Of course," she replied, smiling. But the gravity of the situation quickly set back in. They had kept their promise to Erin—but doing so meant she would need to don the bearer-of-bad-news hat again, difficult as it would be. "I just don't know how I'm going to explain this to Erin and Nikki. It's certainly not going to help them with their already-trampled hearts."

"True," Hananias replied. "But the Lord will be with you, and with them, and his love will heal them in the fastest possible way."

Without warning, Arielle flashed up behind Axel and covered his eyes.

"Like I really need to guess," he said, and he turned to embrace her.

"Am I truly that obvious?"

"You said you'd be waiting for me. If you weren't, I'd be searching every corner of extradimensional space to find you."

24

Closure

Axel, Holly, and RJ darted back to San Diego in a flash. With the early morning sun shining down, they rotated back in onto the ground at the front of the gym, and déjà vu stirred Axel like a stew. He'd stood right there just days before, ready to enter into God's afterlife calling for him. And now, once again, he stood on that very same piece of pavement, having now followed the Lord's lead to uphold divine justice in thrilling fashion. Life in the kingdom couldn't be any more rousing.

He and Holly and RJ walked in through the doors to find their entire northwest San Diego team gathered together. Derek scurried over to give Holly an ecstatic hug, and Taj and Brianna came close behind. Family and friends encircled RJ, and Axel walked right into the arms of Alana as she grinned from ear to ear.

"Hey, hey! So the Lord decided it was time to suffocate that uprising, huh?" Francisco said.

"Took the air right out of it," Axel replied.

Axel soaked it all in as others raved about how the Lord had used them mightily in their areas of service. Marie, Nina, and Derek told of the thousands of people he'd provided care for. Francisco, Taj, and Brianna conveyed stories of his extraordinary feats through them to restore buildings and infrastructure. Jesus stood as the only hero in all of it. No one else could take a single ounce of credit for the miraculous triumphs he had brought about.

A little while later, Ryan walked to the front of the gym. "Greetings in the name of our Lord. I've been monitoring all of your activities through our coordination team, and I think it's safe to say that our God has far exceeded our wildest expectations. I don't think any of us were prepared for the power he's displayed and for the things he's used us to accomplish while reigning with him in the kingdom."

Hoots and hollers of praise to God erupted from the whole crowd, and someone slapped Axel on the back. He grinned and pumped his fist in the air.

Ryan waited for the din to quiet a little before continuing. "We'll now have an opportunity to express that worship directly in his presence. Tomorrow marks the beginning of the Feast of Tabernacles, where everyone on Earth, both humans and Risen Ones, will come together to reflect on the Lord's blessings in a celebration unrivaled by anything else in all of history."

Cheering with whistling and applause filled the air. Axel's head spun as he tried to contemplate what was ahead of them.

"Our task for the rest of the day will be to transport the people of the area to Jerusalem through the other dimensions. The coordination team has assigned each of you a list of people to take. We've contacted them all, and they're anxiously awaiting your arrival to escort them. You'll need to make a number of trips, since you can probably only transport two or three comfortably at a time. There will be Risen Ones on the other end to direct everyone to their tents—which are very nice, by the way. No one will be disappointed with their accommodations."

"Wow, they must have had to put up a lot of them," someone said.

"Millions actually," Ryan replied. "For miles and miles in every direction. I was there yesterday, and it's quite a sight."

"What about packing? Should they take a suitcase or something?" another said.

"Not necessary. The tents are furnished with everything they'll need for the week. Personalized food, drink, beds, clothing, and personal items. The Lord has spared no luxury."

"Luxury? We are talking about tents, right?"

Ryan winked. "In a sense." Many looked at him curiously, but he just continued on. "You'll probably want to have everyone there by two o'clock Pacific Standard Time because of the time difference. That way they'll be able to get some rest before the festivities tomorrow."

After receiving a few more instructions, Axel headed out into the community and began transporting passengers to Jerusalem. The heavenly airspace whirled with activity as Risen Ones from all over the globe made their way toward the Holy City with people in tow.

He completed his list of riders quickly and returned to the gym to see if he could assist with some of the others. Holly stood talking with a member of the coordination team as Axel approached.

"Finished already?" Holly said.

"Yeah, I was able to take four at a time on some of the trips. How about you?"

"Only two more to go. Erin and Nikki. I left them for last so I could spend as much time with them as they need."

He realized right away what she meant, and his heart sank. "They don't know yet?"

"No." She bit her lip. "I've struggled to come up with the words to share it with them."

Axel couldn't conceive of even the slightest bit of counsel for her, but maybe she could use his support when she broke the news to them.

Whoa, where did that thought come from? Emotional drama wasn't his cup of tea. In fact, he didn't like tea at all. He'd much rather down a tall glass of cherry-flavored cough syrup than that stuff. And Holly possessed a tremendous gift for encouragement. He stood completely at a loss for how he might help . . . but something, or someone, kept nudging.

A short time later, he found himself standing beside Holly at Erin's front door. They spent a minute in prayer, and then she rang the bell.

The seconds seemed like minutes as Axel fidgeted beside her. *Why am I here again?* How do you tell a wife that her husband abandoned her? How do you tell a daughter that her dad felt she was "expendable"? Not even a Risen One could make this right.

Finally, Erin answered with a big grin on her face. "Holly! And Axel! So good to see you. I understand you're taking us on a little vacation."

"We are," Holly replied.

"Well, there's no one else we'd rather ride with."

Holly smiled, but Axel could tell she'd forced it.

"I'm really looking forward to hanging out with you guys this week," Holly said. "But we need to talk for a minute. Can we come in?"

Concern flickered across Erin's face. "Sure. Is there anything I can get you to drink?"

"No, but thank you."

Erin led them into the living room, and they sat down on the plush couches. Axel shifted three times before he realized what he was doing and forced himself to sit still.

"Erin, we have some information to give you about Peter," Holly said. "I'm afraid it's not . . . not likely what you want to hear. Would you like Nikki to be here, or would you rather share it with her later yourself?"

Erin's eyebrows turned inward. "Oh . . . I guess you can tell us together." She walked out of the room and yelled for Nikki to join them. Nikki came in and gave Holly and Axel each a hug, and then she sat down next to her mom.

"I'm afraid the news about your husband, your father, Peter, isn't good," Holly said.

Erin and Nikki's eyes fastened upon her. Erin already clutched a tissue in her hand.

"I know this will be hard, but I'll get right to the point. What we've found out is that . . . Erin, he knew he was going to be taken. In fact, he planned it with them."

"What . . . what do you mean?" Erin replied. "He knew he was going to be taken?"

Axel shifted in his seat again. The mood in the room had just flared into emotionally flammable territory. An inkling to make his way toward the door smoldered inside him, but he quickly doused the flames. God had him there for a reason, and no wildfire should drive him away.

Holly continued. "Erin, it was all a phony ploy. From the moment he left, and for the last six months, Peter's been the leader of a worldwide uprising based in Geneva, Switzerland."

Erin stared at her with eyes of anguish. "You're joking, right? I mean, that's the craziest thing I've ever heard!"

Holly just shook her head sadly. Axel didn't respond either. The words escaped him. Nothing he could say would make it any more believable.

"I don't understand. There must be some mistake."

"I wish there was," Holly replied softly. "And I know it sounds absurd."

"But how can you be sure? I just don't—"

"We were there, Erin," Axel said. "We were there to see his fall, just yesterday as a matter of fact. We took him into custody."

Erin looked up at the ceiling and took a deep breath, her eyes tearing up. Nikki bent forward and buried her face in her hands.

"So betrayed . . ." Erin sniffled. "I suspected he wasn't going to church for the right reasons, but I never would've imagined this."

"I'm so sorry," Holly said.

Erin stared off out the window, glassy-eyed, then put her arm around her daughter. "No . . . no . . . please . . . don't be. I asked you to find out for me. You've given us the closure we needed, as miserable as it is."

Nikki shook her head. "I'm sick to my stomach. I was part of that uprising. I listened to all of that hate and rebellion, and I saw all of the evil and blasphemy firsthand, and now to learn that my own father was leading it all." Her breaths became short and fast and pronounced.

Erin pulled her daughter closer. Holly moved to a seat next to Nikki and embraced them both. A minute or so later, Nikki regained control.

"If it helps, I'll find out if you can leave later for the festival," Axel said. "Like in a few days, or maybe bail on it altogether if you're not up to it."

Erin looked up at him. "Thank you, but I've been dealing with this for a long time. I'll be all right. We could use a change of scenery anyway."

"I feel the same way," Nikki said softly.

Holly squeezed the two of them even tighter. "Okay, but you'd better be ready for more love than you've ever experienced before."

They talked and prayed for another hour or so, and then Erin and Nikki decided they were ready to go. Axel was ready to go too. The charge in his emotional batteries had run out about thirty minutes prior.

✷

Nikki took care of a few things in her bedroom and headed downstairs. Her mom had already arrived and grasped onto Holly's arm. Nikki took hold of Axel's shoulder and said, "You're not gonna believe this, Mom. It's truly incredible."

"I'm not going to get nauseous, am I?" Erin replied. "Rollercoasters aren't really my thing."

"You won't have time to," Holly said, smiling, and they rotated out to the other dimensions.

In a blur, they sped off into the expanse and arrived at the coast of Israel in a matter of moments. Holly and Axel slowed their pace, and Nikki's mouth opened wide as the grandeur of the Holy City came into view in front of her. A pillar of fire blazed high into the night over the temple, beaming the Lord's glory and lighting up the area for miles around. The temple stood at the pinnacle of a high mountain, a hulking edifice formed of glossy white stone and glimmering gold, surrounded on all sides by stunning mosaic masonry and walls.

"Oh my!" she exclaimed. The bleakness in her soul had faded just enough to allow the spectacle to move her.

"Staggering, isn't it?" Axel said.

"I don't know if I've ever seen anything so breathtaking."

The sky glistened as the pillar of fire reflected off the gold of the temple and the silver in the city's buildings and walls. Lights from countless tent camps dotted the land beneath them, stretching all the way back to the sea and as far as she could scan to the north and to the south. In the congested heavenly airspace, angels, Risen Ones, and those they escorted moved past, all expressing elated greetings as they went by.

Nikki drank in everything that entered her eyes and ears. She definitely needed a distraction, but this went way beyond that; she'd seemingly entered a completely different world. One laced with the fabric of dreams and wonder. One swept with the splendor of her God.

Holly and Axel then made their way over Jerusalem itself, just to the south of the temple.

"It's truly amazing," Erin said.

"I had no idea it would be so beautiful," Nikki said.

They veered to the right and after a few moments rotated back in onto the ground in the midst of a bustling camp of box-shaped white tents, the canvas of each one worn and weathered.

Music and shouts of joy filled the air, and lights from other camps lined the hills around them. Axel pointed to a tent just down the road where Josh sat out front, and Nikki ran to him.

Josh threw his arms around her and kissed her forehead. "So glad you're here! What took you so long?"

Nikki's lips trembled. "Holly and Axel . . . they had some really awful news to share with us about my dad."

Concern for her filled his expression. "Seriously? What's going on?"

She smiled at him, her heart warmed by his care. "I'll tell you about it in a few minutes."

Axel, Holly, and Erin made their way over and greeted Josh.

"I'll catch up with you guys later," Axel said. "I need to meet up with someone."

"Tell Arielle I said hi," Holly replied with a smirk, and Axel strolled away.

Holly opened the tent's door, and she and Erin went inside. Nikki and Josh sat down on the steps out front, where Nikki laid out the whole awful revelation. He wiped away her tears and held her close. The heartache of her dad's treachery cut like a knife, but Josh's empathy and kindness caressed her wounds, soothing her distress with his words and his touch. The spark between them had leaped to new heights, even in the midst of such a desperate time.

After a while, they said their good-byes, and Nikki headed inside.

She couldn't believe her eyes. The place dazzled with maple-wood flooring, brass fixtures, granite counters, and beds that looked plush and comfortable. Holly and her mom sat conversing at a small marble table. "Wow, I didn't think it would be anything like this."

"You didn't think the Lord would have you come here for a week to rough it, did you?" Holly replied.

"I guess I didn't really know what to expect. So why the rugged exterior?"

"This is the Feast of Tabernacles, to remember the tents the Israelites lived in when they wandered in the wilderness, but obviously housing standards have changed a lot since then," Holly said, smiling. "The exterior matches the symbolism. The interior is meant to spoil you guys. In ancient times this feast was also a festival of the harvest, where the people of Israel celebrated God's blessings."

"Well, regardless of all that's happened, I'm thankful for the blessings he's given me."

The three talked for a couple more hours, and then Holly left for the night. Her mom turned out the lights, but Nikki couldn't sleep, unable to erase the things she'd learned about her dad. The man who'd played Legos with her on the floor and pushed her in a swing at the park when she was little had turned out to be someone else, willing to ditch her to lead a diabolical plot, foolish enough to think he could rise up against the living God. How would she ever reconcile the man she remembered with the truth?

25

Blown Away

Axel's excitement skyrocketed in anticipation of his impending thrill ride as he walked with Arielle on the Haas Promenade overlooking Jerusalem. "It'll be epic, I promise."

Arielle smiled. "I don't know. Sounds pretty sketchy to me."

"Really? What's there to worry about?"

"Probably nothing."

"So let's do it!"

"You know, I was always attracted to your flair for adventure," she replied. "But I could never keep up. You were always going way beyond my comfort zone."

"This one's right in your wheelhouse, though. I don't think you'll be disappointed."

"Well . . . okay. I've definitely been looking forward to doing something together."

Axel grabbed her by the hand and rotated out to the other dimensions, then led her up through the earth's atmosphere and flashed past a reddish planet far off to one side. The sun's light faded fast. Hundreds of jagged, rocky objects appeared and he passed right through.

A split second later, an immense bluish-brown globe with a red spot in the lower right corner came into focus. It loomed larger and larger, quickly eclipsing his field of view. Without hesitation, he darted in one side and out the other, blinded only for a moment by a haze of gassy mist, and then glided to a stop with the galactic night spread out on a canvas before him.

"There," he said, pointing to his left at a desolate orange, white, and olive moon—something of a volcanic wonderland. "RJ was right."

"It looks like a geological nightmare," Arielle replied.

"Exactly, and we're the only ones here."

"For good reason, I would have to say."

Axel squeezed her hand and dashed off toward the chosen orb. He stopped in the sky above it and looked down upon umbrella-shaped plumes of smoke rising from towering peaks and vibrant lava flows branching out in all directions. Axel marveled at the scale of it all. *How could such a small moon have volcanoes higher than any of the mountains I've seen on Earth?*

"Ominous," Arielle said. "Does it have a name?"

"Io. I think that's what RJ called it."

He scanned the area. So many opportunities stood before him. "Let's see . . . not that one. Maybe . . . no, not that one either." His eyes widened as he saw it—the perfect peak. He pointed. "Yeah, check this out." Magma spewed from its cracked and flared opening, and fumes seethed up from its bowels. He rubbed his hands together slowly. "I think we have a winner. That one's definitely ready to go."

"Since when did you become a geology expert?" Arielle asked, laughing.

He put his arm around her and smiled. "Ah, you doubt me?"

"Oh, come on. You have to admit that science was never really your thing."

"Okay, okay, you're right. But *someone* did give me a reason to dive into it a little bit. Quantum physics, actually."

"Really? Well then, I am impressed. I guess you'll have to tell me more about that sometime."

"Gladly, but as far as eruptions go, you called my bluff. RJ had to tell me what to look for. Besides, it's the biggest one around. Are you ready?"

She laughed and shook her head. "Sure, Axel, sure."

He leaned forward and sailed to the summit still in the other dimensions and then inched over the edge into the enormous caldera with her by his side. It easily measured football fields across. He descended gradually with fumes and smoke obscuring his vision and molten matter splattering upward from below. Grievous groans thundered from the belly of the beast, a behemoth in absolute agony. *It won't be long now.*

"Are you sure about this?" Arielle shouted.

"Not really, but I'm looking forward to finding out!" he yelled back.

"And I can see that you're loving every minute of it."

Axel cocked his head to one side. "Yeah, aren't you?"

"Still deciding. I'll let you know when I'm not."

Deeper and deeper he floated into the throat of the volcano with the walls quaking on every side. Fluttering and quivering. The toxic fog became heavier and thicker.

He spotted the lake of enraged lava not far below them. "Let's hang here," he yelled. "We go down much further and we'll be into the soup. I want to be able to see this whole thing unfold."

"I can't believe you talked me into this," she replied.

"You're doing great. Just rotate back in when I do."

Clutching his arm, she laughed. "Okay, but I apologize now for the fingernail marks I'm going to leave in your skin."

Moments later, the chasm ignited below with a deafening BOOM! BOOM! BOOM! Arielle's eyes widened. She threw her arms around Axel's neck and buried her head in his chest.

An angry beehive of scarlet, yellow, and orange matter burst upward. The cavern went blurry, and turbulence filled Axel's ears. He wrapped his arms around Arielle as liquid fire splattered everywhere in a torrent of chaos.

Another monstrous BOOM! BOOM! jolted the air, and even more burning magma thrust forth, immersing him into a massive pot of boiling, bubbling fury.

He rotated back into the physical universe and Arielle came right with him, clasping her ankles around his. The full force of the eruption snatched his body, and blast after blast drove him skyward in a dizzying ascent. Searing lava blistered against his skin. He tumbled and twisted over and over, colliding violently with burning boulders and other fiery debris, holding her close while bouncing against wave after wave of flaming volcanic waste. The commotion blared in his ears. He careened sideways and then rapidly back the other direction, turning and turning and slamming into solid object after solid object, then toppling again and again.

Within moments, everything began to separate. His momentum waned, and the surface of Io came into view, now many miles below. He looked down upon the beleaguered moon, floating high above the explosion with Arielle still in tow. Vivid tangerine rivers flowed out of the mammoth volcano, and ashes floated in a sea of black and grey.

Arielle raised her head and blinked several times. "Whew, that was quite a ride."

"What a rush, huh?" he said.

"Can't deny that, but I think I'll watch from the sidelines next time. Just a little too much jarring for me."

"Yeah, it was even more over the top than I expected." That was an understatement. He'd ridden some thrilling waves on Earth, but after this he knew he needed to redefine his use of the word *thrill.* This venture had raised the bar to a whole new level. Jesus had drenched his afterlife with new kinds of adrenaline rushes, even though the word *adrenaline* didn't apply to his body anymore. "I'm ready to go again."

She laughed and rolled her eyes. "How about if you save that for another time?" she said. "People will be waking up for the festival soon."

"I guess you're right. It's going to be an amazing day for them, and I don't want to miss any of it."

They rotated out to the other dimensions and rushed off, retracing the way they'd come. Within seconds they arrived in the earth's atmosphere and then flew onward into the skies over Jerusalem. They rotated back in onto the road of the camp to find Holly, Derek, and Stein's family walking along.

"Glad you guys could join us," Holly said. "What've you been up to?"

"Oh, we had a burning issue to deal with," Axel replied. "I guess it's almost time, right?"

"Yep. As soon we pick up Erin and Nikki."

✷

Nikki stepped out of the tent behind her mom. Gardens, vineyards, and fruit trees covered the hills dotted with tents on every side. Colorful flowers grew all around, and streams and waterfalls flowed through the area. Other camps swarmed with activity in the distance, and flocks and herds grazed in the greenest of fields.

Only barren desert had rested here just weeks before, and the Lord had now made it all new, now flourishing. Nikki prayed that he would soon do the same for her heart and life.

Josh came walking up the road with the others. He broke into a jog and took hold of her hand the second he arrived. "How's my girl this morning?" he said, looking into her eyes.

"Okay," Nikki replied. "I didn't sleep very well, but I'm here." She wanted him to know how glad she was to see him, but her fatigue, both physical and emotional, kept her from mustering any zeal.

"It sounds like we're in for an incredible day today, and I'll be right beside you every step of the way."

A slight smile cornered her lips. "Thanks. It means a lot to me."

Nikki and her mom grasped Holly's arms, Stein and Josh took hold of Axel's, and Lisa and Josh's sister, Kylie, grabbed Arielle's. They rotated out to the other dimensions and then back in onto the ground of the outer court of the temple. There, they united with other friends and family, each one buzzing with anticipation.

"What an incredible building," Josh said.

"Remarkable, isn't it?" Axel replied. "An unrivaled architectural masterpiece, coated inside and out with pure gold."

"And this massive column of smoke. I mean, where's that coming from?"

"God's glory pure and simple. But if you think this is heavy, just wait until you see what's next."

Nikki hooked her arm around Josh's and followed those in front of her into the inner court, then around the altar and up a wide set of stairs. There, she gazed directly into the temple chambers.

"Amazing!" Josh exclaimed.

Nikki's hand sprang to her lips. Majesty and Holiness sat enthroned before her, none other than the Lord Jesus Christ himself! He wore a golden crown and held a scepter in his hand. Her thoughts swirled, and her pulse pounded. Brilliant waves of light surrounded Jesus, and holy priests stood in front of him. Steadiness drained from her knees, and her head became airy.

She approached the foot of the throne and knelt along with Josh and the others, bowing directly in the presence of her God, captivated and awestruck. Her exalted Creator sat right before her eyes.

And he welcomed her. His love poured into her soul like a flood. She couldn't contain its adoring rush. Tears rolled down her face, and all of her pain fled away.

"Rise," said one of the priests, and she rose to her feet. Jesus's face beamed with affection. He made direct eye contact with her, so personal and so affirming. The God of all creation had met her in her time of need and saturated her with his compassion.

Images sped through her mind. She'd prayed to him since she was a little girl, but now she stood before him, face-to-face, moved beyond awe. *It can't get any better than this.*

Jesus smiled. "My children, you know that I live in you and you live in me, because I have given you my Spirit. You have seen and testify that my Father has sent me, and you acknowledge that I am the Son of God. And so now, continue to know and rely on the love that I have for you!"

Nikki's face lit up as the words fell on her like a blessing. His love beamed so real and so tangible and so warm, and it blew away all of the gloom that had shaded her heart.

After Jesus had spoken with them for a little while longer, the Risen Ones ushered the group toward the gate to make room for the many others who waited to worship.

✷

Axel arrived back at camp around noon and found the festivities raging. He and Arielle strolled among the crowds that danced in the streets, clapped their hands, and shouted cries of joy to God. The tantalizing aroma of meat cooking on grills filled the air, and endless quantities of breads, fruits, and other delicacies made for a feast of epic proportions.

Fervent activity met them everywhere they went. Lions, bears, and other animals wandered peacefully through the camp. Teenage boys wrestled with monkeys, and children rode on the backs of tigers and hippos. Many swam near the waterfalls and in the streams, and the more adventurous dove from cliffs into deep, crystal-clear ponds. Others hiked through the luscious gardens and hills.

Later that evening, Axel approached Holly and RJ. "Hey, I just spent some time hanging out with a guy named Eleazar. What a fascinating dude! He was one of King David's mighty men, and God used him to bring about an epic victory over the Philistines."

"That's terrific," Holly said. She laughed. "You two must have a lot in common."

"Definitely."

"I've met some incredible people also," she said. "Not the least of whom was Queen Esther. Remember? Her faith saved the Israelite people from doom and destruction."

"Very impressive," RJ replied. "But I think I've topped you both. Earlier today, I had a stimulating conversation with Johannes Kepler."

Axel squinted. "Johannes who?"

"Oh, come on. Evidently you didn't pay close enough attention in my science class."

"Sorry, not ringing a bell."

RJ shook his head. "Anyway, he was an astronomer who made important discoveries about light and the laws of planetary motion during his time on Earth."

Axel smiled. "Awesome. Guess I'll have to take your class again so I can recognize all of these scholarly icons."

"Whatever the case," Holly said. "I'm excited that we can expect to have encounters like this for the rest of eternity."

26

Radiance

Hananias reentered the vast heavenly expanse. Dazzling rays shone in every color imaginable. The light oscillated through many brilliant hues, projecting out in all directions from the One seated upon the mountainous throne. The atmosphere dripped with his majesty, and his holiness permeated the entire domain. Thunder and lightning discharged continuously around him, and flames of fire burst forth from before him. Hananias never grew tired of basking in his radiance.

Abiron knelt with his head bowed and hands raised a short distance away. Hananias made his way over and waited as the mighty warrior finished his prayer. "I do not think they will need much more help from us," Hananias said.

"Very true," Abiron replied. "They have come so far. They rely completely on the Lord now, and they teach the people there to do the same. Our God reigns! And he has established a new era on the earth."

"Yes, he has. Especially for you, my friend, with no more battles to fight . . . for a long time anyway."

"I am sure he has plenty for me to do between now and the final rebellion. I am not concerned in the least. And you?"

"More of the same, I suspect," Hananias replied. "People will still pass away on Earth, and I will be here for them. In fact, I sense the Lord calling me right now."

He bade Abiron farewell, and the Lord rotated him into other dimensions of time and space. There, he found himself hovering next to his angelic colleague Cristobel. Jesus stood a short distance away, meeting face-to-face with another new arrival. Light waves of his glory filled the expanse in every direction.

"What do we have?" Hananias said.

"Big drama with this one," Cristobel replied. "He came to Christ during his last day on Earth, after being an enemy of the Lord his entire life."

"Praise God! I love to hear those stories."

"Me too. He's so patient with them."

Hananias never tired of the Lord's mercies. "He chases after them, desperately wanting them to turn to him, even when they throw it back in his face."

Jesus made his way out of the expanse, and Hananias took his cue, moving in next to a blond man who knelt with his head down. The man raised his eyes, and Hananias recognized him immediately. His spirit soared with praise.

"Mr. Erickson, my name is Hananias. Welcome to our Lord's heaven."

"Please, call me Peter," the man replied humbly.

"I am here to answer any questions you might have."

"I don't really have any. I'm just grateful to be here . . . I didn't know if the Lord would accept the sincerity of my prayer."

Inwardly Hananias was still rejoicing, but he remained calm. "I know your story, and Jesus knows your heart. He has determined that your faith is genuine. You have been given eternal life."

Peter's eyes filled with tears. "I surely don't deserve it. I'm a murderer, a blasphemer, and a man who deserted his family. What kind of God do we have who forgives the sins of a man like me? What kind of love does he have that enables him to adopt someone like me as his child, even after all I've done?"

"I think you know the answer," Hananias replied. "A God who *is* love. A God of perfect love, who suffered tremendously to take upon himself the punishment that you deserve."

"Yes . . . and I'm grateful for that. I just wish I wouldn't have waited until the last day of my life to believe it was real. For those last few hours I truly felt his love, and I experienced the satisfaction I'd longed for my entire life."

Hananias smiled. "Well, we are all very glad you are here."

"It sounds like that'll only be for a while, though. Me being here . . ."

"Yes. You will return to Earth at some point to join the others reigning with him in his kingdom."

"I don't know how I'm going to be able to face my wife and daughter."

"I am sure it will not be easy, and it will take time to reconcile fully with them, but if you depend on him, he will lead you. His love covers a multitude of sins."

"I hope so. I just don't know how they'll ever be able to forgive me."

"Jesus has, and in time they will too."

✷

The sun dropped toward the horizon without a cloud in the San Diego sky as Axel and Josh sat on their boards waiting for another set of waves. The ocean glistened like glass, and a few seagulls soared serenely above.

"So how's Nikki?" Axel said.

"Well, you know, she's really strong," Josh replied. "She's trusting the Lord, but I know she's still hurting deep inside."

"She's definitely been through some heavy stuff, but he'll use it for his glory."

"I'm gonna marry her, Axel. I decided when we were in Jerusalem."

Axel reared his head back and laughed. "Man, that's awesome! I'm stoked for you. I know you haven't been dating very long, but it's obvious that she's a great girl."

Josh beamed. "Yeah, thanks. The Lord's given her a really important calling, though, working with Marie and Derek and Nina to care for the hurting teens in our area. She's totally into it, but I just don't think that line of work is for me. I've been praying about what he might have me do."

"And what's he saying to you?"

"Nothing yet, but I think it would be really cool to have an assignment like yours."

"Maybe that's him telling you something."

Josh nodded. "I hope so. The Lord's blessed us so much since he returned. It really bothers me when people abuse it."

"I hear you, big time. I get a little hyped about that myself. We'll see where it goes. Maybe he's planning to use you there. Maybe very soon, or maybe after you've risen."

"After I've risen. That's a wild thought . . . so what was it like? Being in heaven and everything?"

Axel thought back to his first glimpses of the heavenly expanse, the throne room, the angels. "Oh man, indescribable."

The sun set completely over the horizon, projecting spectacular waves of amber, burgundy, and violet across the sky. It was breathtaking to behold.

Axel turned and looked Josh in the eye. "I don't even have the words to tell you how incredible our God is. It's way beyond comprehension . . . the sights, the sounds, and the brilliant lights up there. I mean, you definitely beheld his awesome presence in Jerusalem, and that was amazing, but seeing him in heaven takes it to a whole new level."

"So it sounds like I just need to stay focused on him, on his glory, and he'll lead me to what he wants me to do."

"Yeah, you got it." Axel put a hand on Josh's shoulder. "It's like my friend Francisco once told me: 'God *is* light. In him there's no darkness at all. And he's made his light shine in our hearts to give us the light of the knowledge of the glory of God in the face of Christ.'

Waves of his light, shining into our lives to show us the way. All we need to do is depend on him every moment. Everything follows from there. Exhilaration . . . purpose . . . fulfillment. The riches of following him, no matter where we are."

Foundations

The treasures that God has waiting for his children in the afterlife far exceed anything that human language can convey. While Scripture gives us a glimpse of what we can expect, it provides us with sparse detail at best. The pages of *A Heaven to Die For* contain many afterlife concepts taken from the Bible, but needless to say, much of the story dwells in the realm of what might possibly take place. I have made every effort to ensure that none of it stands at odds with the truth of God's Word.

I sincerely hope this book has encouraged you to seek out the riches of God's eternity in Scripture for yourself, which will assuredly lead to tremendous hope and joy as you drink in his amazing love and grace. Some opportunities to begin your journey lie below.

Chapter 1: Exhilaration

Francisco quotes from 1 John 1:5 and 2 Corinthians 4:6 when talking to Axel about God's light and how God has imparted that light into our lives.

Chapter 2: Connection

Holly's friend Lynne quotes from Psalm 31:14–16 when encouraging Holly to increase her trust in God.

Chapter 3: Validation

RJ sees a vision of the throne of God as described in Ezekiel 1:22–28.

RJ quotes from Colossians 1:15–16 and Ephesians 6:12 when proclaiming the existence of extradimensional realms to his high school science class.

When speaking with his colleague Rusty, RJ cites examples of extradimensional events in the Bible from John 20:19–20, Acts 8:26–40, Luke 9:28–36, Joshua 10:9–15, 2 Kings 2:1–18, and Isaiah 38:8. I first came across these ideas when reading pages 56–61 of Dr. Hugh Ross's book, *Beyond the Cosmos* (NavPress, 1996).

Chapter 5: Aspiration

Abiron's visual appearance is based on Daniel 10:4–6. For more on angels, see Genesis 18, Genesis 22:11–13, 2 Kings 19:35-36, 1 Chronicles 21:16, Acts 12:22–23, and Billy Graham's book, *Angels: God's Secret Agents* (Doubleday & Company, 1975).

Abiron and Axel were dispatched to answer a prayer request and protect believers as portrayed in passages like Daniel 10:4–14, Psalm 91:11, Hebrews 1:14, Daniel 3:28, and Daniel 6:22.

Axel considers that earthly marriage doesn't apply in the afterlife as stated in Matthew 22:30.

Chapter 6: Returning

Axel, Holly, and RJ's return to Earth with Christ on white stallions is based on verses from Revelation 19:11–16, Revelation 5:9–10, Colossians 3:4, Joshua 5:13–15, Matthew 24:30, Luke 17:24, Revelation 1:7, and Acts 1:9–11.

The concepts present in Abiron's discussion of extra time and space dimensions come from Dr. Hugh Ross's book *Beyond the Cosmos,* on pages 75–77 and 168–169.

For more detail on RJ's reference to "Mystery Babylon," take a look at Revelation 18:1–24.

Chapter 7: Conquering

When Abiron describes the previous invasion of Israel by armies from the north, he's referring to chapters 38 and 39 of Ezekiel. Further commentary can be found in John Walvoord's book *Major Bible Prophecies (*Zondervan: 1991) on pages 328–337.

Jesus's march against his enemies with the wall of fire in front of him is based on Joel 2:1–11, Isaiah 66:14–16, Revelation 16:16, Joel 2:20, Hebrews 10:31, and Revelation 19:21.

RJ's reference to priests of Baal and fire from the sky comes straight out of 1 Kings 18:38.

During Axel's flashback to his initial meeting with Jesus in heaven, Jesus's visual appearance is based on Revelation 1:13–16. Jesus quotes from Matthew 25:34, 1 Peter 1:3–4, Ephesians 2:6–7, Ephesians 2:10, Revelation 1:6, Luke 1:74–75, Matthew 17:20–21, John 14:15–17, John 16:13–14, and 2 Timothy 4:7–9 during his conversation with Axel. Jesus's description of Axel's resurrected body comes from 1 Corinthians 15:42–44, and additional information on resurrected bodies can be found in 2 Corinthians 5:1–8, Philippians 3:20–21, Luke 24:39, 1 Corinthians 15:49, and 1 John 3:2.

Chapter 8: Ascending

Jesus's capture of the Beast and the False Prophet is described in Revelation 19:20, Daniel 7:11, and Daniel 12:1.

Jesus's approach to Jerusalem from the south through Edom is a fulfillment of Isaiah 63:1–4.

Jesus's deliverance of Jerusalem, the earthquake on the Mount of Olives, and his ascending the throne are depicted in Zechariah 14:2–13, Joel 2:32, and Zechariah 12:2–9.

Hadassa's reference to Axel, Holly, and RJ as the Lord's priests comes from Revelation 20:6 and Revelation 5:9–10.

Jesus's ride into Jerusalem on the donkey and his ascent to the throne are described in Matthew 23:39, John 12:12–15, Zechariah 9:9, and Ezekiel 43:2–4.

Jesus's earthly reign as Messiah King is declared in Psalm 2:6–9, Isaiah 9:6–7, Zechariah 14:9, and numerous other passages.

The pillar of fire by night and the pillar of smoke by day over the temple are described in Ezekiel 43:5, Isaiah 4:5, 60:1–2, and Zechariah 14:7.

Chapter 9: Restoration

Abiron's departure to participate in the devil's imprisonment is based on Revelation 20:1–3, 7–8.

The land of Egypt will remain desolate during the kingdom as described in Joel 3:18–19, but God will restore the land of Israel to the beauty of the garden of Eden, as it says in Isaiah 51:3, Isaiah 55:10–13, Ezekiel 36:35, and Joel 2:21–24.

Jerusalem will be rebuilt during the kingdom era as stated in Isaiah 60:10–17, and Ezekiel chapters 40–43 give us detailed descriptions of the temple's renovation.

Jesus will reign as both king and high priest as prophesied in Zechariah 6:9–13 and characterized in Hebrews 7.

Zechariah 14:16–19 and Ezekiel 45:13–25 declare that holy festivals will take place during the kingdom age.

Chapter 10: Purpose

God's desire for resurrected believers to serve Christ as his priests in the kingdom is expressed in Revelation 20:6, Revelation 5:9–10, 1 Peter 2:4–5, and Daniel 7:22, 27.

Jesus describes the kingdom blessings he will heap upon his children in Matthew 19:28–29.

Jesus instructs Axel, Holly, and RJ to depend on him at all times as he instructed his disciples in John 15:4–8.

Hananias describes the afterlife rewards that result from faithful service on Earth as depicted in Matthew 25:14–28, Luke 19:11–26, and Luke 16:10–12.

The Lord will establish justice upon the Earth during his kingdom as stated in Isaiah 32:1–2 and Isaiah 61:8. He will initiate it over a period of time at the beginning of his reign, as described in Isaiah 42:3–4.

Chapter 11: Arriving

Axel's witness of sharks swimming with dolphins and orcas frolicking with sea lions is a fulfillment of the prophecy of Isaiah 11:6–7.

RJ's remark about the removal of those who take the mark of the Beast comes from Revelation 14:11 and Revelation 20:4. More information about the Beast and his mark can be found in Revelation 13.

Chapter 13: Investigation

Holly considers the presence of human sin during and after Christ's thousand-year reign on Earth. Verses from Psalm 9:7–8, Psalm 67:4, Psalm 110:1–6, Isaiah 9:6–7, Isaiah 65:20 (KJV), Zechariah 13:1, and Revelation 20:7–9 talk about this. Her reference to the new heaven and new earth, where sin is completely removed and where there will be no more death, crying, sorrow or pain, comes from Revelation, chapters 21 and 22.

Chapter 14: Intensifying

Holly's comment about the Lord destroying everything having to do with war is in reference to Isaiah 2:4 and Psalm 46:9.

Chapter 19: Correction

Axel's flashback to his first visit to the throne of God in heaven is taken from Revelation 4:2–6, 1 Timothy 6:16, Daniel 7:9, Revelation 1:12–16, 1 John 1:5, 2 Corinthians 12:4, and 2 Chronicles 18:18.

Elias's role as a teacher in the kingdom is based on Isaiah 2:3.

Jesus, during his conversation with Axel, Holly, and RJ, quotes from John 15:4–8, Revelation 2:2, Philippians 2:13, John 10:11, Psalm 23:2, Ephesians 6:18, and Colossians 1:10–12.

RJ's comment about the uprising that will occur at the end of the Lord's thousand-year reign comes from Revelation 20:7–9.

Axel's thoughts about the One "who reigned as the Capstone over all creation" is a reference to 1 Peter 2:7.

Chapter 20: Chariots

Axel's ride in the chariot of fire, and his remembrance of Elijah and the whirlwind, are based on 2 Kings 2:11 and Isaiah 66:15.

Chapter 22: Reckoning

RJ quotes from 2 Corinthians 5:7 when talking about walking by faith and not by sight. Rusty's statement about Philip in the book of Acts is in reference to Acts 8:38–40.

Chapter 23: Conquest

For more information on CERN and the Large Hadron Collider (LHC), refer to the online material from the CERN Communications Group, *LHC the Guide*, October 2006.

Axel's comment about the Lord smashing Mundaka like a piece of old pottery comes from Psalm 2:9.

Hananias's reference to the Lord expressing his righteous anger is based on passages like John 2:15–17, Matthew 23:33–36, Deuteronomy 29:28, 2 Kings 22:13, and Psalm 30:5.

Chapter 24: Closure

The celebration of the Feast of Tabernacles during the kingdom age is declared in Zechariah 14:16–17 and Isaiah 2:2.

Chapter 25: Blown Away

Nikki's marveling at the landscape in Israel is based on passages from Jeremiah 31:5, 12; Amos 9:13–14, Psalm 65:9–13, Psalm 72:16, Ezekiel 36:35, and Joel 3:17–18.

The Risen Ones and human believers come into the Lord's presence to worship as declared in Psalm 84:5–7, Psalm 66:4, and Psalm 72:11.

Descriptions of Jesus's majesty and glory as he's enthroned in the temple are found in Psalm 45:6–7, Psalm 76:4, Psalm 84:1–4, Psalm 93:1, Isaiah 4:2, Ezekiel 43:6–7, and Ezekiel 44:4.

Jesus quotes from 1 John 4:13–16 when addressing the Risen Ones and human believers.

The celebration that Axel and Arielle witness in their camp is drawn from Psalm 47:1–9, Psalm 65:8, Psalm 66:1–5, Jeremiah 31:4, and Isaiah 11:6–9.

Axel, Holly, and RJ each met with notable Risen Ones. Eleazar son of Dodai appears in 2 Samuel 23:9–10 and 1 Chronicles 11:12–14. Queen Esther's rescue of the Israelite people is recorded in Esther 4:15–5:14. Johannes Kepler's accomplishments can found online at www.godandscience.org/apologetics/sciencefaith.html.

Chapter 26: Radiance

Peter Erickson's decision to follow Christ is similar to the account in Luke 23:40–43.

Hananias quotes from 1 Peter 4:8 when he states that "love covers a multitude of sins."

Axel quotes from 1 John 1:5 and 2 Corinthians 4:6 when repeating Francisco's words about God's light and how God has imparted that light into our lives.

Resources

Randy Alcorn. *Heaven: Biblical Answers to Common Questions.* Carol Stream: Tyndale House Publishers, 2004.

Donald Grey Barnhouse. *Revelation.* Grand Rapids: Zondervan, 1971.

Billy Graham. *Angels: God's Secret Agents.* Garden City: Doubleday & Company, 1975.

Wayne Grudem. *Systematic Theology.* Grand Rapids: Zondervan, 1994.

Jeff Lasseigne. *Unlocking the Last Days.* Grand Rapids: Baker Books, 2011.

Hugh Ross. *Beyond the Cosmos.* Colorado Springs: NavPress, 1996.

Merrill F. Unger. *Unger's Bible Handbook.* Chicago: Moody Press, 1966.

John F. Walvoord. *Major Bible Prophecies.* Grand Rapids: Zondervan, 1991.

Connect with the Author

www.aheaventodiefor.com